The Elven Monarchy Scribes: Book 2

Brewing Battles

H.L. LAFFERTY

Ladies
of the
Lakes
Publishing

Table of Contents

~Chapter I~
Grieving for Cosaint

"The stranger! The one you took to be questioned, where is he?" The Princess roared lividly at the first guard she met as she entered the palace. She had never demanded anything of anyone, but that was before the man she loved was murdered, her kingdom was attacked during a sacred event and her brother, who had been her best friend, betrayed her. She needed to speak with the stranger and find out what he knew. The guard before her looked terrified. Alveen was still in her black gown, sliced up the side and covered in various patterns of filth from the battle only hours ago. Her hair was a mess and her eyes glowed with anger. She would find out why this happened.

"Your Highness, I do not know. I was not informed. I swear." Alveen stared at him for a moment before moving past him to meet with The Queen. She made her way to the throne room with haste, hoping to find her grandmother there.

"Where is he?" She asked simply with authority. Her face was hard as stone. Without lifting a finger, her magic shot out in front of her and thrust open the metallic golden doors that gave way to the vast display of tree trunk pillars and floating vines, the only light from which the canopy above allowed in. Chandeliers hung uniformly high above from branches, level with the second-floor balcony that wrapped around the throne room for larger events. There was a boundary spell around the palace, so even though many of the ceilings were open to the sky, the elements would not penetrate it.

The Queen stood with her back to the door, clean as can be. She and a few other royals were rushed to the palace before the battle began, Alveen was caught in the middle, unable to escape and forced to fight for her life, which it turned out she was more skilled at, though she would have never guessed.

"Who?" The Queen simply asked, still not facing her.

"The stranger that was thrown through the portal. The one they brought back to the palace to question. I want to question him too."

"Alveen." The Queen scoffed, "What do you possibly think you will be able to ask that we can't?" Her heart raced.

"I may not be able to say anything that you all can't, but I promise I can be a most persuading interrogator if necessary." Her voice was a near growl.

"I will not allow you anywhere near the stranger until you learn to control your emotions." She spun around so fast her gown had to catch up with her. Her face was frustrated. "You are a Princess and you will not be torn apart by these emotions. You will lose control faster than you have the ability to fix your mistakes." She was slowly walking towards the tattered up Princess.

"He has the answers. He is responsible for Samual's death!" She screamed, tears threatening once again to spill onto her blood spattered cheeks.

"No." The Queen raised her voice, but remained in control. "That man is not responsible for anyone's death. Zakarian alone is responsible for the death of Samual, though I can imagine it's easier to blame a stranger verses your own brother whom you've trusted your entire life." She was being blunt to Alveen, but lowered her voice when she realized the insensitivity of her words. "As a Queen, there is no room for self pity or for personal emotion and being the last heir to this throne, Alveen you will have to learn that very quickly."

Alveen dropped to the floor on her cut up knees, cupping her face in her hands to hide the crimson color her face was turning as the pain of loss over whelmed her. "He's gone." She cried.

"Yes. He is." The Queen stated. "So are over thirty others, two of which were kings if you happen to have forgotten that." She kneeled down to her granddaughter, pulling her hands away so she could look her in the eyes. Her eyes were glowing as she met the Queen's stare, so much anger in the peridot lights. "Alveen, Viktor just lost his father and Karolyn her brother.

Those guards? They had families also." She pulled Alveen to her feet. "I know you will not like hearing this, but this is not about you. If you ever wish to be a great ruler, you must learn to put your loss and your struggles behind you and focus on those of your kingdom and of your allies. Don't let Samual be followed into death by you because you cannot control yourself." The Princess stood there silent, unable to talk and think. "Now if you're ready to reign in your anger, I will speak with you in regards to the matter you came here for." Alveen took a deep breath, swallowing the truth her grandmother just laid out in front of her. She tried to relax.

"What have you found out?"

"I'm sorry to say, very little. He claims to not know his name, not know anything about his past. He said all he remembers is waking up in front of a sorceress, he thinks he was meant to be held captive but he escaped the grips of one of the tribe members and dove through their open portal before they entered, and all he knew was that he had to warn us."

"What good that did." She stated. "Do you believe him?"

"I do. I believe it is more than possible the sorceress held him captive and wiped his memory."

"You don't recognize him?"

"Not at all. He has a very different mix of features I've never seen before." The Queen looked at her granddaughter. "I am truly sorry for your loss my dear. I did not mean to sound so insensitive. Samual had come to me only days ago asking to court you so I understand the nature of your relationship." She placed a hand on her shoulder. "And I am only trying to help you gain control because you have now moved to the top of the line as heir to the Cosaint throne. Should anything happen to me, you must lead our kingdom." Alveen hadn't even thought about that. With Zakarian betraying his kingdom he forfeited his right to the throne.

"I don't understand what he did." The Princess stated, focusing on the floor in front of her.

"I have an assumption." She walked back to her throne, gently lowering herself onto the branches that entwined to make the elaborate seat. "Were you aware of his relationship? And that there was a child of it?"

"I was, I have seen her only a number of times but I have never spoken to her. She was with him. When he betrayed us." The Queen nodded.

"Yes. He had come to me only shortly after Samual did, begging for me to accept his relationship with Malika and to accept his child. I refused to accept Malika." She tapped her finger on the arm of the throne. "So I suppose it can be in part blamed on me."

"Why would that cause him to betray his kingdom? And me?"

"Simple. There are no rules in the Dorcha tribes. There is no structure. I rejected for the pure reason of not trusting her, it had nothing to do with her race, though I'm certain he assumed otherwise." The little girl with straight blonde hair and glowing pink eyes entered her mind.

"What of Tanilly? Did they take her with them?"

"Surprisingly not. The guards found her only a short while ago. She is resting in my chambers."

"What will come of her? Her parents abandoned her. She has no one."

"I'm very much aware of that. I have decided that she will be in my care until further notice. The world still believes in a truly pure elven monarch, so all though she is Zakarian's heir, it will be a battle to get her rights to the throne, one I fear I may not be able to win." She sighed. "But that will come later. For now we must ensure she is safe, and not allow her father's decisions to effect her life. I will begin schooling her after the memorial services."

"You've already planned memorial services?"

"Yes. Tomorrow evening we will mourn our dead, and then.." she paused, hesitatingly as if she did not like what she had to say next, "we will move on."

Alveen departed the throne room, bee lining for her chamber. Mysti was not there, she was sure she would be hiding still or with her family. The other royals were busy summoning their kingdoms and advisors to keep them updated on what happened. She went straight to her bathroom, peeling her gown off, tearing scabs that had formed on her legs off with it. Warm, dark blood slowly trailed down her smooth skin. Running her hand over her stomach she felt the grotesque scars still there from the last battle she fought, only that one she fought alone.

A stone mortared wall stood curved in the center of the bathroom, leaving an open walkway leading into the shower, where the floor was entirely pebbles that matched the bay shoreline right outside her room. Walking in, she waved her hand, summoning the warm water to flow through the pipes and rinse off any indication she had just come from battle. The heat burned against the bruises and cuts she obtained as she watched the reds and browns trail in streams down her legs and into the drain. She spent a small amount of time scrubbing areas where the dried and caked on substances needed more than just running water. She tried breathing, focusing on the feel of the warmth against her skin and the steam on her face. But it never failed, every time she tried, the heart ache and betrayal came rushing back in. She finally leaned against the stone wall, sliding to the ground as it scratched the skin on her back, wrapping her arms around her knees letting out a sorrowful wail until she was so tired, she could hardly even cry anymore.

Realizing how tired she was, she dried off and tied a robe around her bare body before she sat in front of the fireplace. Her eyes focused on the flames until her mind went empty. Alveen sat like that all night. She tried lying down on the couch, attempting to sleep, though it repeatedly proved useless so she would turn back to the hot flames and let her mind drift. She would extend her arm and force the dancing flames to move in different directions, just to give herself something to focus on.

Alveen knew it was morning when Mysti entering the room. If her attendant hadn't come in, she would have had no idea the time of day.

"Your Highness, have you been like this all night?" She didn't answer. She was so tired, but sleep wouldn't come to her. "Your Highness." The attendant gently shook her shoulder, pulling The Princess from her daze.

"Oh, good morning Mysti." Her voice monotone and quiet.

"Do you need assistance this morning?" she stood by the mantle observing The Princess she so admired.

"No, thank-you though." She sat up leaning on her arm, still looking into the fire.

"Let me stoke the fire for you. And might I suggest at least changing into comfortable clothing if you are choosing to stay in today?" Mysti knew about her and Samual, she was trying to be the friend The Princess had asked her to be when they first met.

"That's not a bad idea. And yes, I would greatly appreciate that." She stood and walked into the closet, being greeted by her ghastly appearance in the mirror. She brushed through her hair and quickly put a few pins holding her bangs back and made a messy ponytail of her air-dried curls. She emerged in black leggings and an over sized button up plaid shirt. When she came back to the couch, there was tea sitting on the table, steaming against the bright background of the flames. Her curtains remained closed since she had entered the room last evening, making it feel as though it were still night. She walked over and pulled the curtains apart, brightening the room even though the sky above was gloomy. She opened the balcony doors allowing the crisp air to swirl around and fill her chamber. Sitting on the couch with a cup of tea in her hands, she patted the couch for Mysti to join her.

"Thank-you, Your Highness."

"I did tell you I wanted us to be friends, did I not?" She said with a hopeful look in her eyes.

"Princess, I am so sorry." Mysti placed a hand on her leg. "I cannot imagine what you are going through. But I do know, after knowing you for even the short time I have, you are strong. You will overcome this and you will use it to empower you. You will ensure Samual is never forgotten by his kingdom." Alveen was so touched by the kind words, she pulled her attendant in for a tight hug.

It was past mid day when someone came to Alveen's chamber. Mysti still sat next to her, talking and keeping her company. She rose and attended to the door, telling Alveen to relax and let her handle it. When she heard a familiar voice at the door, Alveen rose and met Mysti behind the solid entrance.

"King Luka. What can I do for you?" She didn't smile or sound genuine in any form when she spoke to him. He was standing straight with his hands in his dress jacket pockets. Alveen saw it in his eyes when he looked from Mysti to her that he was concerned. Besides his tired expression, there was no sign that he had fought either.

"I don't need anything Princess. I was only coming to see if there was anything I could do for you. I became worried when I didn't see you at breakfast or lunch." His eyes draped over her, taking in her otherwise unusual appearance from what he had seen since he arrived. He liked her this way.

"I'm fine, thank-you."

"Would you like company?" he insisted.

"No thank-you. I'm sure Queen Karolyn or Prince Viktor wouldn't mind though." She didn't mean it to come off as snarky as it did, but she didn't want to depend on someone else, after all, it was not about her.

"King."

"Excuse me?"

"King Viktor now." He corrected her. It took Alveen a moment to realize what he meant. King Bowen had passed, making Viktor the only heir to his kingdom, and the rightful leader.

"Oh." She paused. "Of course." They stayed quiet for a moment.

"Either way, Princess Willow and King Hunter are spending their time with Viktor. The other queens, Vailion and Lovisa are attending to Karolyn... which leaves you alone."

"I tend to be a very forgettable person I suppose." Alveen felt the depression swelling up inside her.

"I disagree, Princess." He stared into her golden teal eyes as if he were searching for something. "As I said, I believe we can develop a beneficial friendship, and that starts with being there for one another and gaining trust." He reached out in an attempt to hold her hand to show he was being genuine in wanting to comfort his friend. She pulled her hand away, crossing her arms across her chest.

"I appreciate the effort King Luka, but I truly am fine. Mysti is all the company I need right now." He closed his hand into a relaxed fist, placing his hands together behind his back.

"Don't pull away from me, please." The words sounded like he was begging, but his tone made it seem like advice. "I know what it feels like to lose a loved one. I know what it's like to feel lost in this world." It surprised her how easily he opened up to her. He was The King no one talked about or cared to be around because they all perceived him as rude and arrogant. Right now, that rude and arrogant King was trying very hard to gain her friendship. "I haven't always been a King, Princess." With that he bowed deeply, keeping his dark rimmed golden eyes pouring into hers. She slowly closed the door as he turned on his heels and walked down the corridor, disappearing around the corner.

"I don't mean to be the bearer of bad news, but it is getting close to the time of the memorial. We really should get you ready now." Alveen nodded, not saying anything as she walked to her closet. "Anything colorful is appropriate." Colorful? That surprised Alveen.

Sifting through the gowns, she found a few brighter colored gowns of purples and mixed colors that may have been appropriate. Walking towards the back of her gowns, the shimmering fabric caught her eye. The gown Samual had given her peeked from behind the new additions in her wardrobe. She pulled it off the hanger and held it close to her, holding back her tears yet again as her face scrunched up and she felt the rosy heat swarm to her face.

Mysti had to work literal magic to make Alveen look presentable this time. Her eyes and cheeks were swollen and there was little to be done about how exhausted she looked. The few scrapes along her jaw-line and temple were easily covered or healed. Her friend stepped back, admiring The Princess. Alveen looked in the mirror, happy with her appearance.

"I'd like to keep my hair down if you don't mind." Mysti nodded and ran her hands through The Princess's hair making sure it was at least styled and manicured. She twisted a few braids together, pinning them together at the back of her head, leaving the rest of her curls flowing over her shoulders.

"There you are." She smiled to Alveen in the mirror. "I will see you there Princess."

"Thank-you." She called after Mysti who was walking out of the room. "For staying with me and keeping me company. I know I could not have been very fun to be around, but it meant a lot." Mysti smiled, curtsying in response before she departed.

She stood tall alongside the other royals, no matter how much her heart was breaking. It took so much loss for her to realize that her grandmother was right, this was not about her. The full truth of being the next in line for the throne was revealed to her; it would never again be about her, it would be about her kingdom and her people first.

Right now her allies, her people and the kingdom as a whole were mourning the loss of many guards and family members. Men and women that were parents, siblings, best friends and children to those around her now laid on strategically organized logs so those remaining could pay their respects all in one place; Samual being among them.

She couldn't bear to look in his direction. Princess Willow had emphasized that Alveen was not the only one to lose someone, and as harsh as it may have sounded, she was right. Prince Viktor lost his father, their kingdom its King, and Queen Karolyn lost her twin brother and another kingdom its King as well. Samual was her first epic love, he made her feel passion and desire and made her feel strong.

But right now, Princess Alveen needed to be strong for her people. She could not fall apart and cry for days or weeks. She could not allow herself to fall apart in a time of crisis when her kingdom also lost another heir that day. She had given herself a day to mourn, but seeing the reality of the situation in front of her, she realized a day was all she could afford.

Zakarian. Though he had not died, he may as well have. Her heart throbbed with ache from the betrayal of her brother. After so many lectures of how horrible the Dorcha tribes were, after so many words of hatred towards people that had done exactly what he did, something made him give in.

The Banri delivered a moving speech about the strength of an attack like this. Though it is meant to tear us apart and make us weak, all it will ever do is bring us closer and make us stronger. The words she spoke were true, but Alveen had never felt more alone. She no longer had anyone she could lean on or be herself around. She would now be playing Princess every hour of every day.

She was still exhausted from the battle and having hardly slept for obvious reasons. She spent most of the night staring into her fireplace wrapped in her fur blanket, which sounded like exactly where she wanted to be right now.

Today she wore the gown Samual had designed for her, to honor him. As the memorial came to a closing, the Queen placed her hands in front of her palms up and chanted a small incantation, slowly causing flames to engulf the deceased. Each log displayed its own flames, never once joining with the blaze next to it and a few of the individual fires were dancing with blue and green flames. The kingdom stood in silence as the remembered were turned to ash. One by one the flames died down, and Alveen took her part in the ceremony. Blowing softly into her palm, she harnessed the wind around her, elegantly blowing the ashes up in the air and pushing them out over the bay as if all the departed were now one body of glittering magnificence. The Royals all lifted an arm, releasing an extraordinary display of fireworks across the bay as Alveen finished. The bright explosions of color stood out from the star filled sky and the darkness of the evening that blanketed the mountains.

Alveen stepped towards King Viktor, his eyes still on the sky. She reached for his hand, his attention slowly transferring to her. She wasn't sure what there was to say, all she knew was she needed to do something for someone other than herself.

"I am so sorry Viktor." Was all she could get out before tears started trailing down her otherwise masked face. She wrapped her arms around him and he squeezed back with more strength than she imagined he would have used. Holding her, he let out a small cry and she could feel his face grow tense against her shoulder.

"Same to you, Princess." She wanted to offer advice, something comforting, but what could she possibly say to someone who just lost their father, their only remaining parent, and would now be thrust into ruling his kingdom with no one to guide him?

"You will make him proud. You will be a just and kind king. And I will be an ally, should you ever need to call on someone." Alveen managed to get everything out without crying again.

"That means a lot, Alveen." He gave her a weak smile as she headed toward the palace, leaving the others behind.

Everyone would be heading off to bed about now, but she wasn't sure where to go. No matter where she went, she would be alone. After debating with herself and walking aimlessly around the palace she finally retreated to her chamber. Passing by guards who bowed in respect, pillars wrapped in bright autumn colored vines and through a few pointed arched walkways until she finally reached her wing. The usual two guards stood outside her door and bowed as she pushed her chamber doors ajar. Standing in front of the hearth she sunk down into the chair draped with her elk hide blanket. She smoothed it out, thinking about the hunt, grateful she had a few memories with Samual.

An echo rang through her room, startling her, as an uninvited visitor knocked on her door. She strode towards the door, taking a deep breath and holding herself together. Opening the door, memorable golden irises looked back at her.

"What can I help you with King Luka?" The King stood there, serious, looking The Princess over concerned as he had done earlier that day.

"I simply wanted to come see how you were doing. I thought you could use a friend at a time like this." He spoke low as if he were whispering a secret to her.

"Again? Didn't we have this conversation not long ago?"

"Yes." He said with no more of an explanation as to why he was back.

"I'm fine, thank-you for checking." She began to close the door when his hand flew up, stopping her.

"May I come in? I was hoping to speak with you."

"We can speak here. What is it you need, Your Majesty?"

"Please.." He insisted, repeating himself from earlier, staring at her, looking hurt. "Don't push me away. I know you're hurt, I know you don't even know what to think right now, and I know you feel alone. Please." He insisted again, "Just let me come in so we can talk." How did he know she felt alone? Without saying anything, she looked him over and released the door, allowing him to follow her in. The door remained open as he followed her to the chairs on each end of the couch in front of the fire. She hung her cloak in her closet and walked back to sit in the chair. Luka stood leading his forearm against the mantel, looking down into the flames. She only just now realized he hadn't changed into more comfortable clothes from the ceremony, he looked as if he'd come straight here.

"That's a unique color for a memorial, Princess." He took her in, still in her golden teal gown, her hair a mess as it hung gracefully over her shoulders. She didn't meet his eyes when she responded. Her voice shook, giving away the emotion she was trying to hold back.

"He had it custom designed for me when I first arrived." Her face pinched together as she still tried to stop herself from crying and her eyes began to glow the peridot green they did was she was emotional. He quickly stepped over towards her, she stood up, turning away from him and covering her face so he couldn't see her broken heart pouring out of her eyes.

"Then it was the perfect choice." He said simply. His arm reached out to her shoulder and turned her back around to face him. Her cheeks were red when her hands dropped and her makeup beginning to smear. "It's going to be okay." He reassured her, pulling her into his chest, rubbing her back with one hand and holding the back of her head with the other. The physical contact made the shattered pieces of her heart melt together just a little. She needed this, the support of a friend, and she hadn't even known how much.

"Why would he betray me like this?" Luka thought for a moment, realizing she was now talking about The Prince.

"I don't know, Princess." He admitted to her. She cried louder, shaking as her companion held her close. "But I promise, you will get stronger."

"Your Highness, I've come to help.." Mysti entered the room. "Oh, Princess, I apologize, the door was open." Alveen pulled away, wiping her face quickly.

"Oh you are fine Mysti. We left it open on purpose."

"Is there anything I can do for you, Your Highness?" she questioned. Alveen shook her head, rejecting her help at this time.

"Mysti, is it?" King Luka asked stepping forward.

"Yes, Your Majesty." He pulled out a few tea pouches from his shirt pocket handing them to her.

"Would you mind making The Princess some of this tea? It will help calm her nerves."

"Of course, Your Majesty." She curtsied and walked away quickly, leaving the door open.

"You carry tea with you?" Alveen questioned, wanting to laugh at his unexpected behavior. She sat down on one end of the couch.

"I came prepared, that's all." He stated bluntly, giving her a small grin, his eyes still sad as he looked at her. "I remember when I lost my father. Him and I weren't very close, I knew very little of what I was expected to do as a King. I felt more alone than I ever had, despite being surrounded by dozens of guards, staff members and advisors." He looked at her sitting on the small couch in the center of the two chairs facing the hearth. Her back was against the arm of the couch so she was facing him. "I cannot imagine what you're going through, Princess, but I will help in any way I can."

"Have you spoken with Viktor? I feel like he could use your guidance more than I." she stated, appreciative but confused.

"I did, actually. I was with him after you spoke with him earlier." He was facing the fire, still standing behind the chair where he handed Mysti the tea.

"You can sit you know." She stated, eyeing the empty spot on the couch by her. "So, why are you so insistent on helping me?" He held her stare for a moment after the question left her lips.

"Because, believe it or not, you're the closest thing I have to a best friend. And I wanted to make sure you were okay."

"I was only kidding." She said referring to their interaction when she awoke from being unconscious on the field. "On the field, when I woke up. I don't think I am your only friend. I doubt I am your *best* friend. We've known each other a few days." He smirked looking at the ground.

"Actually, it's not far from the truth. I have no siblings. After my friends in the village learned of my position, they all grew distant. I never gained any friends in the palace, just loyal staff. Everyone seems intimidated by me. Not that I blame them." He looked over to her again as Mysti walked in, placing the tea on the table beside Luka. He thanked her as she departed, grabbing a mug and passing it to Alveen. She took it carefully in her hands, pulling her knees to her chest as she took the first sip. "That is until I arrived here, completely unexpected, and I discovered a stubborn, outspoken Princess that can't even be intimidated by dozens of syragons charging at her. I've spoken with you more in the last few days than I've spoken to most of these royals my entire life. You're easy to hold a conversation with, even for someone that doesn't really like that kind of thing." She rolled her eyes at him, taking another sip of tea. "You were impressive, by the way. I've never seen magic like what you can do. And to be honest I thought it was rumor, what you had done to the two here. But after seeing you in action, I believe every bit of it."

"Flattery will get you everywhere, Your Majesty." She replied sarcastically, only to be followed by a lump in her throat as she remembered that was what she said to Samual all the time, and then continued with a confession. "I'm glad you stopped in the entry room when you first arrived." She smelled the drink in her hands. "This is really good." Her statement simple, as the cinnamon and spice aroma entered her nose, the steam warming her from the inside. She sat there silent, she didn't want to admit it to him, but she enjoyed the comfort Luka's presence provided her.

"Your Highness, Your Majesty. The Banri approaches." The guard announced, entering her room. They both set their tea aside and stood. Alveen held her hands together at her hips and Luka clasped his behind his back.

"Ah, King Luka. I didn't expect to see you here." No one replied. "Anyways, I'll get straight to the point." She began, standing near the door still. "Krumvite and Loxley will also be holding memorial services for the guards and The Kings. I wish for you, Alveen, to attend both." Alveen bowed her head.

"When do we leave?"

"Not 'we'. You. I must stay here and ensure the kingdom repairs are finished, and we cannot both leave the kingdom at once. And since you have yet to do this and are learning, I will send Ollahm with you, so you can continue your culture studies."

"Why are you unable to leave? King Luka is away from his kingdom, leaving them with only advisors, same with every other royal here." Alveen questioned, only afterwards thinking it may have come off rude.

"Every other kingdom has advisors, we do not. And I'm sure you remember our conversation, I have a little more to deal with now." She stated bluntly, referring to Tanilly at the end. Alveen thought for a second. It didn't seem like a terrible idea.

Maybe traveling a little and getting to keep busy was exactly what she needed.

"Okay, when must I be prepared to leave by?"

"Tomorrow evening. You will leave with King Viktor. King Hunter and Princess Willow will be along with you as well. From there, you will travel with them to Loxley, and back to Foresi. I will have Caspian and his men ready to escort you home." With that, she walked out of the room.

"Well. I suppose I should begin to pack my things." She walked over to the closet.

"This will be good, it will keep you busy. Loxley is much more modern, yet their ceremonies are traditional. But I have a feeling you will love Krumvite. It is quite enchanting." Luka said as he sat back down on the couch. "You have all day tomorrow to pack, Princess. Come relax." He insisted. Listening to his reason, she walked back to the couch and sat next to him facing the fire. "You can do this Princess." He held her hand on his leg, squeezing it for encouragement. She looked up at him, admiring his encouraging grin.

"Thank-you Luka." She smile and leaned her head on his shoulder, her arms wrapping around his muscular bicep like a pillow. She closed her eyes, exhausted and head pounding from the crying she had done.

~Chapter II~

Krumvite

Alveen woke up, still in her gown, confused as to how she was now laying covered in her bed. She didn't remember Luka ever leaving, but it was probably for the best that he did. She sat up straight, stretching her arms and twisting to stretch her back before feeling the cool stone beneath her bare feet. As she made her way to her closet to change for the journey planned today, she noticed a single flower lying on a table with a note. The flower was unlike any she had seen, with many small spiny bright blue blooms on a single stem. She picked it up, studying it curiously. Then her eyes landed on the note, and she hesitantly picked it up, flipping it over to read what was inscribed.

Princess,

I hope your journey today is safe. I apologize for leaving without word, but I must return to my kingdom before the Krumvite memorial. I will see you there.

He must have moved her from the couch when he left. She was slightly annoyed that he hadn't said anything, but at the same time she was grateful for the sleep she was able to get. At least she would have a companion at the memorial.

She set down the flower and entered her closet, looking for something fitting an underwater civilization.

"I've already packed your things, Your Highness." Mysti approached from behind. "I found some exquisite gowns for the memorials and the ball."

"There is another ball? Do they really think that's wise after what just happened only a few days ago?" Alveen sighed, frustrated.

"The Krumvites value culture and tradition. They use it as more of a celebration of life gathering. Allowing people to dance and be happy in the midst of all the despair." Her attendant explained. "And in many ways I assume it would hold the purpose of a Royal Walk, to show the kingdom that they will not be shaken by an attack on them, but they will be brought closer together." When she put it like that it made sense. Alveen closed her eyes with her hands gripping into her hips.

"What shall I wear on the journey?" She did not look to Mysti when she spoke, she just looked around the closet.

"I would suggest something much more casual." Reaching her arms towards the hangers, she quickly picked all the pieces to an outfit for The Princess. "This should be suitable for traveling." She stepped out, leaving The Princess to dress herself.

She pulled on a pair of fitted jeans and knee high brown boots with a satisfying amount of traction compared to all the fancy shoes she had been required to wear recently. Her look was pulled together with a long sleeve dark red shirt, soft against her skin, and a dark brown leather vest that cinched her waist. She ran her fingers through her curls, using a small amount of product to keep her frizz tamed. The final touch, a golden crown of leaves and vines twisted intricately into a tall pattern resting in a circle atop her spiraled locks.

Opening the closet doors, she smoothed out her jeans over her thighs, admiring her boots. A knock came at her door, making her attention snap to the threshold. She pulled the door open, causing her hair to flip over her shoulder as she was greeted by Viktor, whose jaw was dropping at the unexpected site.

"Prince.." She caught herself, "I mean King Viktor." She said surprised by his presence. He stood level with her, a dark blue cloak sitting on his shoulders, his silver crown resting on his dark hair and matching casual clothing of boot cut jeans and a button up shirt.

"Uh, Hi. Princess." His arms crossed across his chest as a small grin crossed his face.

"What can I do for you?"

"I just came to see if you needed any assistance preparing for the journey. Do you need any assistance?" She could see his eyes were filled with sadness, reflecting her own, but they both managed to put smiles on.

"I believe I've got everything taken care of. Mysti helped and made sure everything was in order." She opened the door fully, inviting her acquaintance in, keeping the door open in full view of the guards. "I appreciate you stopping and checking on me though."

"Of course. Anyways, are you ready to go? The ship is nearly prepared."

"Oh, I was under the impression we were not leaving until later?"

"That was the original plan, however if there is nothing keeping us, I would rather we leave as soon as possible, given the short time frame for the preparations, you understand." He explained only taking a few steps into her chamber.

"Then I suppose once I speak with The Banri I will be prepared to leave." She nodded letting him lead her out of the room.

As they approached the ship, her grandmother awaited her arrival on the shore.

"My beautiful granddaughter," she started, "This casual attire always felt like it was more your style." She pulled Alveen in for a quick hug. "Stay safe on your travels. Remember your etiquette and customs and you will be fine. Krumvite will be enjoyable for you." she paused, "Loxley is a very serious country. So prepare for the difference in culture. Also, slight change in plans. Caspian and his hand-picked guards will be escorting you on this journey as an extra precaution. Ollahm Hilfyro will be staying here, he has other business to attend to." Sir Caspian had become a close confidant of hers since the original attack. He proved to be a trustworthy and strong friend. The centaur stepped up beside her, bowing respectfully. A handful of guards stood behind him, two other centaurs, a fairy and multiple mixed species. She nodded in approval before letting Viktor lead her on the ship.

She approached the wooden staircase leading up to what seemed to be a very detailed deck. Viktor held his hand out, offering his assistance when the stairs dropped off onto the deck nearly two feet below her. She graciously accepted though she could have handled it herself. Taking in every detail of the ropes, sails and doors on the exposed level of the ship, she found herself immersed in wonder.

Hand carved wood working trailed along the railings and balconies she could see from her first step onto the ship. She stood below the largest sail on the lowest part of the deck. A stair case was tucked into each corner of the level she was on, like a double foyer, curved to meet in the center at the top. Below them each were two doors that she had yet to discover what they held. One side rose higher than that, with yet another stair case directly in the center leading up to the helm.

"I'd like to introduce you to Atsalta, my ship." Alveen admired the wood carvings, trailing her fingers over them as she fell into step with the newly named King. Her guards followed behind her, admiring the craftsmanship as well.

"She's beautiful."

"Alveen! I'm so happy you will be traveling with us." Princess Willow burst out from one of the doors below the staircases. "Mind if I show her to her room?"

"I need a room? How long is the journey again?"

"Only about a day and a half." Willow wore black boots with buckles, the material shining much like leather would but somehow it was different. She wore the typical emerald green colored pants that stretched to form to her figure while giving her flexibility as usual and a black v-neck long sleeve shirt, her hair tied back. The King excused them and Willow led her through one of the four doors into a short hallway, all stained the same as the deck, with numerous doors on each side of the hall, each with a golden plaque that said '*Guest of Honor.*'

'Guest of honor?" Alveen asked.

"It's for any other royalty that would ever be traveling with him." Alveen noticed how familiar Willow was with the ship, seeing how easily she navigated it.

"Have you been on this ship before?"

"Oh yes, many times. Viktor and I have always been close."

"What is behind those other doors?" Alveen motioned towards the entrance they came through that shown daylight into the otherwise dim hallway.

"The one next to our entrance is the King and his family's chambers. Across the deck is the ship's crew rooms and our guards. That one leads much further below as they have another deck to themselves. And the last door leads up the stairs on that side below the helm, it's more like a dining hall of sorts."

Princess Willow showed her around the ship while the crew was still preparing to take off. When the time came near, Willow got even more excited, pulling Alveen along until they saw Viktor at the center of the ship, arms extended into the air, lips moving to an unheard chant. Before Alveen could ask what was going on, pillars of light shot out of the King's palms, hitting the top of the center post that held the sail. Slowly, the pillars expanded into a ball of light at the top of the upright beam and a dome barrier crawled downward until it encompassed the whole ship like a giant bubble.

"It tends to get chilly once we go down. Want to grab a cloak before we descend?" Willow asked, guiding her to her chamber again.

Alveen opened the heavy wooden door to see her trunks were already waiting at the end of her bed. The room was much larger than she assumed the ship could hold, she assumed magic had a lot to do with that. The bed was smaller than the one she was use to, but it was still decorated with a lightweight navy canopy, the covers and pillow cases matching the silky blues and blacks. An odd box with stones sat in the middle of the room towards the end of the bed closest to the large window, allowing in the view of Cosaint palace. After studying the box she discovered it was a fireplace, you simply hit a button and flames were fueled to warm your room. Interesting, she thought. It also had a small bathroom with a walk in shower and the essentials, and a countertop with a few kitchen essentials. She was impressed with the temporary living quarters. Alveen sifted through her trunk until she finally found her fur lined cloak, black silk on the outside. She wrapped it around herself before exiting her room, joining Princess Willow and King Hunter on the main deck. Crew members were working hard as the three of them observed, looking up expectantly at Viktor waiting for the order.

"Leave port." They barley heard him give the order, but it was only moments before the boat began to move. The sound of waves lapping along the solid structure filled the air. No breeze penetrated the shield that was in place. Alveen stood and stared over the side of the ship.

"Just wait, this is pretty amazing." Willow said and she joined her.

"Descend." Viktor gave the order loud and clear. The front of the ship dipped lower as Alveen watched the waves get closer and closer to the deck. There was a small part of her that was nervous. Caspian had joined them on the deck, standing near her. She felt a calmness wash over her with him there. The water rose and rather than pouring over onto the deck as Alveen expected, the water crawled over the magical dome, protecting them from total saturation. It was like a wall of glass, you could clearly see everything below the surface of the water. The water ascended the barrier until it engulfed the very top of the posts. Sun rays trailed through the water, decorating the stained deck with dancing reflections. The Princesses looked out into the bay, admiring the species so unlike what she was used to. Mermaids swam around towering seaweed and rock structures. They waved to her, laughing at her astound expression.

"This is.." she couldn't find the words to describe what she was experiencing right now. Lights flashed on from the posts around the ship, giving light to the slowly darkening deck as they descended further from the sun light.

"Unique?" Viktor asked from behind them. She spun around, smiling with awe in her eyes.

"That is certainly one word for it. Consider me officially blown away." Her eyes were wide as she observed the underwater creatures and looked around the dome. The chill began to set in as Willow had promised, the deeper they went the colder she became. Thankfully this fur cloak was doing her wonders right now.

"I'm glad you like it. I cannot wait to show you around my kingdom, Your Highness. It is somewhat of treasure if I do say so myself."

Willow taught Alveen many of the creatures below the surface, explaining a little about them. Alveen couldn't help but drown in the knowledge she was being given, asking questions and showing so much interest Willow couldn't help but giggle from time to time. A chime rang out in the middle of Willow speaking.

"Ah, dinner! Finally." She stood, motioning for Alveen to follow. They made way toward the door that lead to the dining hall. The small hallway was dark and still cold much like the deck, but it soon gave way to an unexpectedly large lit room that held three long dining tables with large hearths on opposite walls. Magic was at play here because there is simply no way this extraordinary room would fit here otherwise. As they walked through the entrance, it was as if a wall of warmth overcame them, shielding them from the chill the depths brought outside. They were led to a smaller table at the opposite end of the room where King Viktor sat, already eating.

"Princesses, it's nice to have your company. Sit! Enjoy." Plates were already at their seats, some of it Alveen did not recognize but she acknowledged that it tasted quite delicious. She spoke with the other royals for a short while after dinner, enjoying the warmth of the fire.

"I do apologize, but I would like to excuse myself for the evening. Thank-you for bringing me along on this journey, Your

Majesty." She bowed, given her casual attire. "I will see you tomorrow." She nodded to Willow as she headed towards the hallway. Expecting the chill to return, she pulled her cloak tighter to her body as she exited the hall.

The deck was empty and it now seemed eerie with only the lights on the posts giving a hint to anything. She could hardly see anything in the water surrounding the ship, making her decision to head straight to her room seem like a good idea. There were no dark encounters on her way to her temporary chamber.

Alveen let out a small sigh as she entered her room. Much like the hall it was protected from the freezing temperatures on the deck. Not that she minded the cold, in fact she preferred it. Pulling her cloak off, she laid it neatly across her trunk to wear again tomorrow. She was able to get a warm shower and comfortable clothes on. Oddly enough she was enjoying these few moments alone. As she dried her hair in the towel they provided, which was royal blue like all the décor. Alveen sat on the edge of her bed staring into the flames she just turned on, making them dance.

A fog appeared in front of her, making her move backwards. She felt a presence. Luka. Waving her arm through it, Luka's face appeared.

"Oh no, did the shield not work? Were you drenched by the bay?" He playfully asked with a grin on his face when he saw her. He summoned her. So that's what this is like. She had never used it before. It took her a second to realize what he meant, her hair was still wet from her shower.

"Very funny, King Luka. I actually just showered for the evening." She felt the cloud in front of her. "This is strange. I've never done this before."

"Really? I would have thought with your power you would have mastered communication at least." She didn't say anything. "It's nice to see you Princess."

"Same to you. What can I help you with?"

"Why do you always assume I want something?" His eyes were playful. She stared into them for a moment, the golden irises peering right back into her. "I just wanted to talk. I enjoyed your company last night, that was all."

"Oh I bet." She laughed rubbing her cheeks. "Having a woman cry on your shoulder and be mean is far from what I would consider enjoyable." He didn't answer, he just smiled and stared at her. "Thank-you for that by the way." He nodded.

"Of course, Princess. And you weren't mean. I've come to think it's quite charming how you are so outspoken. And honest. That's hard to come by these days." She looked to the background, he was surrounded by books and she recognized his face being lit but a fireplace.

"Where are you?"

"My chamber. Why?"

"You have books in your chamber? That many?"

"Yes."

"Well I'm envious."

"I'll show you when you visit." She smiled. She didn't know when or if she would ever go to his kingdom. "So, how is the journey so far?"

"You were right, I do love this. I'm excited to see the kingdom. We should arrive tomorrow night." She pushed her damp hair behind her ear. "Why did you summon me?" She smiled.

"Honestly, I was bored and you were the only person I could think of that I could have an entertaining conversation with." He laughed quietly and folded his arms over his chest. He had a gorgeous smile she hadn't quite noticed before. "Is there something wrong with that?"

"Not at all, best friend." She mimicked his comment from the night before. He rolled his eyes. They talked for quite a while, until she finally wished him goodnight needing to get some sleep. She waved the fog away and turned the lights off, leaving the fire lit as she crawled beneath the heavy silk covers. She blew into her palm, using her air magic to push her curtains closed, leaving the darkness of the abyss out of her vision as she drifted off.

Stretching out, Alveen forced the curtains open revealing an expanse of underwater life, they must have gotten closer to the surface with the amount of light now illuminating the world around them. She dressed quickly, tying her hair into a bun and pinning her bangs to the top of her head before grabbing a cup of tea and walking out onto the deck. She wore a blue long sleeve shirt but didn't take her cloak this time, assuming it would be a little warmer than yesterday.

It was still early, not many others were around other than crew members. They had to be less than fifty feet from the surface. The deck was once again covered in the dancing reflections of rays of sunlight. The water was crystal clear, revealing the sandy ocean floor below where sea life lived harmoniously.

"Good morning, Princess." King Hunter stepped to her side.

"Good Morning, Your Majesty. Did you sleep well?" She asked being polite.

"Yes my dear." He stood in a comfortable silence admiring the water with her until The Princess emerged.

"Morning Alveen!" She said in a giddy tone.

"Hey! Willow, do you think we could do some lessons since we've got all day?" She nodded excitedly at The Princess's request. "Caspian, maybe you can assist as well? Give me constructive criticism?" The centaur stood across the deck, watching out into the water as if a threat may jump aboard any second. He turned to her and nodded with a smile.

They stood with practice swords on the deck, Alveen swinging hers, getting familiar with the weight of the weapon. "Alright, first thing to know is it is all about focus and your feet. Many try to fight and pay more attention to their arms and they do not move their feet, keeping you trapped. You must be comfortable moving and turning." Willow swung her practice sword at Alveen, who blocked without hesitation. "Now step back, but be able to watch where you're going." She swung again, but followed it with faster blows behind. Alveen did as she was told, Willow was pushing her towards the staircase. She glanced down to get an idea of the height of the stairs and fended off her attacker as she hopped gracefully up each step until they were standing at the center of the foyer staircase. Alveen took her opportunity, striking Willow's blade forcing her back. This gave Alveen just enough time to jump up onto the rail, squat down and slide down the railing, flipping her legs over her head, landing gracefully on the deck below.

"Not bad Princess!" King Hunter exclaimed. Willow nodded in approval and she jumped onto the top of the railing as well and did a front flip directly off the top, landing near Alveen. "Now for offensive learning. Learning to attack your opponent or switching from defensive to offensive." King Hunter began to teach her basic maneuvers that would give her a small window to change her position.

Alveen was covered in sweat and the royals of Foresi had managed to land a few blows that would certainly be leaving her with bruises.

"You did well, Your Highness." Caspian spoke joining her as she sat on the staircase. He stood on the other side of the railing. "My criticisms are none."

"Oh Caspian, come on. There has to be something I can improve on."

"There is always room for improvement, Princess." He laughed. "I simply mean I have seen you fight and practice is the only thing that will make you more fluent with a sword." He turned, bowing to her before he commented again over his shoulder, "And from what I remember, you don't normally need a sword." He smiled. Alveen was frustrated, she was trying to become a great warrior, without her magic. King Viktor emerged, letting them know they would be arriving soon.

"We should get cleaned up, I believe we are heading directly for dinner when we arrive. Better get in regal attire to represent our countries." Willow spoke with a sarcastic and exaggerated tone. "But seriously, we do need to get cleaned up." They walked to their chambers and cleaned up.

After a quick shower, Alveen dug through her trunk looking for an appropriate gown for dinner. She found a pale blue gown covered in golden filigree which all crawled likes vines up the bodice to wrap over the sheer fabric that pulled together at one shoulder. Pulling it over her figure, she was satisfied to see it was a sheath gown hugging her waist but flaring slightly at her hips. She admired the single sleeve over her shoulder and began looking for the matching box of jewelry that Mysti surely would have packed. The second box she picked up revealed her golden vine tiara with gold leaf earrings and a bracelet matching the gown flawlessly. Underneath it in the trunk was a thin golden cloak, that would be good for later but she did not need that now. Alveen went to the mirror and twisted her hair in a long fishtail braid placing her tiara between her curls before she headed back to the deck.

"You look like the definition of regal, Princess." Sir Caspian said to her as she stood beside him and King Viktor on the deck. She stood tall with her hands together.

"Thank-you, Caspian. It seems my attendant knew exactly what I would need."

"We're approaching." King Viktor said. As Alveen watched him, it was as if he had aged five years in mere days, and that was saying a lot of an elf. He seemed more mature and like a king than he had before.

Alveen watched as the ship ascended as they were coming to a mountain of glimmering black stone under water. Quickly the wall of water disappeared as they rose to the surface, with land nowhere in sight. She looked around confused. King Hunter gave her a look as if saying to be patient and she would see. As quickly as the walls of water disappeared they raised up around them again. Alveen was surprised she never lost her footing, she barely noticed the movement, that again had to be some force of magic at work. They had gone over the mountain she noticed. But in front of them again was another wall, they were now surrounded by the stone mountains, as if in a giant bowl. The ship moved forward leisurely, and with the wave of King Viktor's hand, the stone wall revealed a giant black iron gate that raised up allowed the ship to pass through.

It was dark, the lights on the post illuminated the deck again as they pushed forward through the murky cave. A light was ahead of them, leading into what looked like more open ocean. When the cavern ended, dropping off below them, the ship was sailing through open water again. Then she finally saw it. The glow of the so-often-talked-about underwater civilization lay ahead. They used whatever magic Viktor had used to protect the ship around the whole city. It looked as if it was in an enormous globe on the ocean floor. As they got closer, her elf eyes could make out the perimeter of the city, which was encompassed with statues of warriors and men and kings. The statues the same height as the glittering castle that sat near the opposite side of the city. They all faced outward, as if they were ready to defend the city at a moment's notice. Waterfalls decorated the city in every crevice, leaving a whimsical mist in many areas. Glowing lights spread across the buildings as the ship came into site. A wide landing strip of white sand expanded from the castle to the side of the dome they were about to enter.

"Prepare for Landing!" Viktor yelled to his crew. Much as going above and below the surface, the surrounding water was pushed aside as the ship penetrated through the protective dome, creaking past the guardian statues, making Princess Alveen feel extremely small and insignificant. Citizens cheered at the return of their new king. The ship continued on through the buildings all made of stones, glass and sand to the front of the castle. This was unlike the palace she was use to, the towers stretched high towards the water's surface, the structure made of glass and mirror like materials, reflecting everything around it, including the sun light through the waves, decorating the town below. Multiple balconies were placed around the castle and there were many windows that showed into a ballroom and other large rooms. Another gate raised leading underneath the castle, where the ship finally stopped.

"Ah at last, home." King Viktor said taking a deep breath in becoming enveloped by the salty air.

"Your kingdom is glorious, King Viktor." Alveen commented. He smiled at her comment.

"Come, I shall give you a short tour of the castle and then we must eat. I hope you like seafood." She did, very much.

The tour didn't take very long. From the ship the guards followed them as they climbed a staircase that brought them to the center of the castle to what seemed to be a lounge area. Smooth stone and driftwood were the main materials used in their furnishings, and lots of glass and gems. A white marble mantel extended toward the expansive ceiling that seemed to never stop. The castle layout was circular, most rooms were in the center with a staircase and hallway encircling them. The only exceptions to this were the multiple wings off the bottom floor which lead to the ballroom, the royal family members and guest chambers, the staff quarters at the back of the castle and the dining hall. Throughout the center tower there were multiple libraries and studies, business rooms, lounges, school rooms and Alveen had forgot the rest when she learned of the multiple studies.

"Through here is where you will all stay while you are here. As on board, you are my guests of honor and you will be treated like such." Viktor pointed to multiple chambers throughout the wing of the castle. "Your items will be delivered to your rooms, but first might I suggest food?" Everyone made their own noise of approval as they followed The King to the dining hall, where a massive buffet of various shell fish and sea foods were displayed along the center of the glass top table. Alveen's guards were dismissed for the evening as the guards on staff protected the interior of the castle. Her guards would be posted outside her chambers and would be assisting with security during the memorial.

"Alveen! Here I saved you a seat." Willow waved her over to sit next to her. Everything here was so light in color and airy. Light blues, whites, greys and tans seemed to be the décor, however the royal guard all dressed in royal blue and black, making them stand out from their surroundings. The chairs were all made of driftwood with plush royal blue upholstery.

"Do you like seafood Princess Willow?" She asked her new found friend.

"Yes, I love it. And Krumvite has the best there is." She said and she began to reach for the delicacies in front of her. Alveen wasn't sure what many of these were but she took note as to how Willow was eating certain things so she didn't make a fool of herself. Over halfway through dinner she realized King Luka wasn't with them. She was curious about when he would be arriving.

"Princess?" Willow tapped her on the shoulder. Alveen was off in her own world for a moment.

"Yes?" She asked snapping her full attention towards her peer.

"Would you care to join me in my chamber tonight? For a girl's night? It's been quite a while since we have spent time together laughing and joking. We could both use that after everything that has happened I think." Alveen thought on this for only a second before accepting. She really hadn't had any female friends other than Mysti. She had spent all her time with Samual or Zakarian. It was time she took some time for herself and enjoyed the company of a female friend.

Evening came and Alveen was still walking around with Willow, talking about the wonders of the world and the things they use to do.

"You'll love the memorial tomorrow. Krumvite has beautiful, joyous ceremonies." She twirled around as they walked. Willow had indulged in a few drinks before they left the table. "Oh! You have to see this. You will love it." She grabbed Alveen's arm and pulled her towards the nearest balcony to oversee the city. The sun was gone, but beams from the moon visible here shined brilliantly, leaving that same dancing reflection over the buildings below. Alveen was speechless, beautiful could not describe the site before her. She stood silently with her friend, swooning over the views that unfolded before her.

"So King Viktor seems much more mature, don't you agree?" Willow asked staring out into the night. She was leaning against the thick rail that wrapped around the balcony. She didn't dress up like the other royals did upon arrival, still wearing her fitted pants, buckled boots and a slim fitting jacket to protect her from the chill the sunless sky provided.

"Um, yes I suppose. I would imagine you wouldn't have a choice to stop your childish ways when you are thrown into such a situation." Alveen explained.

"I was referring more to his appearance." She laughed, scoffing at Alveen's obliviousness. "He is quite handsome." She was looking at Alveen, waiting for a reaction. "You don't think so?" She continued when Alveen's face gave nothing away.

"I suppose he is, I just have not really looked at him in that way. When we reconnected, I felt as if he and I had more of a sibling relationship."

"He was crazy for you when he was younger, that I know for certain. Poor lad." She chuckled with a smile.

"I hadn't noticed any kind of interest since I returned." Alveen stated flatly. Willow pushed the subject no further. "We should return to our chambers. We have a long day ahead of us tomorrow." Princess Willow wrapped her arm around Alveen's waist and walked with her, leaning her head on her shoulder. Guards stood frozen in position outside each chamber door, Caspian being one of them in front of hers.

"You really are my best friend, Alveen. I've missed you so much." The Princess said, sounding like she was falling asleep. They made their way down the corridor hosting their chambers.

"Alright Princess, time for bed. I'll see you in the morning." Willow waved and pushed her weight against the door until it gave way. Alveen stood in the corridor, not quite ready for sleep. She still hadn't seen her room, but the towering windows framing the world outside, drew her to them for one last appreciating scan of Krumvite. Alveen could sense someone further down the corridor.

"Such beauty revealed in the darkness." The voice rumbled her, bringing a smile across her face. "The moon." He gestured toward the water's surface that blurred the object. Luka stepped out of the shadows with the slightest hint of a grin. He must have just arrived. He wore no crown now, allowing for his dark hair to be pushed over atop his head in a messy but stylish fashion. Alveen noticed he looked like he received a haircut since last time she saw him, the sides of his head still shaved short blended to the slightly longer dark locks on top.

"You're here." She only met his look with her eyes, her frame still facing the kingdom below. "I was beginning to think you weren't going to show." He joined by her side, hands clasped together behind his back. He stood tall in a black knit sweater with large buttons, his beard neatly groomed as she had always seen.

"The thought crossed my mind." He paused looking at her, still avoiding eye contact jokingly. "But you are rather fun to be around." He mimicked a comment she had made to him before. Her lips pushed together as she tried to conceal a grin, finally making eye contact with the King.

"It's nice to see you. How was the journey?" She asked facing him now, lowering herself onto the oversized marble windowsill.

"Not terrible. It's the shortest from my kingdom." He sat next to her with his back against the frame of the window facing her, putting his feet up on the sill, crossing them at his ankles. She looked at him and copied, moving to the other side of the window, lifting her gown onto the sill, facing him directly now. "That gown looks wonderful on you." He commented. She looked down, smoothing out the thick fabric.

"Thank-you, I am fond of it. It seems to help me blend in around here." She looked at him. "I am also fond of the attire you have on right now." She smiled, waving her hand toward him.

"Are you making fun of my sweater?" He raised his eyebrow.

"Not at all, honestly. You look very nice. I think it's my favorite look on you so far." He stared at her for a moment, looking for any hint of sarcasm.

"Thank-you." He grinned. "So what are your thoughts so far? On Krumvite?" She leaned her head back and looked out the window, the glow reflecting off her gaze. Luka watched her eyes as the water reflections moved across the unique shade her irises held.

"It's beautiful. Inaitithe had a legend of a place like this. Atlantis, they called it. An underwater civilization, lost centuries ago, sunk in the ocean after they fell out of favor with the Gods. There were a few theories that claimed the city was captured in a large air pocket of sorts, that maybe you could enter it through an underwater cave." Luka sat there nodding, like he wanted to laugh. "There are many holes in the theories, but I always thought it was an enchanting legend. And this place reminds me of that."

"Atlantis?" He asked with an expression looking as if she lost her mind, jokingly.

"Don't look at me like that." She laughed. "Zakarian actually made a comment when I first met King Bowen that he knew of a legend this place would remind me of." She lowered her focus to her hands, fiddling her thumbs together trying to hold back anything that would reveal the ache in her chest and nausea she felt in her stomach. "Looks like he was right. He knew me well." She sniffled quietly, tossing a quick pained smile to her companion. His face relaxed as it filled with sympathy. She hated that look. It made her feel weak. "I should be off to bed. I haven't even been in my chamber yet." She swung her legs off the ledge. Luka rose to his feet, extending his hand to help her stand. "Why thank-you, King Luka."

"Where are you staying, Your Highness?" He joked. She walked down the corridor a few paces and stood in front of a large stone door where two of her guards stood watch.

"Princess." Caspian stated. His eyes went to Luka, as if asking if he was allowed to follow. Alveen nodded pushing the door open. She walked in slowly, first extending her arm out to illuminate the large scones in shapes of conch shells on the walls allowing them to unmask her temporary residence. Luka leaned his shoulder against the door frame, folding his arms as he watched her walk around. He had caught on to Caspian's concern of them being in a room together and decided to be respectful and stay at the doorway.

The white marble floor continued throughout the room, continuing up the wall. A sturdy solid gold frame held her bed, covered in navy and gold thick blankets and pillows. The beds canopy was navy as well, heavy and like silk to the touch. Black glittering stone jutted up from the floor on one side, extending only about halfway up the wall. As she inspected in, she realized it was a fireplace. A window like the one in the corridor outside her door was placed on the last wall, looking out over a sandy ocean floor, giving light to a few nocturnal creatures swimming outside the sphere.

"It's not the most exciting room" Luka commented, looking unimpressed. "But I suppose it will do."

"Are you always so critical?" She spun around, arms folded as she walked towards The King in her doorway. He gave her a glance up and down.

"Yes." He stood up backing away from the door. "Good night Princess." He nodded toward the guards outside the door. Caspian reached in, smiling and pulled the door closed, bowing to The Princess. She returned his salutation and headed for her trunk to change into her night clothes.

~Chapter III~

Masquerade

Princess Willow joined Alveen in her chamber while preparing for the memorial. Princess Willow informed her of a few of the traditions of Krumvite. They would spread the King's ashes and immediately after the ceremony they go directly into the ball, which she was not informed was a masquerade ball.

"I was unaware of that. Hopefully it's not too offensive to show up without a mask."Alveen commented. The royal blue satin fabric of Willow's gown cascaded on the floor around her bare feet. It was simple with no embellishments and the strapless bodice wrapped firmly around her waist. She straightened her short dark locks that framed her face and allowed her attendant to do her makeup.

Alveen finally made her way to her trunk to see which gown and accessories Mysti had packed for this important occasion. She pulled out the dress bag that was neatly folded in her trunk and hung it on the bed canopy. Unzipping it, she exposed the shimmering navy organza fabric of the skirt. Reaching in she grabbed the full gown and pulled it out of the protective layer around it. Sitting off the shoulders were straps of golden appliqué shaped like different kinds of seashells, covered by a thin layer of rushed navy organza that continued split down the bodice and covered the entire skirt. The appliqué wrapped around the shoulders and covered the entire bodice under the sheer fabric, covering the immodest deep neckline the organza gave the illusion of. A slim golden belt was attached to the natural waist line.

Alveen pulled the gown over her head, zipping it from the side. A large mirror sat in the back corner of her room, allowing her to admire herself as she spun around in the ballgown. Willow's attendant had finished her and offered to help Alveen with her hair, which she graciously accepted. The girl pulled a few curls out from Alveen's hair, allowing them to caress her cheek, but pulled the rest of her hair back, braiding the crown of her hair before pulling it back into three layered ponytails. Her eye shadow was a smoky design of golden and navy, like her gown, and her lips covered in a shimmering gold gloss. The accessory box sat on top of her next gown in the truck. It held a short solid gold crown with no gems that slid between her curls, a sapphire ring, and what looked to be a custom set of earrings matching the design and color of her gown perfectly. A knock came abruptly at her chamber door. Alveen opened the door to see multiple guards outside with King Hunter.

"Princess! You are a present for the eyes!" He spoke politely, kissing the top of Alveen's hand before heading toward Willow. "And my beautiful daughter, it is a rare occasion to see you dressed in such finery." He spun her around. "I'm sure King Viktor will be pleased." He nudged her.

"Father!" She proclaimed irritated. Her face was overcome with the rosy shade of embarrassment. Alveen smiled, from their conversation the night before it had come to be obvious that The Princess had an interest in The King.

"Are you both ready to go? The guards are ready to escort us." Alveen took note that her guards were in the entourage outside her room. She walked over to her trunk and slipped into a pair of sapphire hued heels before joining the Foresi royals in the hall.

Caspian and another centaur flanked her as she exited the room, following King Hunter and Princess Willow. "What is your name? I don't believe we've met." Alveen asked her second guard.

"Nikoli, Your Highness." He bowed as he walked with her.

"I feel as if I've seen you before. What is your normal post?"

"Throne room, Your Highness." She nodded understanding why he seemed so familiar.

"Well I'm glad to have you along Sir Nikoli." He fell out of step with her, returning to Caspian's side.

They were directed to the second level, where they lined up on the balcony. King Viktor waited inside for all the other royals. Alveen stood on one end of the balcony between Caspian and Nikoli, with Queen Lovisa and The Princesses next to them. She watched as the other royals joined the group. King Luka finally emerged, standing on the opposite end of the balcony from her. He wore a dark navy military suit with golden buttons and embellishments. It looked nearly black, much like the color of her gown. Alveen couldn't help but wonder if Mysti had somehow known, as she was always too encouraging to have her match Luka. He didn't make eye contact with her, he looked out over the crowd. Alveen did the same, noticing the citizens dressed in their finest clothes. King Viktor now stood in front of all of them at the center of the expansive and ornamentally accented balcony.

"Krumvites! I thank-you for joining the other royals and myself in celebrating the life of the late King Bowen." He paused, composing himself. "He often told me life was to be celebrated, even the losses are to be celebrated. Today we will dance, sing together and love the lives we have be given. Soon, the journey for justice will being." He went on for a short while about how he would carry on his father's acts and be a righteous king to his people, and then Viktor's tone changed, going from uplifting to aggressive and angry. "We will not allow those who have brought this hurt upon our kingdom to go freely. We will not stand by and do nothing. We will get our revenge!" Many of the crowd cheered, but the royals all stayed quiet. Some of them applauded quietly, but before their eyes, the prince once full of humor was transforming into a vengeful king.

A staff member brought out a container holding King Bowens ashes, handing them to King Viktor. He kissed the container as if saying goodbye. "King Bowen will join our ancestors as protectors of our kingdom!" He swirled his hands around the container now sitting on the ledge until all the ashes were floating in the air like a thick cloud toward the edge of the dome. The ashes soon began to take shape of a towering statue of the late King set between the other royals that had passed. Queen Lovisa, Queen Karolyn and King Hunter raised their arms, forcing sparks and bolts of lightning down onto the molded cloud of ashes. The remains solidified into a statue of foggy glass.

"Let us celebrate!" He called out with a large smile. The crowd cheered and shifted as everyone headed into the castle. King Viktor turned around to the royals behind him. "We may want to mingle for a while until they are all settled." Music began to play on the level below them as they all walked back into the castle. Luka and her were the last to pass through the door.

"Princess." He bowed holding eye contact with her, until looking up and down her gown. "You have an infatuation with dressing to match me." He gave her a half smile.

"I have a feeling this is the other way around." She said, and then jokingly whispered as she stepped towards him. "I believe it is you who has an infatuation with me." He raised an eyebrow, "With matching me, that is." She quickly corrected herself, letting out a small laugh as she walked through the doorway. He rolled his eyes, leading her in with his hand on the small of her back. They stood in silence near the door, waiting for the crowd to fill the ballroom before they entered. Luka's guard walked up handing him a small box. The King opened it, putting the lid underneath before pulling out a solid silk navy mask with sharp points leaning outward above and below his right eye, like ice shards. He handed the box back to his guard.

"Well, put it on. Let's see." Alveen encouraged.

"I think I'll wait until right before we go in." Alveen looked around and saw everyone else in their masks already. "Where is yours?"

"Oh, I-" Before she could tell him she had no idea about this and didn't bring one, one of the Krumvite staff members walked up to her, a fairy. Caspian and Nikoli stepped in front of her protectively. Her pink eyes reflected slight fear being confronted by the warriors in front of her. Alveen stood tall between the two of them, waving them to fall back. "What can I do for you?" She smiled.

"I, um.." The girl paused looking between them all. "There was a delivery for you." Caspian stepped forward before Alveen could intervene, reaching for the box in the girl's hand. "It was delivered via cave turtle Your Highness. There was no inscription as to who sent it."

"I don't like the look of this Princess." Caspian reached forward, opening the box. A golden mask sat on red velvet, the mask covered in artistic designs of shells like her gown. She looked up to Caspian.

"I do need a mask, maybe someone from the palace sent it?"

"Princess, why wouldn't they sign something or have summoned us to be expecting it?" He counteracted. Nikoli stepped forward.

"I have to agree, Princess. I strongly recommend not accepting it."

"What could be wrong with a mask?" She asked. Neither of them had an answer, but the looks on their faces reflected their seriousness. "How rude is it to show up without a mask?" she asked.

"It is insulting to say the least. The fact that a royal was not properly prepared for a memorial would not be good." Nikoli explained reluctantly.

"Can I trust that I have two wonderful, strong guards that will look out for me?" She asked. They both placed a fist over their heart and bowed to her. She returned the gesture. "Then allow me to accept this gift. And should something happen, I will count on the two of you to be on alert and protect me, should it come to that." She was not worried about anything being horribly wrong with the gift in front of her. She reached in the box and tied it under her pinned up hair. "Shall we?" She returned to Luka's side as the royals all walked down to the main floor.

"Alright Princess, this is like a grand march, they will announce you each one by one and you will walk through the crowd of citizens. Do not wave, you may nod or walk directly to the front." Caspian explained to her.

"At least someone recognizes I've never done this before." She whispered relieved to get some kind of instruction.

"You could never tell, Your Highness." He stood behind her next to Nikoli. Within the ballroom she could hear the titles being announced, then the door opening to allow one kingdom's royals in at a time. Karolyn in front of her and Luka behind her, she felt empowered being in this group.

"Her Royal Highness of Cosaint, Princess Alveen." The announcer voiced. Gasps and cheers filled the air as she entered the ballroom. Eyes filled with wonder and hope and joy. She heard people yell that it was really her, she had returned. She did as instructed and nodded only a few times to citizens before reaching the front of the room, falling in line with her peers. "His Majesty of Bulgrakta, King Luka." Cheers were less when he entered, the gasps echoed hers though his were filled with fear and intimidation. When the doors thrust open, the handsome king strode proudly and unaffected into the hall. She admired his confidence and security in himself, despite all the negativity around him. She didn't understand it. People cheered still, but a new atmosphere surrounded them. He stood on her side, allowing King Viktor to announce the beginning of the ball.

As the citizens began to talk and laugh over their own conversations, Viktor approached her before she could speak to anyone else. "Princess, may I have the first dance?" Her eyes were shocked, she quickly looked to Willow. She gestured to go on, mouthing that she understood even though her eyes were hurt.

"Um, of course." She took the King's hand and walked to the dance floor under thousands of watchful eyes. Music began to play, taking the focus partially off them as others joined on the dance floor.

"The citizens seem to be in awe by you." He spoke. He was not looking at her, but watching those around them.

"I can imagine it's exciting for them hearing of everything that has happened involving myself." He made no attempt to further conversation so she took it upon herself to question him. "Are you okay Viktor?"

"Of course." He stated, still not meeting her eyes.

"You do not seem the same. I understand the hardship you are going through, and some others may understand it better than I. Vengeance is not the right choice." He spun her off toward one side of the ballroom further out of site. As they danced through the doorway onto the empty patio his grip tightened on her hand and waist. He pulled her close to him, even though she was pulling back slightly uncomfortable.

"Do not tell me you understand." He whispered angrily into her ear, still holding her tight. They stopped moving. "And do not tell me what is the best choice or not. You were always sent away. You never had to deal with your problems." Alveen tried pulling away, but Viktor held her tightly. She took a deep breath trying to call upon a sliver of her magic to shock him, just enough to make him let her go. Nothing came. She tried focusing again, and nothing happened. Like she had no access to magic at all.

"Viktor, let me go." She tried to pull herself away from him. He wrapped his arm around her waist, lifting her off the ground so she no longer had traction. He continued squeezing her until she felt a cruel pop in her chest. She could hardly breathe. She wanted to scream, but the small amount of air being allowed into her lungs was preventing that from happening.

"Or what?" He teased, his eyes were glazed over. Something was wrong. "You'll blow me up? Good luck explaining that one when you start a civil war on top of an existing world war." She used her elbow and jab him in the jaw, forcing him to drop her. Air flooded back into her lungs, her ribs causing a sharp pain with every inhale.

"Caspian! Nikoli!" She shouted, bent over still holding her injury. The centaurs had been watching from a distance, unaware of the danger she was in because the scene before them looked intimate, not threatening. The King stood back up and without a beat clasped his arms around her torso, causing a screaming pain in her chest while also limiting her defenses. Within moments the centaurs were at her side. Caspian pulled The King off of her, knocking off his crown. Nikoli protectively blocked Alveen with his body and Caspian stood in front of him once he released The King.

"Princess, are you alright? Did he hurt you?" Alveen was breathing heavily from her struggle, but she stood upright to hide the worse of her injuries.

"No. I am not alright." She turned from her guards to The King. "What is your problem? I have done nothing to you. Why would you attack me?" Viktor stood there, looking at his hands as if he has never seen them before.

"Alveen, I'm so sorry, I don't know what came over me." His eyes showed his words were genuine, the glazed over look now gone. Caspian slowly reached for his crown to hand it back.

"Your Majesty, where did you get this crown?" He hadn't touched it yet.

"Um, I'm not sure. It was with my ensemble this morning." Caspian looked over the crown, then to Alveen.

"He was cursed. The crown, look. Inside it's inscribed with a spell. Someone meant to overpower him.". Alveen immediately wondered if her mysterious gift was doing the same to her, only draining her magic instead. She reached up pulling the string loose under her hair, letting the mask fall down to the ground. She didn't feel any different. She took a deep breath, trying to summon magic enough to heal her ribs. With a long inhale she touched the sparks inside her and grabbed on tightly. She summoned the energy from the water around the sphere, giving herself the extra energy to heal. She felt grotesque pops as her ribs snapped back into place, letting out a small whimper of pain. Someone tried blocking her magic, coincidentally while King Viktor was possessed with anger? There was nothing coincidental about this. Willow, Hunter and Luka walked out onto the patio, taking in the scene of Viktor with a bleeding lip and Alveen swarmed by her guards

"What is going on here?" Hunter demanded.

"The King. He was cursed." Caspian took his sword and held the crown out to the other royals.

"By vines, look at that. It's inscribed to possess him, it seems." King Hunter looked between the two of them. "What happened?" Alveen looked to Viktor to explain.

"I didn't mean to. I was sort of forceful with her. Like I wanted to attack her."

"Alveen, are you alright?" King Luka whispered walking to her side. She covered her wrist, knowing there would soon be a bruise visible, everything else was under her gown.

"I will be, yes. I don't want to interrupt anyone's fun. Thankfully, we were out of sight so the citizens will not notice the scene." She debated on staying, but someone deliberately tried to block her magic, and possibly even force Viktor to attack her. She needed to speak with Caspian. "Caspian. Nikoli." She called. "Escort me to my chambers please. I think I've enjoyed dancing enough for one evening." She leaned down grabbing her mask by the ribbon and walked away, hearing their hooves click against the stone behind her. The royals all exchanged confused glances, unsure of how to handle the situation. Alveen felt the mark on her waist where Viktor's hand was just forcefully holding her, throbbing with every step. Apparently her art of healing was not as strong as her fighting skills.

Alveen threw her door open tossing her mask on the bed, waiting until Caspian and Nikoli were inside and shut the door.

"Princess, are you alright?"

"No Caspian. I am not alright. Not even a little." She paced in front of the fireplace. "Someone blocked my magic. That mask, I should have listened to you, it blocked my magic." Caspian looked at her concerned.

"What do you mean it blocked it?"

"I mean while I was being attacked by someone I had considered a close friend and ally, I tried to summon magic to shock him enough so I could get out of his grasp and there was nothing. I could not access it, it was gone. When you pointed out his crown being cursed, I untied my mask and after it left my skin, I managed to heal myself and reach into my magic again. That is what I mean." She was upset and stern, her voice like she wanted to yell but she kept her voice low. Nikoli walked to the bed, using his gloved hand to hold up the mask, letting it spin until he saw the engraved words. "She's right. Look here." He held out the mask so Caspian could see. "I've never seen anything this powerful before. I didn't even know you could block someone like that." He said. Caspian pinched the bridge of his nose, deep in thought.

● ● ●

"This is obviously no coincidence." He started. "We must keep this quiet until we find out more information. If we reveal this too soon to the public then our chances of finding the culprit are nearly impossible."

"Who do you think it could have been?" Caspian looked at her, sympathetic as if she was not going to like the answer. "Tell me. I have every right to know."

"My immediate thought is Zakarian. Word of his betrayal may not have reached the depths, making his delivery possible." Alveen stared at him waiting for an explanation. "Sea creatures are for the most part are members of Solas Kingdoms, cave turtles are such creatures. They would not do a favor for someone of the Dorcha tribes." He paused, pacing as he thought. "My other thought is the sorceress, because she does have the power to bend the will of certain individuals. Not many though. Her methods are more of an epic battle though, like the attack on the Night Sky Ball. She is not sneaky and strategic like this suggests." He paused in front of the fireplace, "Or it could be someone we have not even thought of. But those are the two obvious suspicions." A knock came at her door. Alveen stood, inhaling her magic until she felt it tingling in her arm, ready to release at a moment's notice. The centaurs were on full alert as Caspian pulled the door open while allowing it to shield his armored body.

"I just wanted to check on The Princess." King Luka stood outside, his mask off and his face wrinkled with concern. Alveen relaxed a little at the site of him. Caspian looked to Alveen for confirmation, she nodded. "Um, is everything okay? You all look tense." His eyes immediately went to her wrist, it had already started bruising, his face turned pale with anger. His eyes grew dark like clouds, and she understood a sliver of why people feared him simply by the look on his face. "That bitter fool. When I get my hands on him, I swear bruises will be the last of his worries." He headed toward the door with haste, blocked by Caspian.

"Tell him." He said.

"You trust him?" Alveen asked her guard, unbelieving.

"I've had him followed, I don't have any reason to worry." Caspian explained with a pleasing look on his face.

"You had me followed?" Luka looked at him impressed. "I like your guard. He does his job well. I would do the same." He nodded to the guard respectfully. "Now if you'll excuse me, I have business with The King."

"Alveen." Caspian said again, enforcing that she needed to explain the severity of the situation.

"What? What do you need to tell me?" Alveen gestured towards the two chairs in front of the fireplace. Luka exhaled as if he were defeated, but trudged over like his feet were still trying to find King Viktor.

"Viktor wasn't the only one that was cursed." She began. He stared into her eyes patiently. "I didn't actually have a mask for the ball. One arrived just in time, delivered especially for me."

"Who was it from?"

"We're not sure?"

"I take it back, you're terrible guards. You would allow your Princess to take a gift from an anonymous giver?" He rose to his feet in a flash, addressing the guards that stood more than a foot taller than him. He was fearless.

"You're correct. We should have done a more thorough check, however The Princess insisted as she wished not to insult The King." Luka looked at her.

"Are you honestly that gullible?" He closed his eyes for a second, collecting himself once he realized he was being rude in light of what just happened. "I apologize. Anyways, what happened?"

"It cut off my magic. While Viktor was attacking me, I couldn't defend myself with magic. I managed to get away but.. well it doesn't matter. But my magic is back now. As soon as I untied the mask and it left my face I was able to reach in and heal myself for the most part." Luka sat silent for a moment.

"What did he do?" Alveen stood up, shrugging her shoulders when she spoke.

"A few bruises and broken ribs, but I'm really fine. I'm more concerned with who is trying to set a civil war off and why I'm the one that is being targeted." Even his perfectly groomed dark facial hair couldn't hide his jaw tensing up as she spoke.

"You are too good of a friend, do you know that? Defending him while comforting me, when you were the one attacked." Alveen folded her arms, holding back her pain. He cleared his throat looking to Caspian. He nodded leading Nikoli out of the room. Alveen looked confused.

"Whoa, wait. Where are you going?" She pointed to them.

"Giving you the chance to enjoy the rest of the ball, Princess." Caspian walked out, leaving her with Luka who was now standing beside her.

"May I have this dance?" He held out his hand.

"You are so odd." She said, unable to hold back a smile. He motioned for her to join him, still holding out his hand. She rolled her eyes as she clasped her hand in his. He pulled her close and she instinctively wrapped her arms around his waist, taking him by surprise as she rested her head on his chest. He relaxed and wrapped his powerfully built arms around her shoulders as if he were protecting her. "Thank-you." She whispered.

"For what?"

"For being my only friend." She laughed. "Honestly, if Caspian trusts you then I know you are a worthy friend." She pulled back and looked him in the eyes. "and for constantly checking on me and making sure I'm okay. You know you don't have to do that right?"

"Ha, your only friend. That is a joke you know. I've seen the way you interact with people. I've seen those you surround yourself with." She rested her head against him again, making him want to keep protecting her. It made him feel sick that he wasn't there to defend one of the only people he knew he could trust.

"I am very good at political niceness." She blushed, quoting one of the first things she ever heard him say. He shook his head, letting out a small laugh, rumbling against her ear. "I am respectful to others but I do not trust very many. This is all still very new to me, so thank-you, for being my only trustworthy confidant."

"Of course, Princess. Thank-you for being mine as well." He gently ran his fingers up her back, until he felt her body tense. Her ribs had not completely healed. "What's wrong?" He saw her face before she put her 'I'm fine' mask back on. She was still in pain. "How bad is it?" He asked seriously.

"It hurts." She breathed in. "But I will be fine."

"I'm going to get a healer. I'll send your guards back in. I won't be long." Before she could protest he was charging out the door.

"Caspian! Why didn't you stop him?"

"He knows the consequences if he wants to fight another king. I guarantee you he is not that dumb."

"No, he is actually brilliant." She admitted. "You really think he is a trustworthy friend?" she asked.

"I do, Your Highness. And I think his intimidating demeanor will come in handy." Alveen went into the bathroom, washing off the dried blood from where her ribs had pierced her skin and changed into a pair of athletic pants and a tank top for the healer. It didn't take long for the chill of the sea to overcome her, forcing her to put on tall wool socks and a cable knit sweater.

Soon King Luka and the healer returned. He sat in one of the chairs by the fireplace, acting as if he was not watching. The healer requested that she pulled up her shirt, exposing the wounds. She looked at Luka and gave him a plea with her eyes for him to look away. He listened for only a couple seconds when the gasp of the healer pulled his curiosity back to her. Her shirt was folded under her bra, keeping herself covered, but her waistline was a dark shade of purple and black and there were two small puncture wounds where her ribs pierced through her skin before she healed herself.

"You healed yourself nicely, Your Highness. Allow me to finish." Alveen gestured with approval as she stood exposed. It was not very long as her injuries were all superficial now. Luka watched as the colors faded and with it the color returned to his face. He stood by, sick to his stomach seeing her wounds. Knowing he was only a second away from his best friend and could have helped her.

"Are *you* going to be alright?" Alveen asked mockingly. He glared at her, not finding humor in this as she seemed to right now. She pulled her shirt down and wrapped herself in her sweater as she thanked the healer and sat next to Luka.

"Your scar." He stated. His eyes said he wanted to know more, but he didn't say anything.

"Pretty nasty, right? I'm not sure why they haven't been able to heal it. I've been through multiple healing sessions now, but it just…" She paused, feeling it through her shirt. "Won't go away." She gave a forced smile before pulling her chair closer to the fire.

"What is it from?" he asked looking her in the eyes now.

"Syragon." She stated bluntly. "Actually the attack that happened before the royal walk." The matter of fact tone in her voice didn't amuse him.

"You understand how serious this is, right? I know you're just trying to lighten the mood, but you are in very real danger." He said keeping eye contact, making sure she understood.

"Luka, I understand that. I am just trying not to panic and become paranoid. I will figure this out."

• • •

"You don't have to be independent you know. It's alright to have others in your life that you can depend on." Alveen became irritated suddenly.

"I tried that once. And then my brother betrayed me, taking the only person that was actually teaching me about this world and left me with no one but myself." Alveen stood up walking to the door, Luka following. "I know I don't have to be independent, it's just easier and hurts less this way. Plus I have Caspian and Nikoli."

"Are you mad? Seriously? Because I suggested you work with others to figure out this assassination attempt? Because that's exactly what this was. I know what it's like to be independent, so I get that, if you've forgotten." He was heated, raising his voice as he argued with her. "I also recognize a mutually beneficial alliance when I see one, and I recommend you don't let this one go to waste." He pulled the doors open while yelling over his shoulder. "Good night, Princess." She was frustrated and went directly to her bed for the evening. Luka stood outside her door for a moment, confirming that Caspian and Nikoli would be there all night. She may be the most difficult, frustrating woman he had ever met, but he would still do what he could to protect her.

~Chapter IV~
Loxley, LLC

Bright and early, Caspian and Nikoli led Alveen to Atsalta, King Viktor's ship. Despite the recent events, this was her only form of transportation between kingdoms during such short notice. She remained comfortably sandwiched between her guards as staff members loaded the ship.

"Will you wait outside my door? I will inform with The Banri that we will be leaving port soon." Caspian nodded following her, only for them to be abruptly cut off by the familiar king in a fur cloak. "What are you doing here?" Alveen questioned. Luka flashed her a smile.

"You don't honestly think I would allow you to travel with him after what happened, do you?" He returned in a low voice. Alveen folded her arms over her casual apparel.

"Excuse me? You won't *allow* me? Let me make a few things clear, King Luka. First, how dare you act as if you have any kind of authority over me. Second, you could be used to attack me just as well as Viktor could be used again. Lastly, I have guards. Willow and Hunter have guards, what is you being here going to help with?" She asked stepping closer to him, un-intimidated, with every point she made. He couldn't help but smile at the irritable woman standing only to his chest. If anything, she intimidated *him* with her confidence.

"My apologies, Princess. You make fair points, however I believe other than your guards I was the only one that confirmed your well being after the incident, so please tell me who actually cares about your well being." She was silenced for now. He had a point. "Shall we?" He waved his arm gesturing her forward to her chamber aboard the ship. She looked between her guards, defeated.

Luka sat in the chair in front of her fireplace while Alveen stood across the room with a foggy version of her grandmother levitating in front of her.

"Hello Grandmother."

"Alveen, to what do I owe the pleasure? How has your trip been thus far?" She looked as if she were in the throne room.

"It has been eventful." Alveen went on to explain the events of last night forcing her to leave the ball early. "But until we figure out what is going on, I wanted to inform you that we are going to be leaving for Loxley soon."

"You're on the ship after that happened?" She asked impressed. "Is someone there with you?"

"Caspian and Nikoli, and the handful of other guards now. Why wouldn't they be with me?" She asked confused.

"I meant in the room now. I can sense the presence of another." Alveen rolled her eyes looking at Luka giving her a childish grin.

"So nice to hear your voice, Queen Vailion." He spoke as he joined Alveen's side facing the cloud.

"King Luka. I'm surprised to see you traveled for the memorials. You're normally far too busy for such pleasantries."

"I thought this would be a perfect time to make an appearance after all this time." She looked between the two of them.

"I'm happy to see you've made acquaintances, Alveen."

"He insisted on being my extra security based upon what happened." The Queen gave an unbelieving nod.

"Of course."

"How is Tanilly doing?" Alveen switched the subject.

"Very well, surprisingly. It seemed her mother didn't give her much education, but we have discovered she does have the ability to access magic. Meaning Malika must have had even a sliver of elven in her. We will continue training and see how she progresses."

"Where is she now? May I speak to her?" The Queen motioned for the young girl to stand by her.

"Princess!" She exclaimed.

"Hello Beautiful. How is your schooling going? Tell me your favorite thing." She said sitting on her bed.

"I do love it. There are so many books. I think my favorite is reading. I have found so many wonderful stories in the library here."

"Is Ollahm Hilfyro teaching you?" the little girl shook her head that he was. "He is a wonderful teacher. He taught me most of the things I know." She looked at The Queen with her eyes full of excitement. She ran off shortly after.

"Please let me know when you reach Loxley." Alveen agreed before waving her hand through the fog ending the connection.

"I don't think she likes me" Luka said leaning in his chair.

"I don't even like you." Alveen said jokingly. She tried to hold a straight face but a smile appeared on her face, giving away the lack of seriousness in her comment. Luka simply shook his head and grinned, unwilling to return her banter. He walked over to her extending his arm.

"You may want to grab a cloak." Digging through her trunk she pulled out a black fur lined cloak to drape over her shoulders. She held the crook of his arm letting him lead her to the deck for departure. It wasn't necessary that they were there, but Alveen did enjoy watching everything happen.

• • •

Orders were given and after they passed the newly formed statue of King Bowen and sailed through the caverns, they were back diving deep underwater. Creatures swam in all directions as they parted swarming schools.

Luka watched with wonder as predators flocked the sphere. Standing on the deck with him, arm in arm, she realized she felt comfortable again. She felt relaxed and she wasn't afraid, despite being surrounded by dozens of dangerous looking creatures outside the barrier. She wrapped her arms around his bicep, pulling herself minutely closer to him. She wanted to cherish this temporary sense of safety she currently felt.

Within hours, they surfaced, arriving at the next kingdom. Everything seemed to be in pristine condition. Pulling into the port Alveen noticed even all the boats and piers were impeccably clean.

"Get ready for a culture shock." Willow commented passing by her and Luka. They had parted, walking separately down the staircase onto the dull grey stone leading to what looked like an elevator door in the mountainside. Caspian and Nikoli remained on either side of The Princess. When the metallic silver doors opened, inside looked to be a large room. It seemed empty with its white floor, white walls and bright lights lining the ceiling. No one else seemed to think it weird, so she followed along. The doors closed and the oversized elevator raised into the sky, bolting through the vertical tunnel until it reached the top of the mountain. When the doors opened again a modern sleek lobby waited for her on the other side. It was fast paced and everyone was dressed in business attire passing in front of a large white desk. The elf behind the desk stood up without a smile walking towards them. Her hair was cut in a short bob and her green eyes were dull. Her toned elven figure was wrapped in a finely tailored grey dress that held no accents of any kind.

"Welcome to Loxley." The woman spoke before bowing and addressing each of them. "If you would follow me please, Queen Karolyn is expecting you." The woman turned on her black stiletto heels walking like a runway model toward a corridor with windows lining one side. Looking through the glass Alveen was amazed. A valley below held the palace at the center, a tall figure looking as if a dozen sky scrapers were connected. Over the rolling hills below, highways filled with vehicles fancier than anything she had seen before stretched out across the city below. Caspian cleared his throat, encouraging her to move on with the group. She gave him an embarrassed smile.

Passing through a glass door she saw Queen Karolyn in a fitted knee length dress with a high neckline, standing welcoming the royals as they entered. The polished black marble floor reflected everything. On the far side of the room a modern fireplace was inset in the wall over two feet off the floor with a glass front. Everything seemed modern and luxurious; no hints of anything rustic here like every other kingdom.

"Princess Alveen. What a pleasure to have you visiting. I hope you find Loxley to be a pleasant kingdom."

"I was admiring the city on my walk over. It is unique and fascinating." The Queen didn't smile, though she did not sound rude when she thanked her.

"We have a tight schedule as the memorial has to be worked between everyone's daily schedules. I hope you will all not be offended by my lack of presence as you can imagine this recent tragedy has caused a slight upset in our system." She stood on the opposite side of the room, addressing all of them as if she were their teacher. "Princess Alveen, as you are the only one who has not been here I will leave it to the other royals to show you around. The memorial will be precisely before dinner." She started toward the door, "You will be free to go after the memorial dinner or in the morning after." She stated bluntly. "Enjoy your visit." She curtsied and pushed open the glass door. The click of her professional heels on the marble echoed for only a few moments before King Viktor spoke up.

"Well my lady, shall we begin the tour?" He said bowing to Alveen.

"Of course." She replied monotone. Viktor and Willow walked at the front of the group. Queen Lovisa and The Princesses had not yet arrived, leaving her to walk behind with Luka and Hunter.

"Are you alright, Princess?" King Hunter whispered stepping up to her side. Alveen faced him, her eyes felt tired but she knew she had to push through the day.

"I believe so. There's just been so much going on and I did not sleep much last night." She explained, brushing off her exhaustion.

"Understandable." He stated, clasping his hands behind his back as he kept pace with The Princess. "Loxley is a little different than most of ours, much more modern I suppose you could say. They fancy machinery and technology."

"Machinery?" Alveen asked. She hadn't seen anything resembling a machine.

"Vehicles, more so, the most pristine cars, jets, trains, and such. Many of them are fueled by magic and it takes quite a bit of energy to operate one, but Loxlians seem to have perfected that." Alveen thought about the vehicles she saw from the mountain balcony when they entered. "They are all unique, created from the precious metals in the soils in this kingdom."

They were now a few levels lower, closer to the main city but still with enough of a view to oversee the citizens. Alveen understood what King Hunter was saying now. Below her on towering raised roads were cars of the most luxurious designs. She couldn't even think of anything she had seen that looked like these, they seemed almost futuristic. She saw one person get out of a vehicle. There were no steering wheels. How did they drive these things? She wondered.

As they traveled through the city, they finally reached the central palace. The structure looked like a large city was pushed together allowing all the skyscrapers to connect. Everywhere they went there was little décor and no color. Everything was shades of whites, grays, blacks and tans but it all shined and reflected giving a sense of being brand new. Creatures walked around whispering orders to the others following them that seemed to be assistants to each of them. No matter where they visited in this kingdom, the feel of being in an expansive office never ended.

"Where will we be staying?" She asked toward the end of the tour. King Hunter held his arm out to lead her to her chamber.

"We received some of the most beautiful views as guests of the kingdom." After a short ride back up to the top floor of the entrance in the mountain they reached their chambers. They were not much further past where they spoke with Queen Karolyn earlier. The corridor began to curve above allowing the sun to shine through the wall and ceiling leaving no need for lighting. The hall took a sharp left and then a right leading into a marbled set of curved stairs only wrapping to the level above. "The bottom floor here will be for Princess Willow, Queen Lovisa, The Princesses and Myself. Up the stairs your chamber will be the furthest down the hall, and King Luka and King Viktor also have chambers on the top floor as well." She followed The King and his echoing boots up the solid staircase encased with a white railing with the reverberation of her guards hooves behind her. Upon reaching the top floor, the wall dulled a little from bright white to gray and the ceiling above was made entirely of glass, allowing the sun to light their walk. The doors were all silver metal resembling an elevator panel. Caspian and Nikoli stood to the side, waiting for her.

"They are DNA coded. You must scan your hand and eye to be allowed in." He gestured for her to stand in front of the last door. Hesitantly she stepped in front of the reflective door waiting for something to happen. A small screen jutted out from the wall to the right of the door with the outline of a hand. She placed her palm down on the cold screen and a white line traced over her skin. It played an approving tone before sliding back into the wall. Suddenly a screen appeared on the door showing the scan of an eye. Alveen stood closer with her eyes wide open, allowing another white light to scan her retina. Approval granted. The screen disappeared and the heavy metallic door slid to one side allowing her access.

"This is certainly not the usual kingdom around here, is it?" she asked walking into her room. It didn't look much different than the room she was in earlier. The black marble floor reflected the shining sun that poured through the glass around her. The entire glass wall extended in a curved fashion over the ceiling like a large aquarium allowing her the light to see every detail of her temporary quarters. The walls in her room thankfully provided privacy from her neighbors though. Her walls were bright white with a slim black glass-front fireplace and only a few photos of nature scenes on the walls. The bathroom was all whites and blacks as well and the bedding matched the modern décor. A small sitting area was accented with a diminutive display of white flowers and mirrors. As she walked to the glass wall to take in her view, a screen above the fireplace lit up in the wall, revealing Queen Karolyn's face and another outline of a hand.

"Princess, The Queen is calling for you. Place your hand here to allow her visual connection." King Hunter explained, standing back by the doorway as Alveen took in her surroundings. She reached her hand up into the outline and soon Queen Karolyn was in a video above the hearth.

"Princess. I'm glad to see you've made it to your chambers. Did you enjoy your tour?"

"Um.." Alveen was use to technology, she just hadn't seen much of it in this world yet. "Yes, it was wonderful. I admire the work ethic in your kingdom."

"Thank-you. We try to train our young ones in the work environment as soon as possible. Working hard is the only thing that will get the results everyone wants." She explained. "I was actually hoping to speak with you for a moment in regards to the memorial. I need another royal to assist me in the ceremony."

"Of course, whatever I can help with."

"Perfect, we will go over the details tomorrow beforehand. Thank-you Princess. I look forward to speaking with you further." The video ended and the wall took its white color again.

"I believe I'm going to stay in for the evening. Thank-you for escorting me to my room, King Hunter." She curtsied to the older gentleman.

"Of course, Princess. Traveling takes a toll, that is for certain." He walked out of the door and her guards walked in.

"We will stand guard outside, let us know if you need anything." Caspian acknowledged.

"You may come in if you wish. I have plenty of room in here. It would be nice to have some company I don't have to be so formal around." She explained facing the centaur. He nodded and motioned for Nikoli to join.

"So Princess, did you actually enjoy your visit?" Nikoli asked with a smile on his face, his blue eyes reflecting his joking manner.

"It wasn't horrible, it's just a little too serious for me." She explained sitting in one of the black chairs near them. "I really should reach out to grandmother." Motioning her wrists to summon for fog before her, The Banri appeared.

"I see you've made it to Loxley." She said in a relieved tone. She must have looked at the room she was in.

"I have. It's different, you were right. Queen Karolyn asked me to help with the memorial, what would she need me to do?"

"Ah, their memorials are much different than ours. There is no celebration. Just a short speech. It will be a long moment of silence while he is buried in the mountain. She may need your assistance with that."

"Do they cremate or bury whole bodies here?"

"He will actually be crystallized. They turn the bodies into precious gems." Her eyebrows raised showing Alveen that was different for even this world.

"I see." She paused not sure how to continue. "Is Allicent being tended to properly?" The Princess asked innocently enough.

"Yes my dear. He is being taken care of by my own personal attendant." Alveen grew somber for a moment as her thoughts went to Beastil, Samual's alicorn.

"What about Beastil? Who is caring for him?"

"The same. I had to bring in another assistant so they could all be properly cared for." She explained with a slight grin on her face.

"I was thinking of possibly extending this trip." She started, wanting to see The Queen's initial reaction.

"Where?" She said slowly. "And why?" Her eyes held Alveen's attention.

"I was thinking that since I will be visiting all but Irielle and Bulgrakta, maybe since I am over on this side of the world I could make a quick stop in Irielle. I'm sure King Hunter and Princess Willow wouldn't mind. I would need to speak with Queen Lovisa tonight though to ensure the trip is in good timing for her."

"I understand. What about Bulgrakta? I'm sure King Luka would be offended if you did not make a stop there as well."

"I will travel there soon, with your blessing of course. I just believe since I am so close to this other kingdom, I should take advantage and be diplomatic."

"I see no reason why this wouldn't work. You seem to be doing well and I have not heard of any insults yet. You will need to continue training when you return. Immediately."

"Of course, Your Majesty." She curtsied. Alveen wasn't sure of where that idea had come from, but she felt a sudden strong urge to visit and see how different all these kingdoms were.

"Let me know before you slumber what Lovisa says. I will be waiting for an answer." The fog dispersed, leaving Alveen alone with her guards.

"You have a desire to travel to Irielle, Your Highness?"

"I guess so. I hadn't really thought about it until now." She summoned Queen Lovisa, not wanting to go out and find her.

"Princess! What a wonderful surprise." The Queen answered enthusiastically.

"Princess Alveen! Where are you?" The Princesses yelled as they saw her face.

"Hello girls! Hello, Your Majesty. I'm actually in my room in Loxley. Where are you?"

"We've just arrived in Loxley! Will we get to see you soon?" Princess Ava asked excitedly.

"That's up to The Queen I would think." She turned her attention back to Lovisa who was smiling at her daughter's excitement.

"I think we can arrange for that. Alveen, I will be having dinner sent to our chamber within the hour. The girls need to eat and get to bed, they've had a long day. If you wish to come join us we would be delighted."

"Oh, of course. That sounds like so much fun, will there be enough for my guards? I can't wait to see you girls!" She waved excitedly.

"Of course, I always make sure of that." Lovisa smiled.

"Bye Alveen!" Princess Brielle waved with an adorable smile on her face. Alveen waved her hand dissipating the fog again.

"It looks like we have a dinner date." She said smiling to Nikoli and Caspian. "Allow me to freshen up and we can head down." She said, encouraging them to stand outside and wait.

Alveen, flanked by her guards, walked down to Lovisa's room and was greeted with a deep bow from her guards as the doors opened allowing her in.

"Alveen!" The Princesses sang in unison as they ran up to her.

"Hello beautifuls!" She squatted down and wrapped them both in her arms. "It's been so long." She joked. "How was your journey?"

"It was sooo long and boring." Brielle said dramatically.

"We've got seafood darling, if you're hungry." Queen Lovisa walked up and hugged Alveen.

"I would love to. Caspian. Nikoli. If you're hungry, please eat." She turned back to the Queen while they went to get food. "I was actually wondering if after this memorial would be a good time for me to visit? I figured since I am already all the way over here, I would love to see your kingdom and learn about your culture."

"Yes! Oh we would love to have you there! I will summon after dinner and ensure the proper arrangements are made. King Hunter and Princess Willow will be joining also? What about King Luka?"

"I will speak with them tomorrow and let you know before the memorial since it does not seem like it will take up much time."

"That sounds perfect! I am so excited to have you back Alveen." She gave her a quick hug and walked over to the buffet they had set up against the windows in their room. This room was almost identical to hers only there were two bedrooms off the main area. Where Alveen's bed sat in her room, this one boasted a large circular table surrounded by white chairs.

Alveen enjoyed the dinner provided, which was honestly a tie for the best seafood, with that provided at Krumvite. She spent time with the girls, playing games with them and talking about their kingdom and what they would do if she could visit.

"Alright ladies I believe we must be off to bed now. Princess Alveen must be tired as well."

"I am very much so. I will see you both tomorrow?" They came up and hugged her legs before leading Lovisa into their room. The Queen waved as she followed them in. Caspian approached her, ready to lead her out of the room to her own.

"Princess, King Luka is waiting for you." Alveen gave him a confused look as she followed Caspian into the wide hallway towards the marbled staircase where the dark-haired King stood.

"Dining without me." Luka shook his head in jest. "I don't mean to keep you, I didn't see you at dinner and wanted to make sure you ate." He was holding a box with many vegetables and fruits on it. "They don't believe in meat if your thinking what I was."

"I was actually." She laughed. "Oh, since you are here, I was wondering if you would be interested in traveling to Irielle after the memorial? I figured since I am so close I might as well stop in and learn more about culture."

"I think I'll pass." He laughed. "I have no desire to enter a kingdom unless it is mandatory through our alliance." He stated bluntly.

"Suit yourself. I thought you would enjoy the opportunity to spend time with the only other royal you speak to." She was making fun of him, but his hard exterior didn't shake and only offered an eye roll in return.

"You think highly of yourself, Your Highness." He bowed, purposely trying to shake her.

"It must be the company I've been keeping lately." She glared at him, directing her comment to his hidden arrogance. She walked passed him up the stairs. He forcibly had to hold back a smile at her quick wit. She turned when she reached the top of the stairs looking down on him.

"Would you like to join us? We were just going to sip a hot beverage and enjoy the view."

He followed her up the stairs without a verbal response, Caspian and Nikoli behind him. Once in the room they all sat in the chairs in front of the glass wall, watching the futuristic cars speed across the raised streets. The glow of lights illuminated the buildings one by one with the sun disappearing from the sky. Alveen had warm peppermint drinks brought to them as they relaxed for the evening. Luka didn't say much other than the occasional jest. Alveen had come to notice how often he tried to insult her and be rude, which is exactly what everyone else saw of him, only he could never keep a straight face when she would put him in his place. Caspian and Nikoli looked relaxed in body but their faces were still alert as they admired the city below them.

"It's best I return to my chamber now. I will see you tomorrow morning for breakfast?"

"I don't even know where to go around here."

"Then I will pick you up. They don't actually have a dining hall, they do banquets, which is at the palace. However, they have a small area with some wonderful breakfast food." Luka's voice was professional and his face masked any emotion that would suggest this was anything more than a diplomatic meeting over coffee.

"Alright. Then I will see you in the morning."

The guards left to get sleep, replaced by two others that she recognized from training. Once she was changed and finished her drink, sleep was easy for her to find.

In the morning, a knock on her door woke her before the sun did. Bolting from her bed thinking something was wrong she unlocked the door to see Luka standing there with a tray full of food.

"Good morning, Your Majesty. I thought we were going to get food?"

"I had been up for a while and decided to surprise you. Besides, it doesn't seem often that I get your presence alone." She noticed his eyes passing over her with a raised brow. "Did you really just wake up?"

"What do you mean? Of course I just woke up. The sun isn't even up yet." She spoke was a sliver disbelief in her voice.

"I meant you don't look nearly as terrible as I would have expected just rolling out of bed." She looked down at her leggings and t-shirt. It was not revealing or immodest; she was grateful for that. She thought about how Samual had made fun of her for her bed head on the plane when they first met.

"I'm sure my hair looks wonderful." She flipped her head over and ran her fingers through her curls, pulling them up into a messy bun.

"Beautiful." He said as he walked past her. Her scenes were teased with the aromas she was unaccustomed to. Spices from the fluffy cream filled pastries mingled with the gamey meats on the tray, making for a mouthwatering combo. It caused her to close the door and follow The King to the table by the window where he set the tray of inviting delicacies. She eagerly folded a leg under her in one of the cushioned chairs as she reached for one of the chunks of meat. The king sat across from her, leaning back as he looked out across the ally kingdom. Alveen was unsure what to say.

"Thank-you for doing this. It was unnecessary, really."

"What better place to watch the sun rise though?" He asked. They didn't talk much over breakfast. He brought her coffee also, and admired her as she brought her knees to her chest and sipped on the gleaming silver mug. The sun began to peek out over the mountain, allowing the fiery colors to pour in through the glass, draping every inch of the otherwise mute toned room, and reflecting off Alveen's already unique irises. Luka watched her as the heated rays warmed her face and the steam from her drink danced in front of her face, moving ever so slightly as she let out long calm breathes. She glanced over at him. He wasn't smiling or glaring at her. He observed her wondering what made her so much different.

"What are you looking at? Do I really look that funny?" He grabbed his own cup and sat back not giving her a reply immediately. It seemed to be a common trait of his. Excepting no response again, The Princess stared back at him observing in the same way he was just doing. Why did others think him to be everything but what she saw? Was he simply tricking her with his compassion and generosity? She had hardly seen him speak to anyone, let alone other royals. Why her? She was not well versed, she had quite the temper and she knew she pushed his buttons on numerous occasions already, so why did he continue to pursue a friendship with her?

"Not at all. You look mesmerizing." His voice surprised her since he had left such a long pause in their conversation. She raised her eyebrows trying to hide her smile at the compliment.

"I feel as though you are being facetious." Her tone disbelieving yet again. The corner of a grin crept over The King's face as he shook his head in disagreement.

"Not even a little." He spoke low in response, holding her eye contact. She turned back to face the glass.

"The sunrise is beautiful here." She said staring out past the city to the peaks of the mountains. The bright rays of light created a thick curtain over the kingdom below making it hard to watch the daily buzzing below as the citizens began their day.

"Not as beautiful as Bulgrakta's" He said with a raised brow and smile as if he were bragging.

"Cosaint has beautiful sunrises also mister frozen tundra." He laughed outright at her mocking nickname.

"Mister frozen tundra? That doesn't seem very original now, Princess."

"It was the best I could do on short notice. It seems my wit is not fully awake yet."

"I'm disappointed." He looked at her with a serious expression. She threw him a look before scolding him.

"Well, I suppose it's a good thing I don't live to please you then." A fake smile forcibly crossed her lips making Luka chuckle and nod in approval, though he said nothing more about it before looking at the sun. It rested high in the sky above now, telling them time had passed. They sat in silence for the duration of the meal, both ensuring the tray was cleared of anything edible.

"You best get ready for the memorial." He set his cup down as headed toward the door, bowing before he headed toward the threshold, leaving her still sitting at the table.

"Thank-you for this." She said with a sympathetic glance. These little things he kept doing for her were helping her cope with everything that had happened. She knew she was supposed to be strong and not allow herself to grieve too long, but mentally she couldn't always handle it. He made it easier for her. He looked back at her as he walked out, nodding in acceptance of her gratitude.

She enjoyed the sun for a little while longer on her skin while finishing her drink. Going to her trunk she pulled out the ensemble made for today and laid it out across her bed.

The warm water poured over her in a comforting act that soothed her muscles as she stepped into the shower, taking note of the white tile that surrounded everything and the black counter top and floor that transferred seamlessly from the room. Before dressing she pulled her hair back into a tight rounded ballerina bun and let a few air-dried curls hang by her cheeks. Her gown was simple and seemed perfect for the occasion. It was a sleeveless, knee-length thick white satin dress with a high collar and v-neck. A small black belt cinched her waist matching her matte black flats. There was no detail on this dress. A short diamond crown sat on top of her smooth hair. After finishing her makeup, she stood back, pleased with her appearance. Her guards knocked on her steel door waiting for her to open it.

"Princess are you ready to go to the ceremony?"

"I believe so. Lead the way, Nikoli" He bowed and walked on ahead of her and Caspian down the marble staircase. Everyone met in the lobby, waiting for Queen Karolyn. Luka was waiting in a white button up and black dress pants with a silk black tie resting on his chest. In this moment, he looked like a proper businessman and she found she appreciated that just as much as his casual attire topped with his fur cape. They didn't make eye contact as he seemed to still be enjoying the view out the oversized windows and it looked like he was enjoying not being engaged in conversation.

The Queen entered with a stoic expression glued to her porcelain like skin. She did not look any more dressed up than normal. Her blonde bob was straightened perfectly and her crown of white gold rested perfectly balanced atop her head. Her dress was knee-length as well. A white material made up the loose, sheer long sleeves attaching to a pearl white silk bodice with a scoop neckline. Below it a black satin skirt hung loosely at her hips with a minor flare creating a peplum by her knees. She wore closed-toed glossy black high heels making her about Alveen's height now. She didn't bother with small talk or wasting time as she approached the group.

"Alright, follow me." She walked away continuing over her shoulder as if talking to an assistant. "Princess Alveen. All I need you to do is remove the stone when I ask." Alveen wasn't sure what she was talking about, but nodded in agreement as she followed The Queen. Her heels clicked on the floor as she led them all toward the fancy cars that would take them to the ceremony location on the far side of the valley.

Alveen crawled into a pearl white futuristic vehicle along with Queen Lovisa and her Princesses. She watched as the little girls took in the structures flying by them as they swooped through tunnels and around the palace buildings. Alveen watched out the window as the metallic skyscrapers towered overhead.

A large building with a glass dome sat just outside the city, already filled with citizens. There was a quiet hum of conversation as they exited the vehicles. Queen Karolyn lead the way up the staircase and through the threshold as the citizens all clapped as if an award had just been given. The guards followed their royal members down the center of the banquet hall to the stage, standing in front of it while the royals ascended. Alveen stood to the left of Karolyn, waiting for instruction.

The Queen raised her hand, silencing the audience. Queen Vailion was right. There was no speech. Karolyn raised her other hand and parted them above her head causing the roof to disappear off the building. At the center of the mountain in view, a large square stone engraved with a cursive L rested. That must have been the stone Karolyn was talking about. A group of Loxlians walked out carrying a glass casket with King Ronan's body. Shimmering diamonds, rubies, emeralds and sapphires covered the surface of his skin. She turned, having a difficult time concealing her grief as she extended her arms outward and lifted the casket into the air.

"Princess Alveen. Please raise the stone." Alveen nodded and took a deep breath stepping forward and moving her arm forward and to the side, holding it there for long enough to allow Queen Karolyn to put her brother to rest. Once the glittering casket was out of site and Karolyn dropped her hands she nodded the okay to replace the stone. Alveen summoned her magic and pushed it back and dropped her hands, clasping it behind her back as she stepped back into the line of royals. The whole procedure was eerily quiet. Queen Karolyn took a moment to compose herself before standing up straight and turning around.

"Citizens, I thank-you for taking time out of your busy day to help me put King Ronan to rest. Though his passing will cause much disrupt in our daily functions, I know you are all intelligent and together we will keep Loxley strong. For King Ronan."

"For King Ronan." They all raised a hand, chanting thrice in unison before Karolyn dismissed the ceremony. Citizens stood and in a uniformed recession they exited the building.

"That was it?" Alveen asked King Hunter standing next to her.

"Yes. They have a busy schedule here. They do not do the type of celebrations the rest of the kingdoms engage in. They are unique." Alveen nodded.

"I meant to ask you, would it be out of the question if we stopped in Irielle for a day?" Since Alveen was traveling with their entourage back to Foresi before she returned home, it seemed only right that she asked if they would come with her.

"I do not foresee that being an issue. We fly directly over the kingdom. May as well make a recreational stop." Alveen smiled and bowed before approaching Queen Lovisa.

"Foresi will be joining myself. When would be the best time to leave?" The Queen smiled clasping her hands together.

"Perfect, we can leave after dinner. It's a short flight from here. I'm sure Queen Karolyn won't mind lending an alicorn to you for the time being." Lovisa went over details and gave Alveen a time to meet them for departure. King Hunter bowed to her as he left with Princess Willow to prepare the alicorns. King Viktor stepped up to Princess Willow and they began to chat in low tones. Willow's face lit up with him around. She gave off a rather harsh appearance, unapproachable really, but when Viktor was around her, neither of them could help but smile. Alveen watched as some of the Foresi guards went to collect their personal affects. Caspian and Nikoli stood in front of the stage. Caspian ordered the others to prepare for departure and tend to the rooms we had been staying in. Alveen was heading towards the stairs to join her guards when a silk black tie appeared directly in her line of vision. She stopped in her tracks as if her feet had become molded into the floor below her. He was only a foot from her. Thankfully, she had good reflexes otherwise she would have run directly into him.

"You know my kingdom will be the only one left to visit. It would be rude if a stubborn Princess didn't present herself at my doorstep soon." She wasn't sure how to reply at first. She looked over at Caspian, her original intended destination, and he was just shrugging his shoulders with a smirk on his face. It would be rude of her to not go there? Perhaps, but they hadn't had a monarch die, nor were they in the path back home.

"If only I had a reason to go there." She shot at him with a smirk. He folded his arms and looked down at her, his usual long pause and observations taking place before he replied.

"Libraries." He finally said.

"What?"

"Our libraries are the largest and filled with valuable knowledge, more so than even Cosaint. Perhaps among all your research or studying, you could find your way to the frozen tundra, as you call it." Libraries did sound intriguing. He knew that too. She sometimes wondered if had some sort of ability to read her thoughts. Every time she thought that he would never guess what she was thinking or he would never know what to say, he proved her wrong.

"Ah, I see you've figured me all out." She said folding her arms in a mocking fashion.

"Not nearly. It takes an intellectual to know one." Though he had complimented her multiple times before, they often sounded like an obligated formality, other than maybe the night of the Night Sky Ball. Him recognizing her as knowledgeable and intelligent boosted her ego more than she cared to admit, even to herself.

"You've got my attention. Perhaps I will find my way there after I return. I do have some serious research to be done within my own kingdom if you haven't forgotten." He just looked at her as if he wanted to keep her talking, but he knew she had to leave. "I'll see you soon King Luka."

"Safe travels, Princess." He bowed and walked around her going the opposite direction, ensuring to keep his distance close enough without touching her. Her nerves twisted in her stomach.

Caspian led Alveen back to the guest corridors and to the lobby. They waited patiently outside the steel elevator door in order to reach the shoreline.

When the door parted revealing the shoreline and the Krumvite ship, she noticed everyone was already waiting on them. Krumvites scampered around on board preparing the ship, foresian guards reigned the alicorns, preparing them for flight and the other members of the monarchy stood talking with Queen Karolyn who had come to see everyone off.

"Princess! There you are. I have someone I would like you to meet." Queen Karolyn motioned for one of her staff to move forward. A tan and golden alicorn was being led to her. The creature held her head high as she pranced over to The Princess. "This is Cordelia. I understand you are needing an alicorn for the rest of your travels. I think she will be much better fitted in Cosaint." She had a soft smile on her face, this alicorn was one that was close to her heart for some reason.

"She is gorgeous. Thank-you so much Queen Karolyn." Alveen walked to her and wrapped her in an embrace. The Queen was tense for a moment before accepting this form of comfort. "Please let me know if there is anything I can ever do for you." The Queen bowed her head as she stepped back.

"Here are these as well. Some of our best inventors created them recently, they are well tested and improved from those previously used." Karolyn motioned for her staff to hand out metal backpacks to the centaurs, who stood near her admiring them. Alveen was at a loss.

"What are those?"

"How do you think centaurs get around? We can't exactly hop on the back of an alicorn like you." Nikoli laughed, inspecting the bag before wrapping it around his torso. He pressed a button on his chest that led to the consistent sound of metal unfurling. Out of the pack on his back were thin, flexible metallic wings over double the length of his entire body. Alveen stood impressed.

"These are much more durable than those normally used and they should be immensely lighter, allowing for quicker movement in the air." Karolyn explained. Caspian, Nikoli and another centaur guard, Griffith, stood like warriors in their metal wings, flexing their muscles to become accustom to the movements.

"Thank-you. It looks like they will be appreciated."

"Travel safe." She directed at everyone. Viktor began walking back to his ship as everyone else mounted alicorns. Cordelia dipped her head respectfully and knelt for Alveen to have an easier time mounting in front of her golden wings currently reflecting the colors of the fading sun. A beam shot up from the center of the ship, signaling the protection doom would be closing and they would soon dive into the depths to return home.

Alveen watched the others as they left the mountainside one by one, soaring into the sky. She gently petted Cordelia's neck and mane, making her perk up and follow suite of the others. Allicent was strong and forceful, Cordelia was graceful in every sense of the word. Her movements like a ballet. Alveen leaned forward, enjoying the short trip across the sea below her that flashed as the waves caught glimpse of the falling sun.

The fragrance of fresh kelp and salt swarmed around Alveen in a warm breeze before she saw the shoreline of her next venture. Smooth rocks peeked out from the overgrown grassy fields creating one colossal mountain with a single peek in the center of the peninsula they called their kingdom.

~Chapter V~
Shores of Irielle

Cordelia let out a neigh of approval as they flew closer. It looked deserted, but in the best tropical sense. It wasn't until they hovered over the sandbar below that Alveen noticed the lavender hued electrically charged wall between them and the kingdom. Darting directly at it, Alveen braced for what? She wasn't sure. As Lovisa approached it, a small hole seemed to open in the barrier allowing them to gain entry. Bursting through the barrier, structures suddenly became visible. The highest peak with multiple white marble balconies wrapping around the circumference of the mountain. Doors scattered across the ground, the hills and the mountain side made her blink with realization. Their entire kingdom is within the mountain and underground.

Cordelia followed the others as they circled the mountain until they reached a wide section of the balcony that provided the perfect landing strip.

"Ensure our guests alicorns are tended to with the utmost care, though I shouldn't have to tell you that." Lovisa ordered a woman with pink eyes and curly black hair as she dismounted with a kind smile. Each of The Princesses flew with guards that were now assisting them in dismounting as well. "Welcome to Irielle!" She exclaimed facing Alveen, Hunter and Willow. She extended her arms in a welcoming gesture with a grand smile across her face that showed she was happy to be back in her home kingdom.

Lovisa led them to through the white marbled entrance in the mountain, the floor carved of the same materials. Doorways and windows were trimmed in driftwood that was sanded, engraved and elegantly carved. The dining hall was one of the first rooms they encountered in this kingdom. Appetizers were served promptly upon their arrival. Alveen was grateful for that as she had only eaten breakfast with Luka and the small meal during the memorial dinner in Loxley.

They spoke of many things in regards to Alveen's life in the other world. If anything, they all seemed either wildly curious or extremely unimpressed, there was no in between. After dinner the girls began to get restless with all the adults talking.

"Mommy, can we go play?"

"Training first. You know the rules." She leaned down and kissed her daughters on their rosy cheeks before gesturing to one of the centaurs dressed in the traditional dusty blue color of Irielle.

"I suppose I shouldn't be surprised that training starts so young." Alveen commented as the girl's voices faded out of the room with them.

"Anything we can do to prepare them for the trials. We try to take every extra preparation to ensure they win." Lovisa explained from the head of the table. What were the trials? Alveen wondered.

"I'm sorry, I'm afraid I haven't heard of any of that. The trails? What trials?" She questioned, at first only getting silence as a response until Princess Willow finally spoke up.

"The Monarchy Trials. Before taking the throne, everyone is supposed to go through the six trials ensuring they are prepared to lead righteously and with genuine intent." The table became quiet as everyone came to the realization that Alveen had not undergone them. Alveen used the silence to ponder what this meant for her. If anything would happen to her grandmother, where would that leave her kingdom? It was the first time since the battle that Alveen had truly thought about where her place in the hierarchy was. She began to speak softly.

"I'm now the last of my line and next to inherit the throne. Shouldn't someone have mentioned this so I could begin preparing? Or say anything about it at all?" Alveen asked, frustrated that she had been blindsided by this development. "What happens if someone doesn't do the trials or doesn't pass them?" she continued, trying her best to mask the worry in her voice.

"Well...Normally it would go to the next in line." Lovisa added.

"And for me?"

"I'm not sure. It's never happened before, but I would assume Cosaint would end up being ruled over by the rest of the monarchy until you passed the trials, or a worthy heir was presented." Lovisa responded after pondering the question. Her brows scrunched together to reflect her uncertainty about the answer she gave.

"What's all involved in these trials?" If she was going to have to undergo these tests, she should start preparing now, right?

"It's different for everyone. They are magically manipulated to test you for six qualities, but everyone is tested differently in ways that are more challenging for each individual that enters them." Alveen sat back in her chair. If there was ever a time that she was more unsure of her place or her security in her position, she couldn't think of it. She needed to get this taken care of as soon as possible. The last thing she needed was yet another complication to take her focus off everything she needed to figure out still once she returned to Cosaint.

"When can I undergo them? What do I need to do?" Her voice was determined. She knew as she thought about it that there was a very good chance that she was not prepared for this, that she was going to lose, but at least she would know she tried.

"Normally representatives from each kingdom are present to witness it, though I suppose it's not required. The trials take place here, on one of our southern most isles. You're transported there and the transportation spell is only broken when you complete the trials. If you win." Lovisa and Willow each moved their hair, revealing a scarification design engraved into their skin behind their left ear. Willow was close to Alveen so she could see the design well. A simple crown upside down with a reflection in simplistic shapes of mountains and trees. Alveen glanced at King Hunter wondering where his was, she knew it wasn't behind his ear. "We will know. And you will be considered worthy of the throne and to rule over citizens." Lovisa continued as she let her long locks fall back in front of her ear.

"We may as well let her try while she's here. Even if she doesn't pass, she will have time to prepare for when she needs to re-do it." King Hunter spoke this time after he had been silent most of the conversation, his gaze following whoever was speaking as he took in all that was said. Alveen wanted to ask if Zakarian had won the trials or even tried them, but she didn't want to think of him or compare herself to him. He wasn't around. He was no longer worthy of the throne. Willow spoke next,

"I actually lost the trials twice before it considered me worthy." A very real realization of losing and having to redo the trials entered her mind. This had to be done soon.

"Tomorrow. I want to do it tomorrow. Can we extend our stay by one day? We can leave the morning after, no matter the outcome." Alveen questioned King Hunter and Sir Caspian. Caspian nodded in approval. Alveen knew she would have to contact The Banri and get her approval also.

"I see no issue with this. Our advisors are handling things well in our absence. This journey could use a little bit more excitement." King Hunter responded. He and Lovisa both reminded her that she would need to speak with her grandmother.

They finished their meal as the others spoke in quiet tones, but Willow had her eyes on Alveen who was silent the duration of their time in the dining hall. Once they were excused, she followed Alveen down the white marble corridor. Her steps echoed in the empty hallways, even with her thick tread boots she wore. Windows were completely absent here, though sporadically there were doors in the mountainside that led to the spiral balcony that hugged the formations exterior.

"Princess?" She asked. Alveen spun around and gave her friend a weak smile. "You can do it. I know they speak as though you are destined to fail, but even from the short amount of time I've known you, I have faith in you."

"Thank-You Willow." She gave her a quick hug. "It threw me off and was entirely unexpected. I am still curious as to why I haven't learned of any of this yet."

"Honestly, with your return being so recent and working towards learning about everything else, there probably just hasn't been time, that and.." Willow caught herself and stopped mid-sentence. She realized what she was about to say may be too insensitive.

"And what, Willow?" Alveen pushed for an answer.

"Well," she continued. "Technically, Zakarian was the next in line for the throne. He was the one who should have been focusing on this, normally you wouldn't have been prepared for it until after he took the throne." It made sense. And until recent events, Zakarian would have been the next in line. But things change.

"Wait, so Zakarian never passed these?" Willow shook her head as she spoke.

"Nope. He never got the chance to try with his being gone so long."

"Hm. I was curious about that." She didn't say any more other than excusing herself to speak with The Banri about the extension. She reached her chamber, not surprised when she saw the interior. White, marble pillars made up the bed frame and lined the room. The floor was a light grey stone that continued throughout this end of the palace. The white lights reflected off all of the bright surfaces, giving a larger appearance than the room actually was. Her bed was draped in dusty blue curtains and matching luxurious covers were perfectly crisp where she would sleep. She sat on the end of the bed and willed the swirling force inside her to summon her grandmother.

"Princess. Glad to see you've made it to Irielle. Beautiful kingdom, isn't it?" The Queen said as her face because clear in the cloud of fog in front of her.

"That it is. The lack of windows is unappealing though. But overall the kingdom is gorgeous."

"Well I suppose you did not call to small talk. What can I do for you?" She asked, as usual, getting straight to the point.

"Very well. It's my understanding that in order for me to have the proper ability and consent to lead a kingdom I must pass the monarchy trials. Which are held here." Alveen paused. "I was hoping you could give me an extension on my trip and allow me time to try to prepare and pass the trials before my return, seeing as now I am next in line for the throne should anything happen." She stated. The Queen looked at her for a moment.

"You have had no training or preparation, and you feel you are ready for the trials?"

"Not necessarily, but I feel I deserve a chance to try to pass them. Worst case scenario, I fail them and will have to redo it another time after I have had proper training." She answered. She did not plan on passing, but she would be upset if she had not even tried to learn what she as going to need to overcome or face in order for her to become Queen and rule her people properly.

"I see." The Queen thought for a long moment. contemplating the outcomes. "I suppose we could afford to be without you for another few days, however upon your return you will begin training immediately."

"Yes, Your Majesty."

"Do you have any idea what you are about to face?"

"Not at all. Trials of leadership is all Lovisa said. She said she would explain more tomorrow if you allowed it."

"Then I will leave it to her."

"Banri?" Alveen asked out of curiosity.

"Yes?"

"The symbol. The tribal received when the trials are passed. Does it have a significant meaning?" She leaned in hoping for a real answer.

"Yes. The crown reflecting the horizon. It represents growth, and new chances every day to advance a genuine monarchy. In order for a kingdom to grow, thrive and reach its utmost potential, just as in nature, it requires specific traits that each of our kingdoms hold at their core. Once you possess all of these traits, only then will Beannithe know and it will mark you a genuine leader. I'm sure Queen Lovisa will explain it well tomorrow." Alveen nodded understanding.

"Thank-you. I will inform you when I finish." Alveen bowed respectfully and waved away the fog.

Alveen was too anxious to fall asleep, instead she made her way to Lovisa's room hoping to find someone new to converse with. On her way there she passed the Princesses' room and noticed Lovisa was inside. She leaned in and knocked on the door.

"Sorry to interrupt."

"Oh, don't be sorry at all! I'm sure the girls would love to say good night to you, Princess Alveen." Lovisa said looking to the young girls who shook their heads in agreement.

"I would be honored to help tuck them in for the evening." She said with a curtsy. The girls giggled. Alveen adored the twin's beds and the canopys that were at the head of each of them.

"Alveen! Come sit with me!" Brielle called from her pile of comforters and stuffed animals. Alveen sat on the side of her bed.

"How was your day?"

"So awesome! Ava learned a new trick with a sword and beat me! She was so strong!" Hearing Brielle boast about her sister and hearing the pride in her voice made her heart smile. Everyone always seemed to be in competition but these girls were in everything together. "Someday I will be that strong."

"I do not doubt that for a second, Princess. I bet you are immensely smart too, aren't you?"

"Yes! She is so smart! She has to help me with all of my schooling. She has wonderful brains!" Ava said from her bed. Lovisa smiled at the girls before placing a kiss on Ava's head.

Alveen leaned down and tucked all the blankets in around Brielle. "Oh, this is so snuggly!" She said burying her head into her pillows. "Good night Princess."

"Good night to you as well Brielle, and you Ava." Alveen leaned down and gave each of them a hug before going to Lovisa's side by the door.

"Good night mommy." The girls said in unison.

"Goodnight darlings." She said as she twisted her wrist turning out the lights.

"They are so precious." Alveen said as they walked down the hall.

"They truly are. They are a blessing." Lovisa looked at Alveen as if analyzing her. "Come with me, my dear" she said as she led her out to a balcony near the top of the mountain. "I know we have not gotten the chance to become close, but I sense something troubling you. Please know I am a trustworthy companion." Alveen was curious as to what she could have done that led to someone realizing her troubled heart. "The girls." She began as if she was unsure if she wanted to continue. "They were never supposed to be able to happen."

"What do you mean?"

"After my husband and I had married, I was told I would be unable to conceive a child. That I would never be a mother, though I desperately wanted to be. That never kept us from trying though. I can't explain what changed or how it happened, but after trying and trying for so long, we were finally blessed with not one beautiful Princess, but two."

"I am so sorry you had to endure all of that. I ask this purely out of curiosity, but why are you telling me this?"

"Because I see the pain in your eyes, along with the joy, when you look at the girls. As if something troubles your soul. I recognize it. And I want you to know you are not alone. You are strong." Alveen wanted to lie and tell Lovisa she was crazy and didn't know what she was talking about, but something about how she was encouraging her and she was so certain in the way she spoke made her want to confide in her.

"I wasn't even sure I wanted kids. I'm still not. I mean I'm not even married." Lovisa stared at Alveen, who was now looking at the ground.

"I hope you don't take this as an insult, but anyone around you knows you have feelings for someone. Your confidence glows when you are around him, and he has never spoke as much to anyone or been as involved with anything until you arrived. It seems from my point of view you bring out the best in each other."

"King Luka? No, we are simply friends. We enjoy each other's company and we are encouraging allies, nothing more."

"It seems to me that you are fighting this love that wants to help unite the world, and help bring you to your full potential, why is that?" Lovisa was leaning with her back to the railing, hands clasped in front of her, like a mentor or teacher would stand addressing their student. Alveen took a breath in. She was right. Alveen had feelings for The King but refused to admit it for numerous reasons.

"He made it abundantly clear he wanted nothing more than a solid alliance. He has no desire for me, at all. And..." Alveen knew she should just stop talking. She was a future Queen, why would she allow herself this grievance or venting to someone. She needed to be in control. But it felt so good to verbalize her worries and concerns.

"Go on. Sometimes you just need to say it out loud." Alveen could feel herself reaching a break, ready to allow the first of many tears to stream down her wind burnt cheeks.

"And I've already had the man I thought was the love of my life ripped away from me before we hardly had a chance to see what we could be. I don't want to experience that pain again. Besides, Luka needs an heir, something which, besides my healer you are the only other to know, I cannot give."

"The Banri doesn't even know?"

"No. It never seemed like a casual conversation topic. Especially since Zakarian was around and in line for the throne before me." Before she knew what was going on, something happened that she was not expecting. Lovisa leaned in and wrapped her up in a hug. She had not even really hugged her grandmother like this, but here was this other royal offering her comfort and peace. She pulled back but kept her hands on Alveen's upper arms as she looked at her.

"Experiencing loss myself, I understand where you are coming from in mind and heart. But love can give you so many wonderful memories to cherish during the time of loss, compared to closing yourself off and not experiencing any of that the world has to offer." She rubbed one of her arms in a comforting fashion, "You will be happy Alveen. You just need to step out of your comfort zone and make it happen." Alveen pushed her body to The Queen, giving her a warm embrace. Someone she could finally talk to that understood the depth of her troubles for the most part. Someone who didn't judge her.

They finished the conversation confirming that Alveen would indeed undergo the Monarchy Trials tomorrow with a blessing from The Banri. Lovisa walked her to her room before she departed. Alveen quickly changed into comfortable clothes and slid into bed.

The silk blankets wrapped around her as she laid her head back on the pillow. She had no idea what she was about to encounter, but from the sounds of it, she wouldn't come out victorious.

~Chapter VI~
Monarchy Trials

Alveen woke early the next morning to the sound of different birds and alicorns flying over the shore outside her balcony. Her hair slid across the silk pillowcase when she moved closer to the edge of the bed. The sunlight was so different here. White rays of light shot through the doorway of her private balcony reflecting off the marble floor and nearly blinding Alveen. That was enough to wake anyone up, she thought. After taking care of her basic hygiene necessities, Alveen stood with her mind blank. She had no idea what kind of tests would happen today, but her best guess would be to wear flexible, durable travel clothing.

She pulled on a pair of fitted pants that reminded her of flexible jeans from earth. Rummaging through her trunk she found a black, high-neck racerback tank top and a sleeveless zip up vest that had plenty of pockets and a few holsters for small daggers. Around her thigh she wrapped another holster, this one held potions of all kinds. She slid into a tall pair of boots that she had traveled here in and pulled her hair into a tight bun before walking out of her room.

The corridors were silent other than the tread of her brown boots against the glossy floor below her. Salty air filled the space around her from all the open balconies. Alveen decided it was best to head to the training grounds to both mentally and physically prepare, though she had to be sure not to exhaust herrself. Alveen jogged down flights of stairs until she reached the grand entrance that would allow her to leave the inside of the mountain. The guard nodded at her approach and signaled for the doors to be opened.

The white light beat down on her bare arms and face, warming her as she reached the stone walkway on the outside. There were only a few people walking around at this hour, though it seemed much later than what it actually was.

"Princess." Her mentors voice caught her off guard.

"Caspian, what are you doing up so early?"

"I could ask the same of you Princess." He smiled. "Are you nervous?"

"I'm not sure. I wish I knew what it was I should be nervous about." She chuckled, frustrated that she was going in blind.

"Queen Lovisa will explain a little better. Every challenge is always different for each individual because it must be the most difficult for you personally. It will target all your weaknesses and fears. The Banri was silent for at least a weeks' time after she passed her test."

"You were around when she passed her test? How old are you?" He laughed at her question.

"Old enough." A whole week of silence? The Banri didn't seem like much of a talker anyways but Alveen couldn't imagine what could possibly bother someone so much that it had that kind of a hold over them. "So where are you off too?"

"I was going to the training yard to see if they could help me prepare."

"You weren't even going to ask me? Your actual mentor?" He seemed slightly offended.

"I didn't think you would be up. But if you would like to join me, I would not be against it." He bowed his head with his fist over his heart and walked along side her to the training grounds of Irielle.

"It's my understanding many of these tests may be much more mentally challenging rather than physical, perhaps, if you don't mind me suggesting, you should take a more relaxed approached." He glanced down to her fist gripping tight onto the wooden hilt of her dagger. She released it when she noticed how tight she was holding on.

"Perhaps." They reached a small hill with a solid door in the side. Walking in through the open doorway, they took in all the weapons stored here.

"Early risers from Cosaint. I shouldn't be surprised, Your Highness." A middle-aged woman stepped out from behind a wall. She was fit, with upper arms and a back that rippled defined muscles. She wore shorts that revealed matching muscle tone through her legs, gladiator sandals that wrapped around her tanned calves and a soft fabric tank top.

"I was hoping I could use the training yard to prepare for today." She met her green eyes. "What is your name?"

"Rowna. I'm the executive trainer here on Irielle. And take my advice, Your Highness, but you should be meditating or relaxing and clearing your mind before you take on the trials. I've noticed very few monarchs who even unsheathed their weapons upon departure of the trials." She raised her eyebrows in a matter-of-fact way. They hadn't even unsheathed their swords or daggers? What kind of tests were supposed to be happening. "Queen Lovisa told me to be expecting you. She should be here any moment with The Princess of Foresi to help prepare you. In the meantime, you may train in whatever way you see fit, Your Highness." Alveen looked to Caspian as Rowna walked away.

"What do I do Caspian?" Alveen started to feel panicked.

"I would wait for The Queen and Princess personally. If we have no idea what you will be encountering, then I am not one who should be giving advice." Caspian looked at The Princess and took note of her heavy breathing. "Perhaps we should have a seat and relax until they arrive." He extended his arm in a gesture towards one of the chairs in the armory. Alveen shook her head and took a seat. She closed her eyes and tried controlling her breathing. "Very good. Deep breathes Princess." Caspian repeated, standing in front of her. Minutes passed until Alveen was under control again, just in time for Princess Willow to walk in.

"Stressing out already, Princess?" Willow said with a smile. "Better get started." She reached out to assist her fellow royal up off the chair. Alveen smiled weakly letting a breath out as she sent a last glance to Caspian.

"Just breath." He said as she walked away with Willow.

"Alright, so as we've said many times, everyone has different challenges. You may or may not have any physical challenges. So, let's do a quick practice in case you are lucky enough to get one." She was led out of the building to the training grounds. Willow unsheathed her sword without a warning and leapt at Alveen as soon as they reached the unique hillside. The Cosaintian Princess rolled out of the way, pushing herself up to her feet, now fully aware the battle had begun. She quickly reached for her daggers and twisted them in her hands, recognizing the weight. Willow swung again and again, one after another in swift, sharp motions, hardly taking a breath between but her eyes glued onto Alveen's. Alveen stood to defend herself and took a step back as the Foresi sword swung at her, close enough to leave a trail of dark red across her cheek. Willow paused as Alveen lifted the back of her hand to her face and realized she was wiping warm blood from her face. Her insides began to heat up, this wasn't practice. She summoned the tiniest bit of magic just to stop the bleeding before she jumped up towards Willow, spinning violently. As she approached The Foresi Princess, she raised her daggers jabbing and blocking the sword, throwing Willow off balance with the speed of her attacks. Willow jutted her foot out landing a blow to Alveen's chest, sending her flying backwards. As Alveen caught her breath, everything around her slowed, giving her time to take in her body position and allowing her to twist herself around and land in a squat position with her daggers at her sides. Alveen wasted not a single beat before charging toward her friend, sending punches toward her with her daggers sticking out from her grips and with a final spin, the tread of her boot knocked the sword from Willows hands. Her other foot came up and knocked her to the ground, following her with both daggers. Her arms crossed burying the left dagger at the right side of willows neck and the right on the left side of her neck in the soft ground. Willows eyes bulged from her head as Alveen stood back up and reached down to help her up. Quiet clapping echoed from the side of the yard, where Queen Lovisa stood looking impressed next to an equally entertained Caspian.

"Impressive, Your Highnesses." Lovisa said as she approached. Alveen and Willow bowed keeping eye contact. "Now for a bit of mental preparation, shall we?" Lovisa reached her hand out to lead Alveen back to the armory while Willow returned to the field to face her next opponent, this time an Irielle man who stood only slightly taller than her.

As they walked into the armory, a mist covered the air in front of her. "This is going to put you into a trance and help you confront your fears. Most often we have come to face a boggart, a creature with the ability to transform into that which you fear the most." Lovisa's voice faded as Alveen's vision went white as if she had gone unconscious but was blinded by a white light. What did she fear more than anything? She couldn't think of what it could be. There were certainly things she was scared of, but what would this creature think was at the top of that list? In her subconsciousness she walked forward into the blank canvas in front of her. Her footsteps were all she heard, she could see her self when she looked down, but no one was around. Moments passed until she saw a dark red pool ahead of her, contrasting against the perfect white. The pool began to expand, forcing her to step back. After a few steps, it stopped and from the pool, figures began to form.

A coppery smell hit her stomach and she realized, this was blood. In the pool, her mother and father lay. She didn't see their faces, since she didn't actually know what they looked like, but her subconscious recognized who they were. It didn't hit her very hard as she had thought them dead this whole time. Then more bodies appeared. Zakarian, Samual, Nikoli… Alveen took a sharp breath in. This would not get the best of her. More bodies appeared. Tanilly, The Banri, Lovisa, Luka, Willow, Ava, Brielle and Caspian… The pile grew higher and higher. Even the butcher and random citizens she had met and recognized were piled up. Alveen's breath was heavy and she could feel the burning liquid pouring down her face. Her fear was facing the intense deep pain of losing those she loved, and being left with no one at all. Alveen controlled her breathing, taking in the site before her. She needed to overcome this. This preparation would not get the best of her. The bodies started to sink into the pool, and the blood shrank until it vanished.

Fog appeared, ripping her away from the blank canvas and into the dark armory surrounded by Queen Lovisa, Rowna and Caspian. They all looked down at her laying on the ground with concern. She wiped the tears from her eyes and calmed her breathing as she pulled herself upright. No one said a word while she drank water Caspian gave her. She sat in the chair and took deep breathes, relaxing her mind.

"Alveen. It's time." Queen Lovisa said finally. Alveen opened her eyes, the teal and gold glimmering in the darkness of the armory. She stood and followed Lovisa. She felt calm. She felt confident and she felt prepared to lose whatever battle she was about to face, but ready to fight it with all her might.

Lovisa led them to a mountain on the northern edge of the kingdom. All of Alveen's guards waited, along with many Iriellites ready to encourage her through this challenge.

"Remember, if you fail, you will simply be brought back here. Injuries will follow you back." Lovisa assured her. She turned and faced her citizens, while holding Alveen's hand. "Iriellites! Today we will witness a rare tradition of a young Princess wishing to pursue her reign and defeat the monarchy trials." An eruption of applause and chants overcame the crowd. "Today we send with her strength to accomplish these tasks that the center of Beannithe will lay before her, set to challenge the deepest parts of her. Today we pray she will emerge victorious and we will have another heir prepared to rule over her kingdom!" They shouted her name. They wanted her to win. They wanted her to be Queen someday. The Queen turned and faced Alveen one last time. "One last thing, time is different in the trials. When you enter it will feel like you are in there for days, when you return, it will only have been mere hours. Enter in through the cave there and you will be transported," she pointed to an opening between tall boulders. "The magic of Beannithe will address you, and from there, everything will be unique to your tests. We will be waiting, whether you fail or succeed." Lovisa gave her a final squeeze of her hand. Caspian bowed with his fist over his heart, holding it for a few moments to emphasis his respect for The Princess.

Alveen took her first step forward and didn't look back. Her boots dug into the dirt on the mountain side as she reached the towering rocks guarding the entrance. With a swift exhale, she stepped through the barrier and into the cave. It quickly became barren black as the boulders behind her slammed together, blocking her way out.

Just then a white light surrounded by rays of different colors appeared in front of her. A voice came from in front of her and echoed throughout the cave. It didn't seem to be coming from a specific place, more like the mountain itself was speaking to her.

Princess Alveen Of Cosaint. Your magic pulses strong in your core. Beannithe is pleased you have chosen to undergo the trials. The traits of being a Queen require endurance. You will undergo seven challenges to ensure you are fit to rule one of the six kingdoms of Solas.

Seven? They all said six. Why is there seven? What is the seventh? Alveen could feel her heart racing, but she quickly shoved her worry aside and thought to herself, I will finish this. Fail or pass, I must complete it. Whatever Beannithe says needs to happen, will happen. Whatever Beannithe needs to test for me to be Queen, I will prevail. Alveen repeated the phrases over and over in order to keep her anxiety at bay. The voice spoke again.

"Extend your arm." Alveen did as the voice commanded, holding her forearm out. It began to smoke, but she felt no pain. *"You will endure tests of magic yielding.."* A leaf with the letter C was engraved into her arm. Cosaint. *"Survival instincts.."* A small branch forming an F was placed below it. Foresi. *"Integrity.."* A turtle with a K. Krumvite. *"Selflessness"* A wave with an I. Irielle. *"Confidence"* A circle with an L. Loxley. *"Wisdom"* A set of antlers with a B. Bulgrakta. *"And last is circumstantial for you alone, a test of righteousness."* A mountain with a B. For Beannithe. No one else had to endure the last test, everyone else was only given six. What made her different that she needed to pass an extra test

and prove herself beyond the others? Her skin stopped smoking but from her wrist to her inner elbow were symbols of the tasks that lay ahead of her. They all glowed for a moment, then seemed to settle into her skin, dull.

The ground below her disappeared, pulling her down, free falling through a dark tunnel. As she looked below her she could see one rock floating, illuminated only by the light of flames along the tunnel walls. She aimed her body to ensure she would land on the one piece of solid ground she saw and slammed into it with force, landing in the same squat position she did when she fought Willow only minutes ago. The area began to light itself as the flames in the scones that lined the walls thickly roared to life giving off heat.

Alveen's arm stung, causing her to inspect her new inscription. The leaf with a C was glowing red. This was the trial of magic yielding.

The levitating stone below her feet began to shake. Alveen looked below her to see multiple others lying quite a distance down on their sides as if they had fallen from above. She took in her surroundings, looking around to see if there was any clue as to what she needed to do. Looking above, the barren black area from which she had just fallen now looked nothing like where she had previously come from. A ceiling now formed high above her, with a door leading through it. She put the pieces together that she needed to reach that door.

As the thought entered her mind, the ceiling began to glow. Small flaming rocks were hurled down at her. She knelt down quickly and swung her arm up forming a magical shield over herself that deflected the stones for the time being. She needed to find a way up there.

She looked below her again. This stone was levitating, maybe she could move it? With one arm up to hold the shield, her other hand imitated gripping a stone as her fingers curled from the force to move the boulder she stood on. Her face pinched and her muscles burned as she tried to move herself. It wasn't working. She released her magic, thinking. She looked over the edge with an idea. Curling her fingers again she reached down as if she could grasp one of the boulders and summoned her magic. With the smallest effort, a boulder moved, bolting upright and slowly creeping its way through the open area. It was a lot further down than it looked.

By the time the boulder made it level, Alveen was beginning to sweat. She thrust another burst of magic at it ensuring it would be higher than where she stood so she could use it as a step to reach her goal. It worked. Alveen, with her one hand still controlling the shield keeping her blocked from cauterized holes in her body, jumped to the next boulder, shaking slightly on impact. As she gained her balance she felt confident in her ability. She needed to thrust more magic into this if she was going to create the staircase she needed.

One by one she brought the discarded stones to levels she needed. She was almost all the way complete as she still stood on the second boulder. As she started her ascent up the levitating staircase, arrows flung from the sides of the vertical tunnel. Her shield was focused upright, unable to deflected the continuous attack. She quickly took note of where they were coming from. With her free hand she summoned the fire in the torches below and swallowed the walls of the tunnel, blocking whatever mechanism was aiming at her. Sweat began to pour over her, her breathing quickened. She needed to get to the top as quickly as possible or she would not survive the first task.

Grabbing a silver potion from her thigh holster, she took a swig of the concoction she had learned would give her strength and endurance. Exactly what the voice of Beannithe said she would need. With a sudden jolt, she found herself full of energy again. Leaping and holding her shield she reached the top step, still too far from the door. She needed two more. She looked down analyzing what she had. The levitating stones had moved before, but they were her only chance now. She squatted as if she were physically lifting the boulders herself and the first rock shot up toward her with no issues, allowing her to place it where she needed. She was right, she still needed one more.

The flaming rocks were becoming more dense now, forcing her to give more attention and control to her shield, expanding it slightly. The heat was racing into her lungs and she began to feel dizzy and she pulled the last boulder into place. Calling on the strength the potion gave her, she leapt to the final step and touched the wrought iron door handle.

The door didn't open though. The handle began to radiate white light, much like her hand with the shield was currently doing. Her vision was blinded as the door handle exploded and thrust her off the stone forcing her to drop her shield. Everything around her froze, even her body in midair. Her arm began to sting again, forcing her to look at it. The leaf with the inscribed C turned from red to gold and embedded in her skin. The next symbol began to glow green. The branch entwined into an F. She passed the first test.

Her surroundings changed. She remained frozen in the air as trees, bushes, animals and the setting of the wilderness formed around her. Her body felt the gravity again as she descended. She flipped her body around just in time to see she was heading directly towards a branch pointing at her, ready to impale her before she got the chance to pass trial number two. With a swift motion of her hand the branch was throw away, giving her only solid ground to slam into. Her face heated up and she could taste blood in her throat. It took her a minute to push herself into a sitting position as she sent small surges of magic to heal a few broken bones again and her broken nose that slammed into the earth. Using the back of her hand she wiped the blood from her face. This was her test of survival instincts. She needed to find shelter, somewhere to rest and recover before she could take on this next task.

Pain surged through her muscles telling her she needed to rest soon as she walked carefully through the woods. She remembered from Earth and from her hunting with Samual that she should step lightly and make as little noise as possible. She had no idea what kind of dangers could be lurking in this trial wilderness.

It felt as if she walked for hours before she found a stream to follow. She leaned down and drank without hesitation, wiping the blood from her face, leaving some mud in its place. She could feel the gritty sand in her mouth from where the water wasn't entirely clear. Streams came from somewhere, she thought. Following it seemed to be the best option.

The sky still glowed daylight when she reached the waterfall that gave life to the stream. She stumbled up to it, drinking clean water and rinsing her arms and body. She looked down at her forearm to see her embedded C and glowing F, the rest barley visible. What was she supposed to complete here? It had felt like nearly an entire day since she started walking. She needed food and rest, that she was certain of. Looking around she noticed the extra-large trees, one in particular with a glimmer showing from inside the bark. Forcing herself to her feet she walked towards the tree at least thirty yards from the water, hiding behind smaller bushes. This would be a perfect shelter. The bark sparkled in the remaining sunlight. Alveen knew she was weak, but surly she had enough energy to do this.

She braced her feet on the ground and brought the back of her hands together, curling her fingers as if she were prying open a door. She took loud, heavy breathes as the magic poured out of her. The bark began to split, creating a slim entry. She could feel the fibers of the tree being pulled apart and formed into something else entirely. When she opened her eyes, she impressed even herself. The doorway was not the easiest to see and it was slim enough that no large predators should be able to get in. She walked around the bark doorway, giving her a small hall before making a sharp right into what was now a hollowed-out trunk.

As she inspected the inside, she found what was glistening on the exterior. A silver knob, much like the one on the door before. It couldn't possibly be this easy. Alveen reached for it, but her grip did nothing. It became dull, as if it had been there for centuries. Symbols began to glow on the interior around her. Three daggers, a tent, a wave and a flame. They proceeded to flicker, the tent and wave extinguishing and vanishing. The daggers and flame remained. These must be the tasks. The tent, shelter. The wave, water. The flame must mean a fire, but the daggers? She hoped it was food, killing for food and for her survival because she was so hungry right now. She decided for the best results and to increase her magic abilities, she needed to get a little rest.

• • •

The temperature began to drop as the sun fell from the sky when Alveen awoke. She inspected her daggers. She hadn't used them so no damage had taken place. Slowly she stepped out of her hovel and squatted next to the entry. Praying that some type of animal would come soon. She glanced at nearby bushes, unable to identify them. Her fingers dug into the soil, more like peat moss, perfect for growing. She thought perhaps she could summon even just beans of some kind. Burying her fingers in the ground, she channeled her earth magic into the one spot before her, manipulating it in her mind to be an edible plant she knew for a fact wouldn't kill her. Snap peas and cucumbers sprouted before her within seconds.

Like a starving vulture she snapped all the vegetables and took them back into her shelter, eating everything she could. She knew this would not hold her over for very long. She needed some kind of meat to give her real strength.

The Princess decided to gather some wood before it became too dark. She needed some kind of warmth, and a blanket or pelt was not likely to be coming her way. Thankfully, she did not have to go far for kindling and a few large pieces of wood.

Starting the fire was another story. She couldn't just summon fire from nothing, she needed to at least create a spark. She had given up multiple times only to try again as the temperature continued to drop. Her body was shaking from the frigid temperatures, making her task even more difficult. She took her daggers and clashed them together, missing the blades entirely her first strike, until she finally caught a small spark. She missed the first few with her magic, the spark extinguishing before she even had a chance to bring it to life, but once she caught the spark, the small firepit in the center of her oversized tree trunk blazed with warmth that enveloped her. She sat for a while staring at the dancing flames, twisting her hands above it to keep the warmth. Looking up at her symbols of trials to yet face, the flame glowed and vanished from the carving. Only three daggers remained. She leaned against the tree and tried to get comfortable for an entire night of sleep.

Alveen woke a few times, unable to get a deep sleep, and would twist her wrists to bring the fire back to life. The last time she woke she was shocked and unsure if she should move.

A wolf and a squirrel lay curled up on the other side of the fire. She slowly got to her feet, making sure her daggers were in place should she need them. The eyes of the wolf sprung open. He stood slowly, stretched his legs out, baring his teeth as he yawned. He stood looking at her, not intimidated but not ready to attack. With a flick of his tail, he walked out of her temporary home.

She let out a breath as she sank back to the floor. The squirrel still sat across from her.

"You're not nearly as intimidating." She spoke to the small animal. The animal sneezed a few times and then began to swell, and grow. Doubling, tripling in size. Alveen did a double take and stared at the creature transforming in front of her. Its face grew a longer snout, baring fang like teeth, clearly meant to rip the flesh off her body. The round stomach faded into a strong, lean torso, connected to muscular legs. The creatures fur lay flat against its body. It's eyes sharp, predicting the moves she would make.

This was the last thing on her list. She needed to kill for survival. Standing slowly, she made sure to never take her eyes off the monster that had transfigured in front of her. One foot after another, she circled the fire, the monsters keeping directly across from her. It made the first move. With a powerful leap, it bound over the fire. Alveen tried to thrust the flames into its belly, but it didn't phase the creature. With only a second to act she crossed her daggers and thrust them toward the beast. With an eerie howl, the monster landed on top of her. Its blood dripped down over her vest as she blew into her hand and forced the creature off of her. She laid on her back gasping in breathes that the monster had knocked out of her with its blow.

There was no way to get this creature out from her tree, that must have been why it transfigured into something smaller. She had no choice but to field dress it inside her home. The stench of it's inside ripped at her nostrils and turned her stomach. She really hoped this creature was edible. Its fur was soft, unlike its demeanor. Laying the insides off to one side, she began carving the meat to prepare for her next meal and precisely trimming the pelt to dry and use for warmth. She laid the pelt out and piled the internals inside, allowing her to carry them out of her temporary home. Surely this would bring other creatures from far away. But she was done. All she needed was to eat and grab that handle. She dropped the organs on the opposite side of the waterfall, hoping to give some distance between her and whatever scavenger would find it. The pelt now covered in blood was easily rinsed in the pool for her to hang up and let dry inside her shelter. The aroma of meat filled the room, causing a wrenching pain of hunger through Alveen's stomach. She pulled it from the fire and began to rip it apart, nourishing her body. As she looked up to the symbols, the daggers glowed. Relief filled her body. But only one dagger vanished. Two remained.

"Are you kidding me?" she exclaimed to the entity that wasn't there. Two more kills she had to make, survival kills. This was going to take a lot longer than she thought. Her immediate thought was she didn't want anything attacking her in the night again, so she put a protection spell around the tree. It would hide the smoke, the light, the warmth and the noise from inside. It would essentially look exactly like it did before she created a home out of it.

Her skills from hunting back on earth allowed her slight knowledge on how to break down the creature in order to save meat for every other meal she would have. The pelt had not yet dried up to a point that she could use it as a blanket yet.

She decided it best to preserve her magic since she proved herself right and she had no idea what she had left to face. Using her dagger, she found a log about the roundness of her arm and the length of her open hand. She decided to spend her time striking away pieces of it in order to create a large cup to hold water in so she could transfer it with more than her hands. She made herself multiple tools this way. Alveen had remembered Zakarian saying Foresi was known for their woodworking. Perhaps she would learn how to do this all much better once she finished these trials.

She expected for her mind to go crazy soon, having no one to talk to, but she found she enjoyed being out in the wilderness alone. Listening only to the noise of a crackling fire, wind in the trees and animals going about their business. As she sat in her room, she looked up at the two remaining daggers. She wasn't going to need to kill anything else yet. She did a double take. Only one dagger remained. She hadn't killed anything though. What else had she used her dagger for? She did use it to create tools for survival though. Maybe she wouldn't have to kill again.

The roar of the waterfall was sometimes overpowering, but she did not feel frightened enough to not wander from her residence. She gathered firewood multiple times, found perfect chucks of wood to create her next tool from. Eventually she did end up using her magic to make a canister with a handle that she could hang at her side and carry with her. The one dagger remained no matter how many tools she made.

She sat by the fire, roasting a large chuck of meat and covering herself with the now dried and cleaned pelt to shield her from the brisk chill in the morning air that creeped through the entry. An unnerving shriek came from outside. There was no way she was going to walk out unable to see what or where this creature was. It was certainly an aggressive noise and not one of an animal in agony. She closed her eyes and summoned her magic, allowing her to see through the walls around her.

Dozens, maybe over one hundred snarling beasts crawled along the forest floor towards the pool, most of them silent in their footfalls. Alveen was happy with her decision to not walk out before inspecting. They couldn't see her. What should she do though? She waited until they had descended into the unknown depths of the pool under the waterfall.

When she thought the last of them had gone, she walked out of her hiding place, only to be swiped off her feet by the flesh covered tail of a remaining creature that hid in one of the bushes outside. It raced toward her on all fours, forcing her to move quickly; rolling, jumping, doing any maneuver she could to avoid injury. She finally had a second where she stood to her feet and took the offense. A sharp split tongue shot out from the monster's mouth. It was reptilian of some kind, covered in thick plated skin.

As she made her run towards the creature, his tail whipped around again nearly flipping her again. She stayed light on her feet.

The monster reared up on his back legs, revealing a smooth fleshy belly. She wasted no time in plunging her daggers into the creature's stomach, ripping through the muscles, allowing its blood to drench the forest floor below her. She looked around for any others that may have stayed back. No others. She ran back inside. The final dagger glowed and vanished. The handle inherited the glow from all the symbols and Alveen grasped it with her pelt and tools in hand, using the knowledge that she may need these yet again.

The handle vanished and her surroundings disappeared, melting into the white background she now saw. The green F of branches burned as if transformed to solid gold and embedded in her arm before the Krumvite symbol began to glow blue. The integrity trial.

The room went dark and the temperature dropped dramatically, forcing her to wrap her pelt around her bare arms. She could still smell the dried blood from the transfigured creature on her vest as she turned to examine where she was now. There was a chilled breeze, though it was uncertain where in the darkness it came from. A black obsidian floor reflected the four lights that glowed ahead of her, illuminating four identical doors. All of the handles looked exactly as the previous two.

Slowly, all four doors opened. Alveen's heart and chest tightened as she fought the urge to run towards them. Samual stepped out of the first door. He was clean cut with his reading glasses as he had been on the first day on the plane. His navy suit fit his form so well.

"You always said you liked this look on me." His voice rattled her. He sounded so real.

"Samual?" she asked aloud. Beannithe was using her weaknesses, and he was certainly one of them. The next door opened and Luka stepped out. "Are you really here?" she asked The King. His golden eyes locked onto hers, a hint of a smile showing under his dark facial hair. The next door opened. Masgo, Fennryr and Nikoli walked out. Her citizens. Her people. "Nikoli? How are you here?"

"Am I really though, Your Highness?" his innocent voice answered back. The last door opened. She wasn't sure what to expect, but it certainly wasn't who emerged. Zakarian stepped out with a calm expression. One she had seen many times when he was teaching. His eyes were so full of passion, and hers, she could only imagine, were full of anger. She wanted to wrap them all up, she wanted to trust Zakarian and love Samual and help her people and create an alliance with Luka. They all walked back through their doors and they slammed shut, leaving The Princess to do one thing; choose.

Choose between her first love, her brother, her people and possibly her true love. Alveen tossed the options around her head. As much as she loved her brother, after everything he had done and the betrayal he had done her, it hurt to say she would never follow him down another path. Samual. Samual hadn't done anything wrong. He defended her and his people, but so did Luka. Luka defended his own people also. But neither Samual or Luka were important in the overall trials of becoming a Queen. What mattered more than anything? What is the only thing that could make her a Queen? Her people. Her kingdom. With her answer set solidly in her mind, she walked toward door number three and grabbed the handle.

Unlike before, memories flashed through her mind. Every lie she ever told, every time she chose to be honest. Beannithe was judging her past integrity. Where would she stand? Would her good decisions out weight the bad or is this where she would fail?

The transition repeated. Blinding light, her surroundings fading. The burn to tell her the blue would fade to gold and become embedded in her arm, allowing the next to come forth. She passed three trials. She was not expecting to pass any of them. Was there a real possibility that she could do this? It wasn't like a test, she didn't have to pass most of them to become a genuine monarch, she had to pass every single one and she still had four left. The wave on her arm glowed a light blue, telling her the trial of selflessness was next.

~Chapter VII~

The Monarchy Trials

Part II

Alveen sat on the back of an alicorn, behind her warriors preparing for battle. Her body covered in armored clothing adorned with holsters for all kinds of weapons.

"My Queen!" a guard yelled from nearby. "They are coming for you. We must get you to safety." Coming for her? Why would they be coming for her? Wouldn't it seem like a wise decision to put others behind her then. There was no sense in innocent lives getting lost over her, no matter if she is The Queen or not.

"I'm not going anywhere. If they want to fight me, then that's what they'll get." She still had no idea who her opponent in the illusion of a battle was. She pushed Allicent through the crowd of soldiers until she reached the front.

She sat in silence, waiting the on-coming attack. The roar of the opposition grew slowly until they breached the hill top. Citizens. Dorcha citizens, though they looked no different than her own. At the center, the sorceress levitated in front of them, her face covered.

"I see you have decided to surrender." The evil leader spoke.

"I'm afraid for you. I have chosen no such path." Alveen charged forward toward the woman in black. Her magic swirled in her, sending a protective shield around her, ready for an impact from the sorceress. "Just me and you, neither of our people need to die tonight." The sorceresses hand flew forward, sending Alveen flying backward. Her protective cover shielded her from any injury, allowing her to land on her feet and race right back toward her opponent.

She came face to face with her, though technically hers was still covered. Alveen pulled out her sword that appeared at her hip, fending off the attacks both physical and magical. Side stepping out of the way, a magical incantation ricocheted off her blade and back at the Sorceress.

"My people will not die because of me. I would run into the face of death at any time for them." She spoke aloud. A glistening knob peaked out from the pocket of her opponent. She reached down grabbing it, ready for her next challenge.

The wave turned to solid gold and burned into her flesh as the coin symbol of Loxley began to glow. Only three trials left. Alveen was becoming so faint and tired. She grabbed her container of water and replenished herself before her new surroundings appeared.

Alveen stood in her own throne room. It looked as real as if she were back in Cosaint now. People parted, making way for her to ascend to the throne. Her people and her allies stood with frustrated gazes on her. The gown she wore was the traditional burgundy of Cosaint with golden ascents and a fur cape with the Cosaint clasp. This illusion also made it seem as if she had showered and had her hair and makeup attended to, which was certainly not the case. She went along with the charade allowing herself the chance to uncover the task at hand.

As she approached the steps leading to the throne King Viktor stepped out of the crowd. "You are not fit to be Queen. You are selfish and unworthy." That was a blow to her ego and self-esteem. But she knew, if she were to take the throne, that means she would have had to pass all the trials, even in this illusion. Therefore, she could not be selfish and Beannithe saw her as fit to lead.

Alveen turned with a small smile on her face. She would not fight with her ally, no matter his insults. She simply nodded. Then Princess Willow stepped out and spoke.

"You are weak." One by one people spoke out, her citizens and even King Luka.

"You are cowardly and at best, unintellectual." One of her people spoke next.

"We know Zakarian and yourself were close. We have no reason to trust you as our new leader, nor do we want you to lead us. Monarchs have ruled over multiple kingdoms in times of need, and I say now is one." Alveen thought to herself. This is the test of confidence. Its purpose is to waiver her confidence in herself. She would not allow people to speak to her this way, especially when she knew she was worthy of her position.

"Back away." She spoke with venom in her voice to everyone who had made their way closer to her. "I value everyone's opinion. What I do not value is insults, disrespect and lies, which is exactly what you have all just spoken to me." She stood tall, making eye contact with as many people as she could. "I have trained for this position. I am more worthy than you will ever be able to believe. I am not weak, I am not cowardly and I most certainly am not unintellectual, Your Majesty." The last comment aimed at the very real apparition of King Luka. She relaxed her shoulders and put a small smile on. "I know for certain that I will be a great leader, and you will not waiver my opinion on that. My strategies may be different and that may scare some of our allies, but they work and they work well." Alveen clasped her hands together, waiting for another ridiculous attack from the crowd. No one spoke a word. She was unsure what her goal here was, other than to not let them break her mentally, because that was all confidence was.

She turned and continued up the steps where Caspian stood next to the throne. His long blond hair trailed over his bulky torso and his strong hands held the bioluminescent double axe of a throne room guard. "You don't belong here Alveen." He whispered to her. His green eyes filled with sorrow, as if he had finally let out a hurtful truth he had been holding back. She paused. Nikoli stood at the other side.

"You never should have come. Beannithe is not your home. Go Alveen. You don't want this responsibility." Alveen hesitated. She didn't belong here? She never should have returned? Their gentle voices sounding as if they were only trying to be honest with her threw her off guard. She looked between her guards. Was this what she wanted? Was this the position she needed to be in? Was there another option? Questions rang through her head until her stubbornness put them in place.

"This is my home. I will reign justly, fearlessly and strong." She lifted her gown and sat in the throne, facing those that had just ridiculed her and made it obvious they did not believe in her ability to lead. She examined the arm rests as she sat tall and rested her forearms. Just under where her hand was about to rest was the gleaming silver knob she was looking for. The throne room disappeared and this time the room gave way to darkness. She was still sitting on something but the texture changed. In the blackness around her the golden coin of Loxley embedded into her arm and the next glowed.

The last of the kingdom trials. The trial of wisdom from Bulgrakta. Alveen, even in her exhausted state, couldn't help but think of Luka. It made sense. He was always wise. Thinking and contemplating his words before he spoke, taking strategic steps in everything he did, analyzing everything, including her. She had a love for all kinds of knowledge and that's what he represented, the experience kind of knowledge you can't learn in a book. She missed him.

The room transformed into almost an identical replica to the integrity challenge. Darkness surrounded her other than a number of spot lights that shined down in calculated positions to reveal six swords, all with the hilts stuck directly in chunks of stone, leaving the blades free to penetrate the air above them, reflecting the white lights. Alveen was back in her real attire, everything the same as before the confidence trial, even the stench.

She pulled her pelt cape closer together to guard her from the chill this room held. Her footfalls were nearly inaudible as she stepped with caution. As she came closer to the ring of weapons, the floor at the center began to move as if it were a pool of black liquid. Before her, words formed in the native language of Beannithe. She had learned very little in her studies, yet somehow, she could read it perfectly.

The blades before you, each one of a kind
Will lead to either success or demise.
Wise leaders will see an option lay
Out of plain sight where not others may.
A blade per kingdom, four entry to a painful end
The others, success Beannithe commends.

Simple enough, she thought. Four blades lead to an excruciation death, two are the right choices. That didn't seem like very good odds to her. She looked around the room. Were the swords replacing the knob that she needed to grasp in order to reach the last trial? If they were, how was she going to choose? She could think reasonably and think that Cosaint would be a safe bet since that is the kingdom she should protect. However, it could be the opposite as it may be too obvious of a choice for a wisdom challenge. Which other kingdoms would represent something close to Cosaint? Was there anything in the riddle? She read it over and over. Out of plain site. Krumvite was not in plain sight, nor was Irielle or Loxley or Foresi. That was four kingdoms, were those that of a painful end? She was never good at riddles. She continued on through the riddle, piecing it together a dozen different ways.

She had to take a break and sit back to see what she was missing. She stood up and inspected each blade. Each inscribed with the symbol and letter of their kingdom they represent. Each glowing the color of their kingdom. Her hand reached out multiple times for the hilts of Cosaint, Bulgrakta and Irielle, but she couldn't bring herself to grasp any of them with the odds stacked so highly against her. It had to be Cosaint, she thought. That had to be one that would guarantee her safe passage, right? She went around the circle again.

She reached the blade representing Cosaint. Her arm extended as she admired the workmanship. The hilt was wrapped in golden vines and precious rubies. Her hand opened ready to accept the hilt into her palm, inches from grasping it. Her heart beat faster, thumping in her chest so hard she could feel it in her temples. But something caused her to pause. She couldn't help but look beyond it into the dark expanse before her.

A door lay far back in the darkness. No light shining on it, no gleaming handle, just a solid door that looked as if it were ripped off a ruin and placed randomly in the middle of the abyss. She looked between all the swords, contemplating as she pulled her hand back to her side.

She cautiously walked out of the circle of swords, expecting some kind of spell or wall to keep her in, but nothing stopped her. She approached the door and there was no handle at all. For all she knew she could be unleashing something severely problematic to her current situation. Either way, she had to try. She extended her leg, using her boot to push the door open, leaving her hands available to hold daggers should anything attack.

It swung open effortlessly. Nothing came out at her, frozen and braced for the impact of another test. She stood tall, looking back at the swords. Was there anything that said she *had* to choose one? This door was certainly out of plain site. She trusted her instincts that had grown stronger through the trials and walked through the door without looking back.

Black turned to the familiar blinding white as she transitioned. She walked forward into the blank canvas in front of her. Another singe of pain shot up her arm, worse than the others. The antlers black glow brightened to gold and repeated like the others, entrenching into her flesh. The mountain symbol glowed white. The symbol of Beannithe. The trial only she would have to encounter and the trial that tested her more than others in the monarchy trials for whatever unknown reason.

The ball of colorful light appeared in front of her as it did when she walked into the cave in the beginning. She looked at her arm. Six golden symbols. She had passed them all. Something everyone said she couldn't do. They told her it would be impossible since she had no real training or preparation.

This was the last test. If she passed this, she wouldn't have to undergo any of these trials again and she would be declared a genuine monarch, ready to rule her kingdom when the time came.

Princess Alveen. Your performance is most impressive. You show strength, determination, drive, motivation, patience and self-discipline. All traits that make a Queen successful.

The voice whispered to her. She stood tall, awaiting her next and final trial.

Your family has harmed Beannithe multiple times over and chosen to do evil over good. You will need to pass this trial of righteousness in order to be granted the mark of a genuine monarch. Evil has no place in our kingdoms.

That's what this was about. With her parent's disappearance, there was the possibility that at least one of them had to convert to the Dorcha tribes. Zakarian also betrayed Beannithe, not just his kingdom or her as she had been stuck thinking. This test was to ensure evil wouldn't corrupt her.

Bolts of electricity shot out from the orb, burying into her subconscious. Searing pain ran through her skull and down her body. The force knocked her to her knees as the magic of her world shuffled through her memories, her thoughts, her words, her emotions. It searched out hatred and guilt. It searched out unjustly acts. Agonizing pain jolted through her as her mind was torn apart. She couldn't hear herself screaming, but the rawness she felt in her throat reminded her that she was.

She saw times when she was little that she tried to act deceitfully towards Zakarian, but she had learned from that and formed a better character. She saw when she returned and held guilt for Samual and for her friend over the incident causing her injury, but she had managed to move on from those as well.

She no longer harbored guilt, but instead embraced moving on and learning.

She saw the tantrums she threw as a teenager. She saw and felt the anger of finding out she had been lied to, the anger of her brother betraying her. She felt the hurt.

The electrical waves surged through her body, if there was a sliver of any emotion corrupt enough to turn her against her people or this world, it would be found.

Alveen wasn't sure how long it went on for, all she knew was the pain wouldn't leave. Her breathing became labored, her body began to shake violently until finally, the bolt retracted into the orb in front of her. Alveen dropped to the ground on her hands and knees and vomited repeatedly.

The selfish acts of your family have caused much bloodshed.

"What do you mean? Zakarian is the one who betrayed us. My bloodline should not be held accountable for his actions."

Zakarian is not where it started.

"Where did it begin?" she whispered with a raspy voice, horse from her screams. She was trying to act tough, as if having her brain scrambled had no effect on her. Vertigo overwhelmed her, keeping her on her knees with her eyes closed until she regained composure. She was hearing the words the magic spoke to her, but they did not register.

You will not follow in their path. The world recognizes your good heart and your need for justice. You will rule justly when your time comes. Princess Alveen, you are a genuine monarch.

● ● ●
150

With the final word, her forearm and skull felt as if they were being branded. The burning after the torture she just endured was too much. She knew this was too much for her to handle. As she whimpered in pain, trying her best not to allow herself to scream, though the tears streamed down her cheeks, the symbols on her forearms glowed bright gold as if the sun were trying to break through her skin. The heat from behind her ear left the smell of burnt flesh. Her entire body rung with sensitivity, making pain she may have been able to tolerate before, unbearable now. A harsh scream ripped through her surroundings. Alveen looked away from everything going on and tried to control her breathing and think of how it would be over soon. Another wave of nausea washed over her, but as she leaned over to heave, the world went black.

A sliver of light entered her vision as she came about. Alveen's face was pressed against the soft dirt, her body lay limp on the cave floor. It took her moments to realize she had been transported back to the main land cave where she began her trials. The bruises, healed broken bones and pulled muscles made her every movement more noticeable and difficult. The boulders had opened further, allowing her to better see the interior, while also blinding her. Her skull pounded as she pushed herself upright. She could feel the pulsing blood behind the bruises she acquired. Her senses seemed heightened. She could smell the soil around her, the salty air blowing in from outside, the dried blood from what seemed like days ago crusted onto her vest. Her muscles ached as she stood tall.

Examining herself she noticed she still had her pelt draped over her shoulders and her canister with the hook through one of her belt loops. Beannithe must have wanted to allow her souvenirs. The pelt felt wondrously soft under the skin on her neck, a complete contrast to the mark now behind her ear. She raised her hand to feel the crusted over dried blood from the scarification she won. Her reward and honest mark that she had completed the monarchy trials triumphantly. The Princess took small steps towards the light before raising her forearm up to inspect it. She could very faintly see the seven symbols, though they were hardly noticeable even to her knowing eyes.

She squeezed between the boulders, emerging from the cave and walking down to where Queen Lovisa, King Hunter, Princess Willow and the two Princess of Irielle stood waiting, along with Rowna and a handful of others, including her own guards. Gasps poured over the gathering of people as a blood covered Princess approached them. It was obvious she was in pain, no matter how much she tried to mask it. With every step she tried to send slivers of magic to different areas of her body, healing herself. Her headache wouldn't subside, no matter how much she tried to aid it.

"She won." Willow exclaimed with shock in her voice. Her eyes examining the pelt, the blood patterns and bruises, but resting on the dried blood behind her ear.

"That's near impossible." Rowna commented.

"Some of us were destined for things greater than we have yet to know." Lovisa said as she approached Alveen with Caspian, Ruslan and Griffith. "Congratulations. It seems we may have all underestimated you."

"I think I underestimated myself." Alveen commented. Lovisa extended her forearm, grasping Alveen's elbow for a formal congratulations. Static shocked her when their skin connected.

"It happens when you pass." Lovisa explained turning her arm upright so Alveen could see her marks. She only had six.

"I've never seen any of them, on any of you before."

"You couldn't have. Not unless you passed." Lovisa looked at Alveen's arm. Her brows pressed together curiously. "Seven? No one has ever under went seven trials before."

"That was what I thought when I entered, but apparently I'm the lucky one." She said between heavy exhales.

"Let's get her to her room. She's in need of healing. Draw her a warm bath please." She directed to one of her female guards. "Ruslan, go with and ensure everything is ready." Lovisa guided Alveen to a nearby chair, pulling the pelt from her shoulders, allowing the sun to warm her from the constant coolness she had been in. "We will get this washed and turned into a proper cape."

"No. Please. It may be washed, but just a clasp and proper tanning. I wish for it to keep the shape." She said dazed. Her toned bicep sported a large slice from the creatures' tail during the survival trial, the dried blood still decorating it, though the wound itself had begun to heal.

"Very well." Lovisa handed Rowna the pelt to be tended to along with the canister and all her weapons. Alveen was still trying to control her breath as Lovisa moved her limbs for her. "May I replenish the potions in your holster?" She asked. Alveen nodded. "Rowna will sharpen the blades as well. Let's get you up to the room."

Alveen managed to stand tall and walk to the entrance door with no more than a limp and a fierce look on her face. Blood still covered her cheek from both the swipe from Willow's blade before the trials and the blood she managed to wipe on her face during her survival instinct trial.

Passer byers gave her feared looks. Apparently, they didn't know or hadn't heard about the events of earlier that day. Caspian strode alongside the newly named genuine monarch.

"Princess?" he whispered still looking ahead. She raised her eyebrow and looked at him, acknowledging him. "Are you well? I know these things take a severe toll on the body and mind. If there is anything I can do.."

"Caspian?" She spoke quietly with a small smile. "I'm okay, honestly. A lot happened to me, but I concluded there was a reason behind it. I needed to face each of those trials. It will be a while until I'm... normal." she explained, "but it was all with justifiable reason." Caspian nodded in understanding. The maturity of The Princess beside him amazed him. He would be honored to fight along side her.

When they reached the room, Lovisa's staff had done an excellent job preparing everything. Caspian stood watch at her door, ensuring her he would be right there should she need anything. Other than feeling exhausted, The Princess felt okay after everything that had happened. In fact, she felt stronger. She had triumphed over things not a single person thought she would overcome, not even herself. She went under extreme torture that others didn't have to do because of her bloodline running dark. She just needed sleep.

The room was dimly lit with candles to give a calming ambiance, along with the scent of cinnamon. She thought of Luka and how he smelled of firewood and cinnamon twisted in a masculine cologne. She thought of how his presence was strong enough that it was pulled from her subconscious to be used as a trick in her integrity trial. Did she truly have feelings for him on a deeper level than she realized? It was too much to wrap her mind around at the moment.

Alveen peeled the crusted clothing off her body, leaving them on the white marble floor of her bathroom before she stepped into the open shower to rinse off. It felt like it had been a week since she showered. The warm water poured over her chilled skin, covering the floor with red and brown marbled designs streaming around her feet. She ran her fingers through her hair now clotted by dried blood. Her fingers felt greasy as the first few layers of dirt washed away, unveiling her soft curls as she rinsed out suds from her shampoo. She leaned against the cold wall, breathing steady as her body warmed. Her legs wouldn't be able to hold her much longer she realized. With her eyes closed and forehead against the stone wall, she turned off the shower and walked over to the inlaid tub in her floor.

A few stone tiled steps led into the body forming sculpture, allowing her to be fully submerged in the steaming water that gave off a calming aroma. They must have put healing oils and soaps in the water she guessed by the scents that rose with the vapor around her. It didn't take long for her to drift off into her first real deep sleep.

When she woke the bath had lost its warmth. The suns were low in the sky that she could see from the bathroom window. A warm breeze caressed her skin as she dried off and walked into her room. Food was prepared and set on her table by the fireplace, which was roaring and had already warmed the room. Clothing sat freshly washed on her bed, along with her canister and pelt. With her towel still wrapped around her body tightly, she lifted the canister and noticed it was oiled, accenting every grain in her masterpiece and protecting it from the elements. Her pelt had a fresh gloss to it with a beautiful tan hide on the back and two large golden clasps with a golden cord for her to hang over her shoulders. She smiled at her prizes, lying them in her trunk so she wouldn't forget them.

After Alveen changed into the provided silk pajama suit in the traditional sky-blue color of Irielle and twisted her hair into a long side braid, she sat at the table in front of the hearth and enjoyed the light vegetables and seafood provided for her. A cider like concoction sat in a silver goblet for her to sip on. A knock came at her door.

"Come in." Alveen jumped to her feet, on the defense. Caspian entered with his fist over his heart.

"Queen Lovisa is here to see you, Your Highness." Alveen relaxed. The Queen walked in with a long sleeve, floor length sky blue satin night gown on.

"How are you feeling?" The Queen asked after Caspian took his post, closing the door behind him.

"Alright I suppose. I expect I could be feeling much worse. The oil in that bath did wonders."

"A specialty of my healers." She nodded in understanding, "Helps put you into a deep sleep, advancing the healing properties, and works quickly while you are relaxed. I see it didn't heal all wounds though" she brushed her finger-tip along her own cheek bone. Alveen felt her cheek. A scar from where Willow had cut her. Alveen chuckled.

"I'm sure Willow will be proud that she stuck such a blow." Alveen took a deep breath, sitting back in her chair. "I'm sure it will heal with time, like all things."

"I hope you don't mind me asking, but what was your seventh trial? I have never heard of any monarch, ever in history, having to undergo such a feat." Her face was innocent and curious. Alveen felt comfortable around Lovisa. She hesitated before talking to her. Should she just keep this all private she wondered? No. She needed to verbalize it.

"A trial of righteousness." She said quietly, meeting eye contact with The Queen.

"What happened?" she hesitated, "If you want to share. I know from experience they can be horrible tests and I do not wish to make this any harder for you."

"No, it's alright. I don't mind." Alveen took a breath, thinking. "The magic told me I came from an infected, corrupt bloodline. One that had caused much bloodshed with its selfishness. Though I had passed all the trials, the magic would not allow a ruler with the ability to be evil to be branded genuine." She stopped speaking, deep in thought.

"Zakarian." Lovisa said. "He never underwent the trials."

"It was more than him, it said." She wasn't sure if she wanted to get into the conversation, but now was as good of a time as any, "Lovisa? Did my parents ever undergo the trials?" The Queen thought for a moment.

"Your father did, yes. Your mother did not, from what I remember." Lovisa's gaze went from deep in thought to understanding. "Dear, you are not your parents or your brother." She nodded in agreement.

"I know. That was what the magic needed to know. That was why I passed. Because I am nothing like them." Alveen could feel warm tears pooling in her eyes, but refused to let them spill over and she blinked them back.

"What happened?" Lovisa asked in a small voice, as though she could tell it was not easy. Alveen searched for the word, a description of what happened and she could only come up with one.

"Torture." She let out a forced smile with a tear and a fake chuckle. "But it needed to happen. I understand why it had to happen, and that makes it a little easier now. It was by far the hardest of my trials. It was the only one I wanted to give up during." Lovisa stood and walked to her, wrapping her athletic, sore figure in a warm motherly embrace.

"You are so strong. I am so happy my daughters get the chance to watch a wise, mature and disciplined Princess come to reign. You are going to do amazing things." She reached into her night gown pocket, pulling out a gold cuff. "It goes around your upper arm. There is good magic in it. From the first world. It helps fend off the negative forces." Alveen reached her hand out as Lovisa extended the gift to her. "The trials have lasting damage on us all, this makes it a little easier."

"Thank-you." Alveen inspected the golden cuff. It was surprisingly light weight. No gems embellished it, but engravings and carvings decorated the surface. Mountains, trees, waves, flames and swirling designs to represent wind. Lovisa squeezed Alveen's arm gently before walking out.

"Get some rest. You can leave in the morning."

When Lovisa left the room Alveen thought it best to summon her grandmother and give her the news herself. She sat in her chair and with a deep inhale, the fog appeared in front of her with her grandmother's face.

"Congratulations Princess." She said as she saw Alveen's face with clarity.

"I assume Lovisa spoke with you already?"

"King Hunter actually. I must say I am as shocked as anyone. I did not think you would pass having no preparation or knowledge of the trials." What praise her grandmother was good at giving, she thought sarcastically.

"I have to believe that maybe that's why I succeeded. Because I did not over think it and dealt with the struggles as they were presented. I did my best to not anticipate anything."

"This tells me you will make a fine Queen someday." The Banri was not one for small talk, "Well I am happy to see you handled it well. I shall let you get some rest and I will see you upon your return from Foresi. There is still much to learn." The fog dissipated.

The breeze from her balcony drew her outside. Her room was near the very top of the mountain giving her a spectacular view of the rolling hills, mountains and coastline that made up the kingdom.

Alveen closed her eyes feeling so surreal and small as she sat so high above the world. Taking a deep breath in she tried to enjoy being in the moment with no one else around. Until that familiar fog covered the view in front of her. She waved her arm to view whoever was summoning her. Golden eyes and perfectly groomed facial hair that rested on a sharp masculine jawline met her relaxed stare.

"Luka. What can I do for you?" She spoke as if she were ready to be finished with the conversation. She was just feeling so content. She could now feel the mixed emotions rising to the surface. The last thing she wanted to do was tell him how obviously important to her he was. Important enough to be brought up as a weakness in her trials. His ego didn't need that boost.

"Hello Princes. Nice to see you."

"I just saw you a couple days ago." She stated bluntly.

"You look awful. What happened to your face?" he must have been referring to the slice across her cheek Willow had given her. She chose not to heal it right away, in all honesty because she kept forgetting about it. She rested her hand on it and healed it before replying.

"Has anyone ever told you how rude you are, or do you just not care?"

"Many have told me, quite frankly, no. I don't care." He paused looking directly at her as if he was about to challenge her. Alveen was not use to him being so defensive. This was the side others saw. "If you haven't noticed Princess, it is only my honesty that is ever precepted as rude. Which means those who think so simply can't swallow the truth." Did he honestly just say that?

"Are you sure they are honest facts and not just your obnoxious opinions?" She retorted defending herself. He allowed a sliver of an approving grin slip across his lips, his eyes reflecting that he enjoyed getting her worked up. She was a challenge to him, she questioned him enough to make him question himself. He was never bored with her holding conversation.

"My opinions are always based upon facts; therefore, they hold the same ground." He leaned forward, giving her a better view of those molten eyes. She glared at him, eyes like daggers, but it only lasted seconds before her composure broke and a smile shown as she released an irritated chuckle.

"You're infuriating. That is my factual opinion."

"Likewise, Princess." He smiled and sat back in the chair he was in, intertwining his fingers together over his abdomen. He wore a button up sweater and she could tell he was near a fire with the flushed colored his cheeks were and the flames casting a glow on his face. "Are you going to tell me what happened?" She rolled her eyes but lifted her freshly washed curls that hung loose of her braid and turned her head to reveal the raw scarification behind her ear in the shape of a crown reflecting the shape of the trees and mountains.

"I won." Was all she said. His eyes got wide as he stared at her, impressed. "I am officially considered a Genuine Monarch." She forced her tone to mock arrogance again.

"I wasn't even aware you were to be undergoing the trials. Normally a representative from each kingdom is there. No matter." His smiled, melting her heart like fire does a candle. "I'm proud of you." He said with affection glittering in his eyes.

"Do the guys go through anything like that? To ready them for becoming Kings?" She asked thinking of how every Queen or soon-to-be-Queen had the mark of the trials, what about the men?

"We do. The trials are almost identical to yours." She didn't want to mention how different hers actually were. He rolled up his sleeve and showed her the barely visible marks on his forearm of the six kingdoms. "Let's see yours." She didn't want to show him, but she knew if she didn't that would be even more suspicious. She rolled up her satin sleeve, waiting for his comment. His eyebrow raised. "Apparently your trials were unlike anyone's." He said. "How are you holding up?" He asked with sincere concern in his tone. She bit her bottom lip trying to keep her composure.

"Better than I thought 1 would be. It was all for just reasons." She stated. He caught her tone of not wanting to go any further into conversation about it. She changed the subject. "Do you get cool tribal inscriptions?"

"Yes." Was all he replied.

"Are you going to let me see?"

"I think that would be indecent, Princess." He smiled and blushed slightly on top of the flush color already adorning his cheeks.

"What?" she exclaimed, "Where could they possibly be?" She asked intrigued.

"Upper back." He stated. "But that would mean I need to remove my shirt for you.." he trailed off as if he was intentionally trying to tease her.

"Ah, and that would very much so be indecent, Your Majesty. I apologize." He laughed at her understanding.

"That was a joke you know. We train shirtless all the time." Alveen felt stupid. Did he really just try to make something indecent out of nothing?

"Seriously? Why would you do that to me? I felt like I had crossed some unknown boundary."

"To see you blush." He said with a sweet smile as if it were the most obvious statement. She rolled her eyes.

"I did not blush." She wanted to add more like, '*you don't appeal to me at all*' so he wouldn't try anything like that again, but she knew as soon as the thought entered her mind that he would be able to tell that was a lie. He was certainly a handsome man. A handsome man that had made his intentions clear in the beginning, a mutually beneficial alliance was all he would seek with her.

"Your cheeks say otherwise." He called her out.

"It's windburn from the ride yesterday, not to mention I am sitting out in the open on top of a mountain. Don't flatter yourself." He studied her for a second before replying.

"You're lying." He still had a smug grin on his face. How did he always know? He was not letting her brush this off or get away with the idea that she might have some kind of attraction to The Bulgraktan King. It was obvious she would have to turn this conversation on him, putting him on the defense.

"And I suppose your cheeks are only reflecting the heat from the fire you sit in front of?"

"Just as much as yours are from the wind, Your Highness." She had no comeback. She let out a sigh of defeat. "I should probably let you get some rest for your journey to Foresi. It's quite a bit longer than your journey there."

"I have so much appreciated this conversation, King Luka. Perhaps we can irritate each other another day?"

"I look forward to that day." He bowed his head and the image of him was whisked away by the breeze that blew her hair to the side, allowing a chill to shudder down her back.

They left early the next morning to ensure a safe arrival so Alveen could return home only a day behind schedule.

"Safe travels, Princess. It has been an honor getting to know you again. You will make a fine Queen someday." Lovisa wrapped her arms around Alveen before she pulled herself up onto Cordelia's back, positioning herself in front of her wings again. The young princesses smiled and waved as Alveen blew them friendly kisses.

"I will miss you girls. You'll come visit me soon, yes?" She asked. They looked with excitement to Lovisa.

"We'll see. You girls have much training to undergo." She answered. With King Hunter and Princess Willow at the front of the group, the alicorns were all in formation on the balcony, ready to lift off the mountain and sore into the royal blue sky ahead. Warriors waved to them as they departed. Cordelia ran gracefully up the balcony until the wind lifted her wings, taking them soring into the clouds above.

~CHAPTER VIII~
FINALLY IN FORESI

The endless sea soon gave way to a dense forest. As they approached the seaside cliffs, she ducked behind her alicorns head blocking her face from the change in wind whipping around her. All the alicorns instinctively maneuvered into a single file line, bee lining for the towering lush trees ahead. King Hunter rode at the front of the group, waving an arm. His movement forced tree trunks and foliage to bend and warp, forming a tunnel at the edge of the cliff. Alveen kept her eyes open, unafraid of whatever was to come.

As they entered the trees she could see that's all it really was, a tunnel made of the trees themselves, much like Cosaint.

Branches intertwined above, leaving no opening for natural light, but the walls held many torches that lit their path like a runway. Humidity washed over her, entering her lungs and bringing beads of accumulating water down her arms. Warm mist coated her skin as they flew closer to an opening. A few more flaps of the alicorn's wings brought them to a clearing she now saw as the base of a large waterfall. The alicorns slowly landed on the outside of the tunnel and trotted towards the large pool ahead of them. The waterfall was hidden under the canopy of the trees. At the bottom it collected into a crystal-clear pool which showed her every rock and plant below.

Princess Willow's alicorn stepped forward, this time she clasped her palms together in front of her. She twisted her wrists outward and curled her fingers as if she were forcefully pulling them apart. Before her, the waterfall began to split as if she were opening it like a curtain. Everyone was still mounted and soon in the air again, diving into the next tunnel. It turned out to only be about a wingspan long.

Steadily flying through the opening, a veil of majestic beauty surrounded her. The entire kingdom of Foresi was in the tree tops. Staircases wrapped around tree trunks bigger then the redwoods back in the realm she used to call home. Every few branches there were massive leaves perfectly wrapped to look like teardrops. It turned out those were rooms for their citizens. A family would live in a cluster of these teardrop shaped rooms.

"Beautiful isn't it?" Willow asked, meeting her pace as Alveen gapped at her best friend's kingdom.

"It is unbelievable." Alveen said as her eyes sparkled reflections of bioluminescence that was beginning to shine. Below them, mist and fog covered the foliage on the forest floor.

Cordelia followed the herd of alicorns ahead until the trees became further apart, revealing what seemed like open sky until investigated closer. A single tree towered in the center of this clearing, its massive roots system creating rooms on the forest floor. The alicorns all dove down directly towards the ground where a clearing was, and a throne at the very base of the tree. The throne was carved out of the tree itself. The craftsmanship second to none as Alveen admired the designs intermingled throughout the arms and tall back.

"Welcome to the center of Foresi." King Hunter declared to Princess Alveen and her guards. "I understand this will be a short visit Your Highness, but I do hope Princess Willow will show you things which are unique to our kingdom in order for you to gain a better understanding of our culture. We are vastly different from the rest, as I'm sure you had no problem seeing." He stated. Alveen nodded. What he said was true. King Hunter and Princess Willow were much more outspoken, determined, confident and radiated an overall strength compared to the others.

"We are not that different. We simply have survival engraved into our genetics." Willow commented as she dismounted. "But I would be happy to show her some local pubs and some of our hidden beauty." She chuckled. King Hunter did not find her comment funny. "Oh, come on, I was just kidding father." He waved his hand at her to dismiss them.

"So where to first, Your Highness?" She contemplated for a moment.

"I suppose we will start at the top." She said leading Alveen and her guards back to the alicorns that paced at the end of what Princess Alveen assumed was their throne room that they landed in. They followed along.

"Why is your throne room the only thing on the ground?"

"It's a symbol of humility. It's a way for us to say to our people, 'we are not above you. We will always put you before us.'" She explained as she examined the many lights above her.

"I like that." Alveen commented. She knew she didn't have too, but she wanted Willow to understand that she appreciated their alliance and this kingdom.

The centaurs all unfolded their thin metallic wings, preparing for a short flight and the alicorns trotted forward ready to depart the ground yet again. Willow aimed them all directly up through the canopy, passing branches and vines until they burst from the top of the trees and glided on the wind that skated over the highest branches. Willow led them to the mountain top only minutes from where they left the ground.

Dirt covered the ground they landed on, free of trees leaving an unobscured view of the kingdom. There wasn't much too see since it was all in the trees. Every so often you would see lights or children bouncing around atop the canopy, but for the most part, the light just glowed through the tree tops as if the kingdom itself was a lantern. Leaves swirled in glamourous formations in the sky above as Alveen sat at the edge of the cliff they stood at, admiring yet another glorious kingdom of Solas. They were on the highest peak now, the only spot higher than the kingdom itself. Everything around sloped downward into the valley.

"Come. There is a pub that I think you would enjoy." Willow began walking toward the trail where the alicorns grazed. Cordelia lowered herself for Alveen to ascend. Following Princess Willow, the alicorns and guards glided through the open atmosphere. Willow took a sharp dive toward what looked like a treetop field. Cordelia's reflexes were miraculous as she followed gracefully, landing only feet behind Willow.

"This is pretty cool." Alveen admitted.

"I do favor this place. I am not a fan of leaving any of the alicorns in the stables all day. This place makes for a perfect stop." Tables were placed along the edges of the small field filled with alicorns playing and grazing while their owners ate and enjoyed quiet conversations. The sky was crystal clear, no clouds blocking the stars and galaxies above them. Willow had gone over to one of the workers requesting food and drinks.

"Are we not eating in the palace?" Alveen asked.

"We could if you want I suppose. I thought you would enjoy a change of pace though. Especially since you leave only tomorrow."

"Very well." Alveen smiled in understanding. Only one more day away from her routines. After that Ollahm would be her constant companion and Caspian would begin his training. With Zakarian gone she wondered who would be working with her on magic control. She would soon find out, she thought to herself. No need to think about it now.

A young boy with fairy-like features brought food over to the branch entwined table that Willow had chosen. Alveen recognized nothing in front of her. All Foresi delicacies she assumed, much like the other places she had been. One by one she tried everything on the saucer in front of her, never to be disappointed.

"You must have been starving Princess." Willow laughed.

"Surprisingly, hungrier than I thought. This was all delicious though, and I honestly don't even know what any of it is." Willow leaned forward as if she were about to explain it and Alveen stopped her. "I don't think I want to know." She chuckled, fearing whatever it was that she ate.

"I'm ready for sleep." Willow stated, walking over to the grazing alicorns in the center of the rooftop. "You coming?" Alveen followed her along. "We have some archery training before you leave Princess. Best to head in early." She explained, taking flight again, only this time, diving soon after the hooves had left the ground, swerving sharply through the tree trunks until they reached a branch extended out, flat on the top as if it were made to be a runway.

"We can walk from here, Sylvesto will care for them this evening." Willow hopped off the alicorn and handed the reigns to a tall, lanky blonde man. He was certainly part elf, but she couldn't determine his other features. Alveen petted Cordelia's mane and rested her forehead with hers before she followed the Foresi Princess into the palace inside the tree trunk. "He takes very good care of them, nothing to worry about." She assured Alveen.

Carved out of the tree was a large door-less entry, leading to an open room with spiral stairs on either side. The floor was glossy in the moonlight, allowing the age rings to contrast on the floor below her feet. "Caspian can show you to your room, he has been here a time or two before." She waved as she ascended the staircase to her left. Caspian stood tall before her leading her up the right staircase. The carved railing was silky under Alveen's fingertips as she trailed them along. On the second landing of the stairs Caspian pushed open a solid door that lead to a corridor with half a dozen identical doors.

"Last door on the left is your room, Your Highness. I will be across the hall if you need me." He spoke while he walked and pushed open his door.

"Thank-You Caspian. Have a good evening." She smiled to her mentor.

He responded with a smile and a nod, waiting for her to go into her room. The door opened effortlessly. These rooms were not like those of the citizens of Foresi. These rooms were carved inside one of the expansive branches, holes in the walls carved perfectly allowing views of outside. The walls, ceiling and floor all glossy as if a protective layer was glazed over them. A small branch chandelier hung in the center of the room. The bedframe, end tables, benches and even the fireplace were all one continuous design of wood carving. The deeper Alveen investigated the furniture she realized they had carved them when they carved the room. They were not separate pieces, it was all the original tree. The skill it had to take for them to plan this perfectly impressed her.

Alveen's trunk sat at the end of the bed on the large bench. As usual, she pulled on fitted comfortable pants and an over sized shirt to sleep in.

"Alveen! You don't need beauty sleep! Get your lazy bum up!" Alveen opened her eyes, curiosity filled her mind. Who would be talking to her like that? It took only a few seconds to realize it was Princess Willow. "Hello? I know you can hear me. Get up."

"I'm up! I swear I'm awake." The door burst open and an all too anxious Willow strolled in with a grin on her face.

"You sleep so long. I was worried you were under a sleeping spell or something."

"Very funny." Alveen rolled her eyes as she swung her legs out of bed. "Am I allowed to change in privacy?" Willow walked out, pointing up at the sun.

"Days passing quickly, best get a move on Princess." Alveen looked out the window. The sun hadn't even risen yet. Never the less, she was up now, no sense in trying to fall back asleep. Sliding on a casual outfit that she could also travel in, Alveen opened her door to see Caspian holding back a smile leaning against the wall.

"What is so funny?" She questioned her guard with a smile.

"Good morning to you as well Princess." He said bowing with a fist over his heart.

"Do I look terrible?" She asked.

"No, no. I was merely entertained by the Princess's tactics for waking you."

"You and me both."

"You must have become close for her to become that comfortable around you." He stated his observation.

"You could say that. This world-wide journey has certainly helped us grow closer, as she emphasized in the beginning that we were." He nodded but gave no response as they walked down the stairs to the glossy foyer they entered last night.

"It is about time." Willow spat sarcastically. "I'm only joking. I just wanted us to have as much time as possible before you leave this afternoon."

"I can appreciate that."

"To the training ground!"

"Whoa, can we have food first?"

"Oh right, that would be a good place to start. Follow me." Willow quickly jogged out of the entrance in the side of the tree and turned, jogging down the staircase that wrapped around it. Caspian and Alveen had to speed up just to keep pace with her. They had to have wrapped the tree over half a dozen times before they reached another doorway reveling the dining hall. Much like the other rooms, the floor and ceiling reflected the age rings of this gigantic tree. The side walls the same glossy wood that her room was. The biggest difference, other than the size, was this furniture was all moveable, made separate from the tree itself, though it still looked as if it was all made of carved branches. The table was covered with plates of similar foods to what Alveen had tasted the evening before, and a few that she recognized. The familiar scent of cooked pork brought excitement to her chest as she searched the table. She sat next to Willow and filled her plate with many different foods ensuring she was ready for whatever Willow had planned for them.

"Alright. Ready to go?" Willow stood and without waiting for an answer, she headed out the door. Alveen quickly ate another bite before following her toward the training ground.

"Pick your weapon of choice." Willow said while gesturing to a wall full of archery equipment. Long bows, recurve, compound, crossbows and a few others Alveen had never even seen, let alone had the knowledge to use one. A dozen different types of releases and bow accessories were laid out on the table in front of the bows, allowing Alveen to scan over them.

She pulled down a few compound bows, testing their draw length and poundage until she found one that was perfect. She twisted a few accessories into place and grabbed a matte black trigger release and a quiver of arrows matching her draw length.

Willow lead them to an area in the forest where only a few trees stood in the clearing, but targets were strewn everywhere, from ten to over one hundred yards away. Alveen would be lucky if she shot anything over forty, where she had become comfortable shooting with her bow. Caspian approached her before they began to shoot.

"Princess, a word of advice. Gravity is quite different here than what you were accustom to. Keep that in mind much as you would consider the direction of the wind." As he stepped back Alveen realized exactly what he meant. Back on Earth, gravity would drag the arrows down, meaning when you shot a further target, you needed to aim high to ensure it would land where it needed to. Here she hadn't yet shot these far distances. This first round was going to be all about her figuring out how the elements here would affect her aim.

"Guests first." Willow had her wrist and fingers wrapped in a green release as she held her bow, arrow nocked, down by her side as she waited for Alveen to find a target.

Approximately thirty yards out she saw a small red target near a bush and decided to aim for that to see how her arrow would react. She exhaled, pulled her cable back and used the one sight pin to aim perfectly, unlike what she would have done before, where she would have aimed high. Letting out half a breath, she released and hit perfectly in the center of the target. Thinking back, she realized all the sights only had one pin, maybe that was all she needed.

Alveen finished her set of three arrows with precision. Princess Willow expressed her appreciation of someone who knew the skill of archery as they went to retrieve her arrows before allowing Willow to shoot her set.

"Why do you aim so close? There are many targets to choose from." Willow jested with her regained Princess friend.

"Where I was before, we actually only shot maybe half the distance of your furthest target, and that was only if someone was seriously skilled." Willows brow raised,

"Are you kidding me?" She asked almost appalled.

"Gravity. It acted much differently than it does here. Even the target I hit would have required a high aim so the arrow dropped to where we needed it." She explained. Willow was intently listening. She had never heard of such a thing before. She took stance as Alveen stepped behind her.

"Now watch how the master does it." Willow said with a smirk. Quick and accurate, Willow drew back her own compound bow and released her arrow at a target nearly fifty yards out, hitting her mark. She repeated herself aiming further and further.

When Alveen shot again she decided to aim for the furthest target. She was surprised to discover that her eyes could effortlessly see that distance. She knew that would not have been the case before. It must have been another heightened sense from the trials, she thought. Imitating Willow's graceful draw back, Alveen prepared herself, leveled her breathing and released her arrow through the trees and into the stump, only slightly below the center of her target. Another released quickly behind it, splitting her first arrow down the center.

"Robin hood." She exclaimed. It was not a common occurrence for her to do that back on Earth.

"What?" Willow asked.

"Robin hood. When you split your first arrow with another? Do you not call it that here?" She asked. Willow gave her a quizzical gaze.

"No. They are just called split tips." Willow smiled shaking her head and they retrieved Alveen's last set.

"Princess." Caspian, Nikoli and Ruslan addressed her as they returned to their shooting location. "Everything is ready for departure. Whenever you are ready to go. It's a short journey through the mountains." Caspian explained.

"Thank-you Caspian. Let me put my equipment away and then we shall be off." Alveen faced back toward Willow.

"It was wonderful being able to spend so much time with you again." She said to The Cosaintian Princess.

"Likewise, I'm so happy we still got along as much as we use to." Willow extended her forearm, ignoring the static shock when their forearms touched. It was going to take Alveen some time to get use to that.

"Summon me if you need anything? I'm only a mountain range away." Alveen chuckled as she hung her bow up and took off smaller accessories, placing them in their appropriate spots.

King Hunter awaited her in their throne room standing in crisp brown trousers and a long sleeve green shirt. Alveen's guards were all ready to go with some of them mounted already and others finishing up clasping their own set of wings.

"It was an honor to travel with you Princess. And an honor to share such an important milestone in your reign." He kissed the top of her hand and his brown eyes met hers. "You are destined for great things." She bowed toward her royal host.

"So I keep being told." She smiled. "I'm sure I'll see you both soon." She turned her back and pulled herself onto Cordelia, who was patiently waiting for her.

"Caspian knows the quickest way out of Foresi and through the mountains. Stay at his back and you will arrive home by nightfall." King Hunter waved. Alveen looked to Caspian who nodded in agreement and waited for her signal that she was ready.

Caspian lifted off the ground with Alveen closely behind and the other guards trailing her. Much like on their flight there, many of the trees formed tunnels of sorts giving them quick entrances around the kingdom. Streams and creeks flowed underneath them along the forest floor as they sped through the shade of the canopy. Alveen could feel the random bursts of warmth from where rays of sun ruptured through the branches above.

They finally emerged from the forest, being drenched in rays of sunlight that warmed their faces, backs and legs. Alveen looked around her. The mountain covered in towering trees behind them poured out all the streams and creeks into a large lake between it and the oncoming range of mountains covered in autumn enriched tones. They were the boundary and entrance to Cosaint.

Princess Alveen admired the glorious mountains she would one day rule over. The waterfalls drained into the valley below where thick trees lined what she assumed was yet another river leading to the lake they so recently flew over. As time passed, they finally reached the barrier for the kingdom. A large dome expanded high above, connecting with the mountainsides effortlessly on every ridge. The blue hue and random electrical charges were the only thing that made Alveen look up. Much like when they entered Krumvite, they simply flew through the barrier, allowing it to warp around them and seal back up behind them.

Rounding the next formation, she finally saw it. Home. Alveen had never traveled in this direction to know that her entire kingdom was on a mountain top. Parts of it, where the village was, had plateaued off, but surrounding it was the steep incline of a mountain on the side closest to them. She recognized that they would be landing in the training grounds, on the far side of the kingdom. Soaring high above she could see the palace glimmering in the sunshine, so deceptive to what it really looked like inside. All she could think of was her warm fire, her elk skin blanket and her bed. Traveling had taken quite the toll on her. She admired the topography for a while longer. She looked behind her at the mountain range they had maneuvered through. She had never seen them before even though they were right in her back yard. Trees must have blocked the view from the area she had been comfortable exploring. It was like a painting staring back at her, un-touched and un-damaged. She would have to take the time to admire it more often.

"So good to be home!" Nikoli called out with a smile. Alveen returned it as she wrapped her arms around gently around Cordelia's thick neck to brace for landing. They spiraled through the tree tops and branches, coming to a graceful stop on the grassy field.

"You are a magnificent flyer, Cordelia." Alveen said giving her a scratch along her neck and up to her ears. She hopped off planting a kiss on her snout. Cordelia stepped closer, finding comfort in Alveen's appreciation.

"I see Queen Karolyn has taken favor to you if she passed Cordelia on to you." Queen Vailion said as she passed the guards, walking over to greet her granddaughter. King Hunter must have let her know they were on their way home.

"Passed her onto me? I was under the impression she was just being lent to me for the time being."

"Oh no dear. This was King Ronan's alicorn. She meant to pass her on. She spoke of it when she was last here." Alveen looked back at the tan and golden alicorn rubbing against her and wrapped her in a warm hug.

"Well, I hope you, Allicent and Beastil get along."

"Dinner was already served as we didn't know when to expect you. You will have a hot meal waiting in your chamber." She turned and addressed the guards, "you will all have a hot meal sent to your homes as a token of appreciation." The guards nodded and all but Caspian departed.

"Princess. I've received plenty of rest. I don't mind staying on duty for the evening." He said to Princess Alveen. "Assuming that is, that The Banri still wishes for you to have guards at all times." He looked to The Queen.

"Of course, Caspian. I would be delighted. Could we have Caspian's meal brought to my chambers as well?"

"I shall have that arranged." The Banri nodded and began walking back to the palace.

Alveen led Cordelia into the stables across the village, waving to the citizens as she passed by. It took everything in her to be nice to everyone as she was now exhausted and just wanted the comfort of her own room, her body still ached, even with the multiple healing sessions and her own magic healings.

When she reached the stables, other guards were tending to their alicorns. They bowed in respect as she passed by walking to the private area of the stables that was meant for the royal's alicorns.

"Hey there boy!" She said as she approached Allicent, her original alicorn. His white coat looked to be freshly groomed as the sun hit it from the nearby window. She tied off Cordelia while she greeted the others. "Beastil, how are you today?" she asked expecting no reply. She reached her arms in and petted both of them, giving them some much needed attention. Caspian stood nearby, remaining in his post.

"Caspian, would you mind leading Cordelia in here. I would love the extra hand in case they aren't fond of each other."

"We could do that, or I have another suggestion Your Highness." Caspian pointed to the stable room with an alicorn Alveen hadn't seen in a while, Zakarian's. "I'm sure she would love company, and it doesn't look as if she's gotten the best attention since Zakarian's departure." Alveen hadn't even noticed the white and brown alicorn standing back in a corner still as can be.

"That poor baby." Alveen walked over, ensuring to close the gate behind her to Beastil and Allicent's room. When Alveen walked over the alicorn walked directly up to her, nudging her arm with her nose. "Oh, you are just needing attention and love, aren't you?" She petted her nose and neck, noticing that she was in dire need of a bath.

"I will get one of the royal stable hands." Caspian said as he walked to the main area of the gigantic building. These stables housed many of the citizens alicorns, though there were many that did not require one or simply didn't want one. Caspian returned with a young boy, muscles much more defined in his arms than she would have expected from someone his age.

"Princess, this is Elias. He will be tending to Remia today once we are finished. I will instruct that we find someone to handle her and Cordelia." The young boy bowed and looked up to her.

His eyes reflected the light, much like that of an animal. That would explain his muscle definition, he must be a werewolf.

"Do you have much experience with alicorns, Elias?" she asked politely.

"Yes, Your Highness. I generally tend to the whole population. Those of us on staff take turns caring for everyone. I would be honored if you would allow me to tend to Remia. I'm sure she's in need of exercise and attention. I shall also tend to her hooves, mane and tail before the day is through." Alveen nodded, happy with Elias's answer. Cordelia was carefully led in, making sure her and Remia got along well and would be fine in the same room. At first, they stayed on separate sides of the room, looking at each other, but they moved around until they were closer and seemed to have no issues. They left them in the same room while Alveen tended to Allicent and Beastil, just to see how they would do but making sure they had full supervision.

"Your Highness, this bedding is in need of being changed as well. Do you mind if I prepare the room next to it and put Cordelia in it while I tend to Remia, then put them both in the other room while I clean this stall?" Elias asked. "Many owners are quite picking how the placement of their alicorns and insist on knowing every detail." He explained when Caspian and Alveen looked at him curiously.

"Of course. Please do what needs to be done to ensure they get the best possible treatment. We don't want anyone getting sick from laying in dirty bedding." Elias nodded and began working on the room next to Cordelia and Remia. Wagons of fresh straw were brought over.

A brush hung up nearby so she decided to use it to bond with Allicent and Beastil since it had been a while. Tomorrow if her schedule allowed, she would come back out and spend time with Remia. It looked as if people just forgot about her and no one thought to tend to her while they were tending the others.

After they were fully brushed, Alveen decided it was best that she go to her chambers for dinner, a shower and finally, her bed. The meal was nothing compared to the buffets and banquets they had come from, but a warm meal was all they needed right now. Caspian stood with his bowl, watching out the balcony. He ate fairly quick and then bowed with a fist over his heart as he went to take station outside her room so she could shower.

Alveen sighed as she relaxed her muscles under the warm water. She still ached from her trials and the traveling had made her exhausted. As she dried off, she went to her closet to find all her clothing had been washed and returned already. Mysti was a miracle worker. Alveen pulled on a comfortable pair of leggings with a long shirt, crawling into her bed enjoying the crackling and warmth coming from the hearth.

~CHAPTER IX~
RETURN TO COSAINT

Just as Alveen had assumed, morning came and courses were back in her schedule, which meant she was back in her gowns. She had enjoyed being able to wear normal clothes for a change while she was away.

Mysti was in her closet helping her pick the next glamorous gown to wear. With the weather becoming cooler her closet had been replenished with not only plenty of shawls and jackets, but also long sleeve dresses. Together they pulled out a sheath black gown covered entirely with gem-less applique, but wrapped in burgundy embroidery. The gown was thicker than what she was use to. A v cut neckline enhanced her features and black velvet sleeves warmed her arms as she pulled it on. She opted for only ruby earrings today and a matching ruby and obsidian crown that must have been recently added to her collection. Thankfully, she was granted the opportunity to wear black boots under her floor length gown.

● ● ●

"Thank-you Mysti. I will see you this evening." The girl nodded as The Princess walked out of the room. Outside her doorway was Caspian and Ruslan, ready to escort her to the library where Ollahm awaited to start the lessons.

"Caspian, was anyone found to fill the position to tend the alicorns? Remia and Cordelia?"

"We have a few candidates coming in this morning. Elias is one of them. He seems to have formed a bond and wishes to make the post permanent. I did see to it that Remia was well tended, and she was." Alveen let out a sigh of relief.

"Thank-you Caspian. I know it was very short notice, but I was worried."

"She looks much better and she seems much happier. I think it was a wise choice placing another alicorn with her. I expect soon she will be at a healthy weight."

"The suggestion was from a wise guard."

"I must meet this guard you speak of, he seems to know what he's talking about." Alveen shook her head as she smiled to her mentor.

"He gives very sound advice. He has yet to steer me in a wrong direction." She placed her fist over her heart, he returned the gesture, bowing his head. Caspian and Ruslan effortlessly opened the stained wooden doors entwined with gold that led into the library. Alveen felt a calmness wash over her. She loved learning and being in this room.

"Banphrionsa! It feels like its been so long since we have been here together." Hilfryo chuckled as he approached, holding out the crook of his arm to escort her to the familiar table in front of her favorite fireplace in the palace.

"I am ready to get back to my usual schedule, that much is for certain. I must say I loved visiting all the other kingdoms."

"Except Bulgrakta, if I am correct?"

"Yes, I have not made it to Bulgrakta just yet. I'm sure royal business will take me there soon."

"Congratulations by the way, Banphrionsa!" The professor spoke with a jolt, as if he had completely forgotten about the trials. "May I see?" Alveen moved her manicured hair out of the way, revealing the genuine monarch symbol, a crown reflecting mountains and tress. "I feel as a proud father would. I must admit, like many of the others, I was not confident that you would pass."

"I wasn't even confident that I would. I figured there was no way I was prepared enough and I was expecting to fail." Alveen adjusted in her seat before continuing, "but once I was in there, it seemed so natural and I thought that I better give it my best shot while I was there."

"Exciting, Princess. Now surely you understand there is much more to learn before you will be ready for everything."

"Of course."

"Before we start, let me ask. What were some of your favorite things during your visits?" Alveen sat back and thought for a moment over the last couple weeks.

"I am truly fascinated with Krumvites transportation and the kingdom as a whole. I admire the work ethic and hard works that Loxlian citizens do. Irielle just felt magical to me, the ambiance there is like no other and Foresi honestly, reminds me of Earth. The woodworking is far superior no doubt, but the values they have and the kingdom as a whole is simply magnificent."

"Ah yes, there is much to learn of Krumvite. Loxley will make more sense once we get to the economic portion of our training. We deal mainly in trades here, I understand your old world had currency everything was bought with? We have some here, but not much. Many things you'll find we can handle with trade, within or outside the kingdom." Alveen nodded in understanding. "Now, with recent events we will be having a few more lessons than normal and I will be taking on new subjects with you." He stood and grabbed a few books walking back, "I will be leading you in magic control, nature manipulation, magical defenses and potions. I understand you know some of these already. We will need to start teaching you the native language so you can preform specific spells. Teleporting, transfiguration, the lot. Much of what you do now is offensive/defensive magic, and much of it is simply bursts of extraordinary amounts of magic. I am not saying this is easy by any means, but with your abilities, we must hone in and teach you to control every sliver of magic within your being." Alveen was excited that she would finally get real lessons in magic. Other than Zakarian's few minor lessons to her, she hadn't received a real lesson. Most of her magical abilities had been instinctual.

"Is that what we're starting with today?"

"Yes. As in every area, you must study and learn of origins and learn the why and when before you should be doing anything hands on. So we'll go over the native language and I would like you to take this book with you," he pointed to a large red canvas covered book with gold inscriptions, "to study and read before bed.

Find things you find fascinating and things that interest you so we can go over them. Write down any questions you may have." He reached for a small stack of books. "These are all potions. There is a book on healing, abilities and alchemy. Before you leave today we can go over the ingredients and their main purposes, also something I would like you to study." Hilfryo continued his lesson going over the importance of different herbs in this realm, different ingredients such as specific barks and elixirs. Some more advanced potions may call for certain animal or species saliva, tears, feathers, fur and such.

Alveen was captivated learning all of the potions. She knew a handful from the books that Zakarian had given her. Simple ones like the strength and energy potions she used in her trials.

Hilfryo allowed her a few breaks, one of which they brought a meal into the library for the two of them and the guards. He would switch between he native language where he worked on her pronunciation and writing. The native alphabet was extraordinarily different from the common one she used.

"and with that, I do believe I have stuffed your brain full for the day and given you plenty to ponder. Take your books and study them Princess." He stood and bowed and rested a hand on her shoulder, looking at her with pride. "Remember, we don't do tests. This is all knowledge you will need in your future. I do not doubt that you take this seriously by any means, but just remember everything I teach you, you will need to recall and some may be in very serious moments. Study well." Caspian stood tall by the door with his hands straight down his side.

"Well done Princess." He said as she approached him, ready for dinner. "Ruslan was called elsewhere." He explained before she got the chance to ask.

"This must be immensely boring for you. I'm sure you would rather be at the training grounds or doing something much more exciting."

"This is rather exciting to me. I was never given the opportunity for this knowledge when I was young. It was during one of the first wars with the Dorcha tribes. I was sent to train when I was very young and never looked back." He explained. "Knowledge like this is priceless and precious. It should be cherished and preserved. Though I may not be able to preform magic on my own, I may need it if I stand with an elf in battle or if I am with a magic yielder in a dire situation." Alveen had never thought of that. Caspian stood there and was learning just like her. He was taking in everything as he was standing guard. This was exciting and completely out of his normal comfort zone. To him, there was nothing boring about any of this. Alveen was never bored with her learning, but she knew others weren't so fond of staring at books and studying.

"I do plan on returning this evening to do some personal research, if you would like to have time to rest. I will remain in the palace until then. I will actually be in my room studying believe it or not." He smiled.

"I would very much appreciate that, Banphrionsa. I shall return to your chambers later this evening then to escort you to the library. You will still have your usual guard outside your chamber." Alveen nodded in appreciation as they approached her corridor that lead to her chambers. "Here, allow me to take these." He reached for her books, "so you can head to dinner with your grandmother. Your studies will be waiting when you return."

"Thank-you. You can place them on the chair in front of the fireplace." She turned and walked away toward the throne room.

The Banri was untalkative during dinner, as she found she was often. They sat in a comfortable silence as they enjoyed a native dish that consisted of toast covered in a bright colored relish and a bowl of odd tasting soup. It smelled very fishy. She compared it to catfish in her mind. Tanilly arrived a little late but sat next to Alveen.

"Princess Alveen! Welcome back!"

"Thank-you Tanilly. How have your classes been going?"

"Um, good. I got a new teacher." She said not sounding very thrilled about it.

"Oh, I'm sorry, I forgot my teacher was helping you while I was gone. Hopefully we will be able to share him soon." Alveen explained, squeezing Tanilly's hand.

"I have a lot to learn still." She sounded disappointed, and unhappy with herself.

"It's okay. I still have a lot to learn too. We will both get there soon enough." Tanilly smiled and nodded as she began to eat her soup. Dessert was a small pudding with fresh cookies placed delicately on top. The Banri stood and excused herself for the evening, leaving Alveen to fiddle with her pudding until she finished it before heading to her own chambers.

It felt lonely with Zakarian gone. She missed him every day, but she was wise enough to understand that his return would not be for the better of the kingdom, or for her. Willow was so far away, she thought about summoning her but she didn't have much to say at this moment. Caspian had become a close confidant, in fact she had the thought already of making him her head advisor when the time came that she needed one. He was one of her mentors and he seemed to have one of the best work ethics she had ever witnessed. Just as she was thinking all of this walking down her corridor, she decided to summon Luka. He seemed to always be able to make her smile.

When she first met him, she was the farthest thing from interested. He seemed arrogant, but he was polite to her. He seemed mature and wise yet, somehow not at all what she was looking for. Yet with the trials bringing him up as an equal of importance to her people, her brother and the first man she loved, maybe she was wrong. Though it was so close to the passing of Samual, the loss still raw, she owed it to herself to not miss any opportunities, political or romantic. For now, she would continue as a beneficial alliance, showing no further interest than that of a friend.

"To what do I owe the pleasure, Princess Alveen?" A wide smile sprawled across his face when he saw her. He wore his fur cape, hood up over his messily styled hair. Snow swirled around him and his cheeks and nose were a rosy color from the wind. His casual personality decided to show itself.

"I find you to be a source of laughter for me in my free time." She stated as if it was nothing important.

"You're in need to laughter? What's wrong?" His brows pinched together but he still smiled.

"Nothing actually. I just found myself in need of company. My guard is taking a well-deserved rest and I am stalling my studies since my nose has been buried in books all day."

"Ah, so you are using me for companionship." He raised his brow and laughed at his way to yet again, make something indecent. Alveen tried holding back a smile but it never worked. A tinge of pink crossed her cheeks as she stared at The King, on his home ground. The snow suited him.

"It would appear so." She said shyly. "How are you today?"

"I am admiring the glistening snow at sunset and I am talking to someone I don't hate having a conversation with. So, I would say I'm having an alright end to my day. What about you, Princess? How was Foresi? Anything exciting happen that I missed?"

"Not really. I was rather irritated upon my return. Turns out no one had been tending to Remia, Zakarian's alicorn. She looked awful. But Sir Caspian went out of his way to help find someone to permanently tend to her and my newest addition, Cordelia."

"King Ronan's alicorn? How did you manage that?" His attention was fully on her now, shocked.

"I guess I made quite the impression on Queen Karolyn."

"I am quite envious. Cordelia is a beautiful creature. Graceful if I remember correctly."

"She is very much so. She made hours of flying seem effortless." They spoke for a while about her studies and of her guard, Caspian.

"I'm not sure he likes me. Remember in Krumvite, he would not leave the room."

"He is very protective, with good reason. He has become one of my closest confidants since the incident." Luka shook his head.

"I guess I will have to try harder to make a good impression if I ever want to spend time with you outside of political events."

"Now why would you want to do that King Luka?" She tilted her head, interested to hear his answer.

"I told you already, you're one of the only people I don't hate having conversations with." His answer was spoken as if it were blatantly obvious.

"I suppose I should be happy and take that as a compliment?" She asked, use to his outward rudeness.

"It is, really. I am much better at complimenting someone than you would believe though."

"I don't doubt that. I believe you have many skills you refuse to share with the world."

"You know me so well." He stated. "Well, as much as I do love our chats, I treasure the opportunity to learn so I will not keep you from your studies. I expect you to know all the potions and the entire native language by morning." He winked with his exaggerated expectation.

"I suppose you'll never know if I do."

"Don't challenge me, Princess. I will summon you before the sun rises."

"I'm normally awake then. So, it is you who shouldn't challenge me, Your Majesty." He couldn't get enough of her stubbornness and her strength. She was like a mighty ice wolf, unafraid of the snow and cold and struggles to come. He was viewed as someone with a heart of ice, cold and strict, but she was seen by all as a Princess filled with fire and passion. She was determined and mindful and intelligent. Someone he knew he needed on his side. It was odd that she mentioned feeling lonely and needing company, because he had been feeling the same way. He sat in his fortress alone in his dining hall, other than being surrounded by guards, which he often ordered away. His people feared and respected him. He needed someone who challenged him to be better.

"Then I shall see you in the morning, Your Highness." She didn't believe that he would summon that early, though she was normally up.

The fog dispersed as she walked through it, joining her books in front of the fire. She quizzed herself on ingredients for potions, even tried tying in her native language lessons. Before she knew how much time had passed, a knock came at the door. She placed book marks in the books and piled them on the carved table in front of her.

"Is it that time already?" She asked when she pulled her door open to see Caspian.

"It is, Your Highness." She walked to her closet and pulled on a sweater over her gown.

"Then we shall go before my eyelids become too heavy." She led the way to the library, unsure of where to start. She raised her hand summoning the few magical books she knew of in the library. From the second floor, the books floated down, landing gracefully on the table in front of her. The fire was low in the hearth and the chill from outside was beginning to creep in. before sitting down she walked around the table and stood in front of the fire. She reached out, palm exposed to the low-lying flames and blew slightly toward her palm. She controlled the air, adding oxygen to the fire, allowing it to roar back to life.

"What is this personal research we are doing, Princess?"

"Are you helping me, Caspian?" she asked with a smile.

"If you do not object."

"Of course not. I am trying to do research on anything that would have allowed the syragons to attack when it was not a double moon. I don't feel enough is being done to figure out why it happened and how to prevent it from happening again."

"That makes sense." He nodded. She handed him a book.

"Here, if you want to start with this one. We need to find something with moon manipulation, or about sorceress powers and abilities. Something that will tell us a little more. We also need to figure out the portals. Portals are generally between realms, not to teleport on the same world. We need to know how they managed such a feat."

"That's a lot we need to know and find."

● ● ●

196

"I anticipate this to be the first of many long nights of research. You are not obligated to be here every night with me."

"I am though. I am assigned as your personal guard. I may as well assist while I'm here." Alveen turned back to her book, flipping through the pages as she scanned the paragraphs, speed reading.

Hours passed and they found nothing. The little information they found on the Dorcha tribes, was guesses at best, other than the night the syragons were created. No one really knew where the tribes resided, because they seemed to always be moving through the valleys, sometimes disappearing completely. There was a known location for the syragons lair, Alveen remembered the mermaids in Palace Bay telling her about it. It was not close to Cosaint though. It was south of even Foresi and Irielle, in a deep area of the sea. There was one encounter written of a search and report team of warriors traveling there from Krumvite to see what else lied around it. They had found the lair but It was empty, perhaps the lair moves as well. No information they found on that night provided any answers.

"These books seem to repeat themselves rather than give new information." Caspian observed.

"I am finding I am running into the same issues."

"Banphrionsa, might I suggest we try again later tomorrow evening? You still have courses, I believe you are doing magic yielding tomorrow, which you will need energy for." She groaned, upset that they found no answers.

"You're right. Let's save our places in these pages and take them to my chamber so we do not lose the books to someone else."

He nodded in agreement, closing the books and piling them in his arms.

Alveen could barley keep her eyes open by the time they reached her chamber. "You can just set them next to the others. The guards are still on duty outside, might I suggest going back and getting more rest. Those few hours are not enough when you are mentally tired." She explained. He nodded in agreement and headed to his chamber, which they had moved into the castle so he had quicker access to aid The Princess if she needed.

Alveen changed into her usual bed ensemble, hanging her gown in a specific location Mysti had showed her to ensure it gets cleaned. As soon as her head hit the pillow, Alveen was fast asleep. No thoughts or nightmares kept her awake.

~Chapter X~
Family Secrets

She woke early as she normally did. It was still multiple hours before her courses started, so she took care of her normal morning hygiene and pulled her hair into a messy bun, pulled a thick headband over her head, allowing a few loose strands to hang by her face. She looked over her freshly washed face and brushed teeth before heading out to sit in front of the fireplace. She stretched her legs, arms and back before taking a seat. Her arm outstretched she shot out a burst of magic causing the fire to roar and crackle as it warmed the room.

The door opened slowly, forcing Alveen to her feet in defense. Mysti walked in with her breakfast.

"I didn't mean to frighten you, Your Highness." She giggled.

"No worries." She laughed in return, trying to peek at the food. It looked delicious and a cinnamon scented breakfast tea sat next to her meal. "Mmm, this looks like exactly what I need." She stated as she sat in front of it. Mysti had brought her food in also, setting it down next to her. "Have a seat Mysti, dig in." Alveen was by far the most lax of all the royals Mysti had ever worked with. She was also the most kind and caring. Mysti admired how Alveen had manners and was polite to all the staff members around her. Fog appeared in front of the fire facing Alveen. "He did not." Alveen spoke aloud, she hadn't believed Luka would summon her early as he threatened. Alveen accepted the summon.

"Well Good Morning, Your Majesty. To what do I owe this pleasure?" Alveen said, sitting back and folding her arms. Mysti had a huge grin on her face looking between Alveen and Luka.

"I want you to know I am not normally a morning person. I prefer sunsets and evenings." Luka looked tired, his messy hair standing up in all direction, noticeably not styled and he wore a plain black v neck t-shirt.

"Well I prefer sunrises and morning walks, what does that have to do with anything? I thought for certain you were only threatening me with an early morning summon." Alveen grinned at his obvious unpleasantness.

"I do not make threats, Princess. I make promises." He was not smiling and clearly not happy to be awake at this hour.

"I will have to remember that. Do I need to let you get back to bed now?" Alveen asked with sarcasm.

"I am already awake, no point in returning to bed now. Now I will be unpleasant to deal with all day."

"So, it will be like any other." Alveen stated, giving him a joking glance.

"Princess, you test my patience far too early." He chuckled as if he were trying to sound tough still in his tired state.

"I'll talk to you later, Your Majesty."

"I hope so, Your Highness. I expect a summon late this evening, so I can witness you in a horrible mood as well."

"As you wish." She raised her eyebrows as if saying she accepted his challenge. Little did he know she already had intentions of staying awake long hours to do more research. The fog dispersed again, melting into the fire.

"King Luka summons you regularly now?" Mysti asked with an enormous smile. She shook with excitement.

"We talk as friends. Often." Alveen commented.

"He fancies you, Princess. He would not have allowed you to see him so disheveled this morning if that were not the case."

"I don't believe that." Alveen pondered the thought for only a moment, "I'm pretty sure it is his ego that couldn't handle being on the losing end of a challenge he himself made up."

"Perhaps your right." Mysti did not look like she believed the words she said. "Are you going to summon him late this evening?"

"Probably not." She said.

"But why!? It is so romantic."

"I don't like being told what to do, or expectations to be thrown at me. Therefore, he will wait and probably anticipate my summon, because he is competitive, and I am not. And he will end up summoning me at a late hour, frustrated because I did not play along with his game."

"So, your goal is to frustrate him?"

"Yes. If he indeed is interested in me, then he will put in the extra effort. And if I have noticed anything, it is that he and I are complete opposites in many areas, so that may make this extra difficult for both of us, *if* there is any kind of attraction." Alveen spoke as she stuffed her face with the glorious warm breakfast before her.

"I don't understand your methods but whatever they are, they seem to be working."

"My methods are that of a beneficial alliance, remember? Not to crawl into The King's bed." Mysti blushed at The Princess's comment.

"What do you wish to wear today?"

"Honestly? What I am wearing now."

"Your Highness, please be serious." Alveen smiled and joined Mysti in her closet.

"Okay. I think I want something like.." she shuffled through the gowns until she reached a metallic gold gown. The sleeves were fitted to her arms and even had holes made for her thumbs, an effort to keep her hands warm no doubt. The top was a scoop neckline and the bodice dropped down to her hips, loosening up to a floor-length silk skirt that looked like liquid gold.

The legs had slits in each side, making her excited that she could wear brown leggings and tall boots with this dress. "This one." She pulled it out and slipped into it.

"Crown, Your Highness?" Alveen walked to the island where they were all stored and searched for the crown she wore for the royal walk.

"There" Mysti retrieved the crown and matching earrings, metallic gold leaves that hung down.

"Perfect, now this seems more elegant so I'm going to spend more time on your hair and makeup today, if you don't mind."

"Not at all, we have time." Alveen said sitting gracefully at her vanity. Mysti curled and pinned strands of hair, leaving a few strands hanging like Alveen had it earlier. Her hair was piled in an elegant array atop her head, holding her crown perfectly in place. Mysti turned her around and began applying her makeup, more than she normally wore.

Alveen admired herself once Mysti had finished. Sparkle filled golden eye shadow covered her lids, dark eye liner and mascara made her teal and gold irises pop even more than normal. He skin looked flawless and her lips were layered with a shimmering nude lipstick.

"I've impressed myself today." Mysti said resting her hands on Alveen's shoulders as she spun her around to approve her look.

"I feel weird saying this, but I love this look."

"Gold and black do look wonderful on you." Alveen gapped at Mysti, she intentionally tried to make her dress for Bulgrakta's colors again. She couldn't argue though.

"I would be irritated if you weren't right." Alveen stood and went back to her books until her lessons were to begin.

"Caspian is here, Your Highness." Her attendant allowed the well-manicured centaur through the door as Alveen approached.

"Ready for your lessons?" He asked politely.

"Of course."

"I do love this look on you, Your Highness."

"Thank-you, Caspian." She wanted to roll her eyes at how well she sported the colors of another kingdom.

That day all her training was going over things from the day before. They worked little on magic yielding as Hilfryo figured out just how much she had been learning on her own. He was impressed with her abilities for having such little training.

After her lesson Caspian suggested getting out of the palace to walk around since she had her nose stuck between pages for days now. "You need fresh air, Princess."

"Can we go to the training grounds? I think I need a little exercise as well." She asked, leading him there anyways.

"Of course." Kids ran up to her hugging her legs and telling her she looked beautiful.

"You look like a Princess of the sun!" one little boy said to her.

"I like your gold dress, Princess Alveen." A little girl mentioned. Tanilly was within the group. The Banri must have decided it was best that she spend time around normal kids her age.

"Princess! I've missed you!" her niece yelled to her.

"Tanilly! Oh, I am so happy I get to see you again!" She picked up the young girl and hugged her tight. "You know what I think?" Tanilly shook her head, making he long blonde hair twist around her shoulders. "I think we should spend a whole day together. What do you think of that? Maybe tomorrow? If The Banri says it's okay?"

"Yes! I would love to spend the day with you!" She wrapped her arms around her.

"Okay, I am going to go try to train with Sir Caspian for a little while. I will see you for dinner?" Tanilly shook her head, her pink eyes glowing with happiness. She waved to the kids as she stood tall walking to the training grounds with Caspian at her side.

Once they reached the grounds Alveen went for a weapon.

"Nope. Today you work on flexibility and hand to hand combat, Princess." She stood up stepping away from the weapon chest. "Spend time stretching." He walked into the armory while she stretched her back again, leaned to the side stretching her arms and legs. Caspian returned with weight belts. "Here, put these on your ankles and waist." He dropped them into her arms, forcing a grunt out of her, not anticipating them to be as heavy as they were.

"Oh my, I do not think I'm going to like this." She said as she strapped the weights to herself.

"Kick." Caspian ordered. Alveen followed his instruction, awkwardly at first. "Jump. Backward kick. Swing Kick. Squat jumps." Caspian listed different moves and maneuvers, Alveen followed immediately.

This didn't continue for long before he listed different gymnastic maneuvers like back handsprings, flips, splits. She felt like she was doing a routine. Alveen landed on her back a few times, not being use to the extra weight.

"Hand the weights back." Alveen unstrapped the weights, hands them back and feeling like she was walking on air. "Now do it again." He listed out combos of flips and kicks. Alveen used power, this time anticipating the extra weight that was no longer there. She was quicker, more flexible and now she was feeling her muscles crying out.

"Enough for today."

"I would have to say I agree." She said as she sat on the weapon chest. Caspian brought her a canteen of water to replenish.

"I'm impressed, your hair and makeup don't look a bit phased." He laughed.

"My attendant is a miracle worker as I'm sure you've noticed." She could feel the sweat in almost every other area of her body. The chill in the air made her fresh sweat cold against her skin.

Walking back, she cooled off and managed to dry off also before re-entering the palace. "Will you be joining me yet again for a night of research?"

"I'm afraid not. I have to attend a guard meeting this evening. But you will have to inform me on what I miss out on." She bowed and placed her fist over her heart.

"Enjoy your evening, Sir Caspian."

"You as well, Banphrionsa." He walked back towards the training field as she entered the palace watching the suns become lower in the sky.

Alveen went directly to the library for the evening. Up the stairs on the second level she decided to search where the few magic books had come from. Shelves upon shelves were books on different spells, different uses of magic until finally she came upon a book about the basics of sorcery.

Flipping through the pages, she learned of how sorceresses summon their magic through themselves, transferring energy, but they could not harness the element like elves could. They were in between a witch and an elf, unable to control the elements but they still had a magical ability in themselves that was greater than that of a witch. It went on to explain how all Solas creatures had magic in them, but many did not have enough to truly harness it, like a centaur. It aided in quick healing and sustained energy but they could not expel the magic like others could, making a difference on the world around them.

Sorceresses used moonlight as a main ingredient in any potions and the center of many spells. Sunlight weakens them because the only external power they can draw from is the moonlight, which the realm had many of.

Alveen walked down the stairs, still staring at the book in her hand, excited that maybe she finally found something. As she reached the last flight of stairs, her gown caught under her boot, sending her face first down the stairs, the book flying from her hands. She thrust her hands out in front of her, levitating off the ground before she actually hit the floor before her. A loud crash rang out near the mantel. Alveen got to her feet, heart still racing from the impending damage that could have been her face.

"Oh, no, no, no." Alveen ran over to the mantel. The book had flown from her hands and slammed into a large globe, breaking it, and sending the book into the flames. Alveen reached in with her magic and held the book floating mid air until the embers all went black. The pages were so old that many of them burnt quickly. She grunted in frustration. The one lead she may have had. She looked back at the globe that she had admired many times. This was not a good evening for her. She bent down to pick up a broken piece to fix the globe. As she tried reattaching the large chunk that had broken off, she noticed the globe was hiding something.

A scroll lay in the bottom of the hollow sphere, twine wrapped around it. No seal or anything showing it would have come from a certain kingdom. As she pulled it out, it looked as if it came from a simple cottage with the type of paper and twine. She looked around to see if anyone else was in the room and called out to be certain.

"Hello? Is anyone in here? We're locking the doors for the evening." She lied aloud. No one answered. She paced in front of the fire, unrolling the paper, reading it.

Dearest Killian,

I wish I could apologize for what I've done, but the truth is I'm not sorry. You have been my closest confidant all these years, but I fear with my magic gone I am no longer who I use to be. I've heard of ways to regain my power and control, but it comes at a price. I will return for you. We will be happy again, away from that wretched daughter that stole my magic from me by simply being born.

Be warned, should you ever betray me, I will wipe away all the precious memories of her and Zakarian. You won't remember your name, your children or anything about us.

See you soon my love,

L.

Alveen froze, reading and re-reading the letter. Was this letter written to her father? The one whom everyone thought burned in a house fire? As sad as it was to think, she didn't know either of her parents' names. She had always been told it was part of her dangerous childhood so she never thought to ask.

'her and Zakarian' she read. Was that referring to her or Zakarian and someone else?

'wretched daughter that stole my magic from me by simply being born'

Who was that referring to? Could it be that this was her mother? She said his children, not our children though, so maybe it was a mistress or someone who had loved her father. Alveen had so many assumptions she wanted to make. So many things she felt certain about, but it could just be that she was hopeful that she found some evidence that her parents might not be dead.

Another question reeled in her, was this related to the sorceress or was this another puzzle all together? Alveen sat in front of the fire, warming her hands, going over the words from the book and the letter, seeing if anything made sense or matched up.

Fog appeared before her. Luka sat in his chair with an amused grin on his face, until he saw her glazed over stare and absence of a smile.

"Alveen?" Her heart jumped a little when he just used her name. When he was comfortable and concerned and casual with her, so she could forget the weight that was on her shoulders. "Alveen, are you alright?" He moved closer to the fog, as if that would give her comfort. Should she tell him about this letter? Should she wait and do more research? She wasn't sure.

"Yes, I'm okay. Just been doing a lot of research and thinking." He looked at her, full of disbelief. "It's frustrating when you cannot find the knowledge and information you are looking for." She eyed the book on the table and the letter, out of Luka's site. Her brows pushed together, reflecting her feeling of being confused and stuck.

"Yes. I have found that to be extraordinarily frustrating." He continued looking at her, watching her eyes, observing her body movements as if trying to figure out what she wasn't saying to him. Not only did her facial expression make it obvious that something was not right, but he could feel it. His chest tightened when he saw her look of sorrow. Sorrow, not defeat, not confusion as she was explaining. He saw sorrow and hurt. "What, may I ask, is it that you are looking for?"

She knew this much was alright to share with him. "I'm trying to figure out how the syragons were able to attack that night and how they managed to open portals and travel within the same realm. So many unanswered questions and theories and no one seems to be trying to look into it and prevent it from happening again." This time she was frustrated. The Banri didn't seem to be researching. Did she know something that she wasn't telling them? Did everyone know more than her? "I feel as though everyone knows something I don't." He looked at her for a moment, recognizing that she was right. No one was trying to dig deeper and figure out the why and how behind everything that had conspired, they simply sat back and accepted what happened.

"You're right. No one seems to be doing anything. My opinion is that they all think it was a fluke. It would not happen again."

"They're wrong." She stated, looking into the fire as if it were the horizon. "That attack was calculated, to the very place of the portals opening. They blocked the palace, they threw a stranger out where they knew people would be, and they attacked where they knew they would do the most damage."

"I agree. I've actually been doing my own research, though I'm sure not as extensive as yours." Her eyes finally met his. For a split second it was as if she forgot what they were talking about. His eye contact with her calmed her instantly and melted her as a candle melted the snow.

"You have?" a small grin peeked out from the corner of her lips, making him feel a little better. He still knew she wasn't telling him everything. "Have you found anything?"

"Not much. I did find a spell that they may have used, I actually found it in a witches and warlock grimoire. It's for harnessing moon light. Perhaps if they did do that, and harnessed enough of it, they could have caused a faux double moon, giving them the opportunity to move around."

"Does that sound like something that is possible?"

"It seemed tedious, even for a sorceress. It would take years to harness enough to do something like that. So even if they did it once, it would be years before they can do it again." He stated, not sounding worried.

"That does seem like a reasonable feat. But what about the portals?"

"My only thought on that, is that they traveled to a different realm, only to travel back here. I'm not sure how they came up with such precise locations for the receiving end. Normally those take time to set up. They could have had other magical help from outside out realm. There's many possibilities."

"None that I can find concrete information on in my library." She looked around and rested her face in her hands.

"Is that where you are? I wondered. It's beautiful." He looked around. "Not nearly as beautiful as you look though. I love the color on you. Brings out the little bit of gold in your eyes." He made eye contact with her, giving her a sweet and innocent smile. She blushed, his compliment catching her off guard.

"I knew you had skills you kept hidden." She whispered in return. "Thank-you. I'm told gold is my color."

"Gold and black." He corrected. She rolled her eyes, pausing and looking at the letter again.

"Luka?"

"Yes, Princess?"

"This may seem like an odd question, but do you know my parents' names? Zakarian never told them to me and I never really thought to ask." She looked at him, waiting.

"I do. I never met them, but I remember reading about them in hierarchy books." She hadn't even thought to look in a book. "Killian, was your father. He was actually younger brother to King Ronan and Queen Karolyn. Lyra, your mother, was obviously daughter of Vailion and her late husband of Irielle, Lovisa's uncle."

"Wait, so Queen Karolyn is my aunt?" She gave him a different path to talk about, while she was taking in that L, could very possibly be her mother. Talking about her, a wretched daughter that stole her magic. It would explain why she was so powerful and no one could understand why or how. She would bet her mother didn't tell anyone about it for fear of being branded an outcast. She would have failed the monarchy trials not being able to pass the Cosaint, magic yielding trial. She wondered if both her parents were still alive somewhere and what became of them.

"Yep. You didn't know that?"

"Apparently not. I need to really look through these books. Are we related?" an important question.

"Ha, No. Our families have never married. Your family has married into old lines from Irielle and Loxley. Our life lines are so long that there are very few marriages."

"So, we haven't run into any incest yet?" she laughed but looked disgusted.

"No, there have been many offspring so if there has been any inter-wedding, it would be through marriage and not blood. Our monarchs live for millennias, unlike many of our citizens."

"So soon we will have to open up to the possibility of marrying into non-pure lines, correct?" He looked at her, wondering what her angle was.

"It's been discussed, but we have not reached that point yet." She nodded as he decided to change the subject. "You know, Princess, Bulgrakta has the largest library in this realm."

"Being as your main value is wisdom, I would certainly hope so." She forced a laugh, still not convincing him that she was alright.

"You're welcome to come visit and spend time scavenging through the shelves here."

"It's a grand gesture, honestly, but I do have more training to undergo and I actually have a date set for tomorrow." She tried throwing him off to see what he would say.

"A date?"

"Yes. Is there a problem with that?" He didn't smile, or joke. "It's with a little girl, if that makes you feel any better. More of a play date. Me trying to be a good role model and all."

"You tricked me. Very well played, Princess."

"Mm, but now I know information that I know you won't say out loud. So, I do appreciate that." She winked at him and he bit his lip, shaking his head.

"I said nothing."

"Which told me everything." She grabbed the burnt book and tried to look through it. "Besides, you couldn't resist not talking to me this evening. I knew if I didn't summon you I would still get the chance to see your face."

"You think you know me so well?"

"Not really. You are hard to figure out. It's easier when you're casual as you have been today. But I know competitive spirits, and I am not one of them. I knew you couldn't resist calling me out as if you expected me to be in bed at this hour." She wasn't smiling anymore; her face gave way to a stressed expression.

"Alveen?" He asked softly, pausing when he couldn't help but wonder what he could do about whatever was bothering her. "Are you okay? The words you say and the banter is normal, but I can feel something from you. You're hurt. Talk to me." He said. Was she really that transparent?

"I just found out information that makes my position a little more difficult. That's all." Another fake, forced smile landed on her face for a second. The letter was about her, she thought again. It had to be, unless she had an older sister no one knew about which was highly unlikely.

"You know, one of the benefits to this alliance you and I have, is that you don't have to do things alone. I understand how hard it is to face struggles with no support and with no knowledge of what's next. I want to help you and I hope in return you will someday want to help me if I am in a similar situation."

"Mutually beneficial alliance." She said with a small smile.

"Exactly." He said with a sympathetic grin.

"Well, as an ally do I have you word you won't repeat what I'm about to tell you?"

"Of course. I wont repeat it. I did not lie when I told you I am worthy of trusting. Loyalty is the most important trait in a person." She took a deep breath and held up the letter. "What's that?" She started to tear up but cleared her throat and forced the water works back for right now.

"It's a letter. I found it during my research today. From L, to Killian." She sniffled as the tears threatened to spill over again. "I had an assumption based on the contents that it was about me, but I wasn't sure. Until you confirmed their names. I could be wrong, but it makes too much sense."

"Will you read it to me?" He asked, his tone not demanding. She read the letter to him, her voice breaking a few times before she finished. She set it down on the table. He stayed silent for a moment. "I don't know what to say, Alveen. I'm so sorry."

"I have no idea who they are, if they're still alive or how this stupid letter even managed to find its way inside a globe inside the palace."

"It could have been a gift. From Lyra, to Killian. Maybe he had it placed in the library instead of their home. No one ever found his body, right? The letter said she'd be back for him. Maybe it was a cover, so they could run away together. Though it is cruel that they would leave their children, it is a possibility." Luka was always analyzing things. Leave it to him to analyze a letter that broke her heart.

"It is possible. Or maybe he betrayed her and didn't want to go, and she burned his house down and kidnapped him, wiping his memory." Alveen spat out. A realization came to her as she rambled.

"Well." Luka paused, "That's certainly another possibility." Her eyes widened as she thought of something. The stranger. He claimed to not know his name, or remember anything. But surely someone would have recognized him if it were her father.

"Is it possible to put a strong, almost permanent cloaking spell on someone?" She asked walking over to her spell books, the fog following her.

"I haven't heard of it, but that doesn't mean it isn't possible. Why? What brilliant theory dances in your mind?" The way he said the last part, as if the spark in her eye when she got an idea was the most beautiful thing he witnessed, made her blush, and for the first time since they're conversation started, she let out a real smile.

"The stranger, the first one through the portal. He claimed and still claims to not know his own name, or anything of his life. His memory completely wiped." Luka began to follow her train of thought.

"But if it were Prince Killian, someone would have recognized him, so you are thinking if she wiped his memory, maybe she was able to wipe away his identity or cloak him somehow?"

"That is exactly what I am thinking. Even Banri said his mix of features is unlike anything they've seen. Maybe it's because it's not real." Luka stood up from his chair and ran to a shelf, both of them ravaging through pages, looking for some kind of spell or potion.

An hour passed with them tossing back and forth ideas or spells and potions they found, but none of them were right. They decided to call it quits for now, though they would follow up in a couple days to touch base.

"We are keeping this secret until we have all out information for this theory, yes?" Luka confirmed.

"Yes. Because if I know my grandmother, she will try to rip apart this theory. My hope is to be able to know the solution and try to reveal the true identity of the stranger in my dungeon before she has a chance to ask questions. If I am wrong, nothing will happen and she can't question me, but If my theory is correct..."

"Then all she will be able to do is listen." He concluded for her.

"Exactly." She smiled. "I think I need you as a study buddy more often. I feel like this is the first time I actually got something accomplished." She let out a sigh, falling back into her chair. "Sleep well, King Luka."

"You as well, Your Highness." he ended the connection. Alveen stood, collecting the few books she hadn't looked through

● ● ●

yet, hoping the librarian wouldn't be too upset that she left a stack out. She took the burnt book with her as well, not wanting anyone to think she vandalized her sacred space.

Walking out of the library the corridor was dark. Two steps out of the doorway and a hand clasped over her mouth, pulling her back. The assailant wasn't much taller than her she took note. She sent her elbow plunging into her attacker's ribcage, and again in the stomach, dropping her books with a loud echo through the hall. She pulled herself out of her attacker's arms and spun around to face whoever it was. She pulled the light from the orbs in the library and sent it to light the corridor, lighting the face of her brother.

~Chapter XI~
Attack around the world

"Zakrarian." She whispered, as if she didn't believe her eyes. He knelt on the ground, coughing up blood from the force of her hit. The once clean-cut man she looked up to, stood before her now in black jeans and boots and a long sleeve red thermal shirt. His facial hair grew out but was unkept, his eyes were bloodshot and his hair was now past his shoulders, disheveled. "Guards! Caspian!" Alveen screamed. She stepped back, bracing herself for a fight.

"Alveen, It's me."

"I know exactly who I'm looking at. Last I knew you were not welcome here, traitor."

"I don't want to fight you." She didn't give him the kindness of responding. She thrust out with a kick, sending him into a wall, slamming his head backward. He was weak. Weaker than she had ever seen him. She pinched her brows together, curious, but not stupid. She blew into her palm and pushed her palm out toward him to hold him against the wall, without harming him.

"What did she do to you?" Alveen questioned with authority.

"Alveen. Please. Listen to me. There's going to be another attack."

"Why would I believe you? Why would you give away a plan? You betrayed us. You chose your side." She said angrily, forcing the air to squeeze him tighter.

"I didn't know what I was getting into. Mom. Dad. They..They're alive, Alveen. And it was the only way to be with Malika." She didn't know they were alive, but she had a good assumption.

"By leaving your daughter. And your people. And your sister. And killing your best friend." With the last words she squeezed even tighter, she was angry. Tears crawled out onto her cheeks. "You killed Samual!"

"I wasn't myself. I swear. My mind, it was manipulated. He was supposed to be a sacrifice for the greater good." Zakarian had taught her that no magic could bend someone's free will. He taught her that, so she knew what he was saying was a lie, right?

Footsteps pounded down the hall and the palace guards got closer.

"Don't lie to me." She squeezed hard again, making him cry out.

"How can you torture your own brother like this?"

"You are not my brother. My brother was selfless and wise. The man I see before me is weak, cares only about himself and is fearful. My brother didn't murder people or allow his own kingdom to be slain as he ran away like a coward!" She was screaming but controlling her grip on him.

"Princess! Are you alright?" the first wave of guards consisted of Nikoli, Ruslan, Griffith and a handful of others. Alveen realized she didn't get any of the information about the attack, she was so wound up in her emotions.

"Where is the attack happening?" She demanded. The guards all swarmed around him, ready to grab him.

"Everywhere. And it will be soon. Brace yourself, Princess." Zakarian took a breath in and when he exhaled, his whole body faded and turned to fog, disappearing from her grasps.

Alveen looked dumbfounded, staring from her hand, to the wall to all the guards who looked just as confused. None of them had seen anything like that before.

"Dark magic, My Banphrionsa." Nikoli commented, stepping away. Alveen dropped her hand.

"Lead a search through the palace and the kingdom. If he's still here, we need to find him." The second wave of guards came, Caspian among them.

"Banphrionsa, what happened?" He asked, guiding her like his child to safety.

"Zakarian." Was all she said. "Somehow his body turned to fog and disappeared. But he was real, he was here. I felt his hand over my mouth and I felt my elbow hit him. I could feel the weight of his body in my grasp. And then it was just gone." Caspian guided her to the throne room where The Banri waited for them.

She repeated what happened to her. Explaining that he claims there will be another attack soon, but all he said was the attack will be everywhere. She explained that he claimed to have turned to evil because mom and dad were there, and Malika. He said they were alive.

"That does not help us prepare. I will warn our allies to brace for any kind of attack and let them know of the attack here and the advanced magic to expect. Caspian. Please lead Alveen to her chambers. I would like two guards in her chambers at all times and at least two outside." She ordered with frustration on her face. "You are a magnet for evil, my dear. You must be important to them in some way." She dismissed them, not addressing that her parents could be alive. She was right in keeping the letter from her grandmother. It was firmly tucked away in the side pocket of her pants she wore under her golden slit gown.

Caspian gathered Nikoli, Ruslan, Griffith and a female centaur to help with the guard. "Nikoli and I will remain in the chamber. Ruslan and Griffith, on the balcony. Stella, there will be two normal guards on her chamber door, I would like for you to guard the corridor, checking windows and anyone who goes in or out of her hall." They all nodded in approval, understanding their assignments. Alveen walked with her entourage toward her corridor.

Mysti waited in her chamber, flinching when Alveen walked in with four guards. Alveen nodded toward the closet, walking in to change. Mysti followed.

"Your Highness?"

"I am required by The Banri to be under heavy guard. Zakarian somehow managed to get into the palace, and literally vanished into thin air before our eyes. Caspian and Nikoli will be in the chamber at all times, and Stella will be guarding the hall." Mysti's eyes were wide. "I just wanted you to understand what was going on. Please be careful when you are not here. Stay with people." Mysti nodded, still looking a bit nervous, but helped Alveen out of her dress and placed her crown and earring back in their place. Alveen slid off her boots and leggings and quickly slipped into something comfortable. She would have to stick to her leggings and t-shirts now that she was to have two male guards in her room. Thankfully she had a bathroom and closet, both with doors.

"Thank-you, Your Highness. For caring the way you do." Alveen nodded and hugged Mysti. It seemed days were becoming more and more dangerous without them even knowing. Mysti left the room, passing Nikoli who stood at the door. Caspian stood between the door and the fireplace.

"Just pretend we aren't here." Nikoli said as Alveen looked between the centaurs on the balcony and the two in her room.

"Yeah, that will be easy." She laughed. She sat in front of the fire, leaning back and letting out a long breath.

"Princess, how are you holding up?" Caspian asked, walking towards her, standing by the fireplace facing her on the chair.

"I think I'm doing well for finding out my parents are alive, and evil, and for just nearly squeezing the life out of my own brother who betrayed me and killed the man I loved along with important allies of mine." She chuckled at the insanity that filled that statement.

"It's okay if you are not fine right now."

"I appreciate that Caspian. Unfortunately, I do not have the luxury of being not okay." He nodded and went to stand back at his post. Alveen curled up in her elk blanket on her couch, enjoying the warmth of the fire.

She had drifted off quickly, but became hot part way through the night, causing her to wake up and move. She stood up, noting Nikoli and Caspian still stood by the entrance to her chamber. Alveen walked over to her balcony and stepped outside, the crisp night air thrusting itself onto her skin that felt as if it were nearly burned. Her temperature dropped slowly as she stood in bare feet with Griffith and Ruslan.

"Is everything alright, Your Highness?" Griffith asked.

"Yes, just got a little over heated near the fire, that's all." Alveen took a deep breath in, enjoying the sensation of the cold air in her lungs, and let out a deep breath, admiring the steam from her mouth. The sky was cloudless, revealing planets stars and things she wasn't even sure what they were called. She admired it until she felt cool and relaxed again. She waited a minute taking a few deep breathes, focusing on the cloud of breath before her. The future was going to hold many surprises for her. She went back inside going to her bed, snuggling up with her pillows until morning.

When morning came Alveen must have been allowed to sleep in, because the sun had risen before she did. Mysti sat by the dying down fire with Alveen's breakfast. The exchanged pleasantries as Alveen ate. Today was her day to spend with her beautiful niece, who didn't know they were related quite yet. Alveen decided to dress nice again since Tanilly seemed to enjoy it so much.

"Caspian, can we send someone to retrieve Tanilly? I have a surprise for her to start the day." He nodded and opened the door, taking the task upon himself since Tanilly knew him.

"Are you ready for her?" Alveen asked her attendant.

"Yes, are you letting her help you also?"

"Yep, so we can relax until she gets here." Mysti leaned over and opened the trunk she brought with her this morning as Alveen has secretly requested, revealing a dozen gowns for Tanilly to choose from for herself. She cleared a spot in the closet and hung them up. Each had a small bag attached to it with shoes and a hairpiece.

"Princess!" A flash of blonde hair and pink eyes darted across the room, tackling Alveen on the couch.

"You know you can call me Alveen, right?"

"Oh no. Hilfyo says I am always to address royals with their titles." Alveen understood that.

"I have a surprise for you." She stood up covered Tanilly's eyes and walking her to the closet. "Today, you are going to play princess with me in the palace." She uncovered her eyes so the little girl could see her assortment of gowns. "and I was really hoping you would help me find something to wear also." The young girl jumped and squealed with excitement as she looked at each dress, custom made for her. Little did she know she would be able to keep them all when the day was over.

"I like this one for me." She pointed to a dark green tulle ballgown, the skirt in folded layers. The bodice was covered with hunter green lace with capped sleeves. The bag consisted of dark green lace flats, a simple green headband with a gemstone flower offset, a small pair of studded emerald earrings and a belt to match her hairpiece. Mysti curled her hair and pulled it into an off to the side hairstyle.

"You look beautiful. That is one of my favorite colors." Alveen said and she spun the little girl around.

"What color do you want to wear Princess?" she asked sweetly.

"I'm not sure, what do you think would look best on me?" Alveen leaned on the island as Tanilly shuffled through the large gowns, her face reflecting her contemplating which choice was best. She stepped back and looked at Mysti, pointing to the gown she chose. It was the gown she wore for King Bowen's funeral.

"Beautiful choice." Alveen slipped into the large organza ballgown, admiring how the skirt looked like a night sky and how detailed the bodice was. Tanilly helped Mysti choose a tiara and earrings also. Teardrop sapphire earrings and a gold and sapphire crown were the perfect accents, even the little girl knew. She chose a pair of golden filigreed flats to complete The Princess's look.

"Are we ready to start our day now?" Alveen asked, holding her hand out to the little girl. She nodded, hopping up and down in her dress. "Alright, now we need to be very proper princesses, right? Keep your hands together in front of you and you have to walk with your head up." Tanilly mimicked Alveen, making her smile. "Perfect." The guards surrounded them as they left the room. Tanilly looked intimidated. "It's okay sweetie. They are just going to help make sure we're safe, that's all." Stella stood at the front of the group, leading the way, Caspian and Nikoli to the sides of them and Griffith and Ruslan behind them.

"Where to Princess?" Stella asked Alveen.

"I think we will go to the palace garden." She wanted to stay near the palace but she also didn't want to keep Tanilly cooped up inside. Stella nodded and led the way to the yard between the palace and the bay.

Tanilly skipped through the now dying flowers, without a care in the world. Alveen snuck around a path, cutting in front of Tanilly. The little girl let out a gasp when Alveen scared her. The dying petals regained color, blooming back to their peak. Her face fell, like a puppy in trouble. The flowers around her bloomed back to life. Alveen looked around, standing up to see this little girl just brought an entire garden back to life because she was scared. Just like when Alveen was angry or sad in large scales, she couldn't control the bursts of magic that came from her.

"I'm so sorry Princess Alveen. Please don't tell anyone." Tanilly looked terrified at what she had done. Alveen reached her hand out calmly.

"Why are you apologizing? This is beautiful." Alveen was nervous that a girl this young had come into her powers and no one was helping her control them and even more nervous that she thought they were bad.

"The Banri doesn't want people to know I can do magic. She says people will try to hurt me." Alveen reached out for her, pulling her in for a hug.

"Sometimes people try to steal beautiful and amazing things because they cannot have them for themselves. But, if you learn to control this, you can protect yourself." Alveen created a small cloud letting it rain over where they stood, and quickly created a shield, a dome to protect them. Tanilly looked up, inspired.

"Will you teach me?" She whispered. Alveen nodded.

"First, you need to learn to control your breathing. When you get scared, or angry, or upset, you must remember to breath." Tanilly took a deep breath in, copying the way Alveen was breathing. "Good job. Second, try to hold it. Instead of letting it go from where ever in your body, try to picture little rivers of magic in your arms that pour into your hands. Focus on your hands." Alveen took a deep breath in and formed water spheres in her hands. Tanilly excitedly copied her again, only instead of water, flower petals ripped from the stems around them and swirled in spheres in her hands. She gasped, shocking herself. "It's okay. You can do so many amazing things. Don't be afraid of this. The Banri is right to keep is secret from the other kids, but don't be afraid of it, okay? I will help you as much as I can. You have to promise me one thing." She said looking seriously into her pink eyes.

"What is it?"

"You must only use this magic for good. There are rules with magic. You can't hurt others, or steal or do anything bad with it, otherwise it can be taken from you. Do you understand?" She asked letting her water sphere pour into the flower bed nearby. Tanilly pushed the petal spheres together and pulsed her hands, caused the spheres to explode in a brilliant shower of colored petals and sparks.

"Yes. I will be a good elf." She said. "That's what I am, right? Otherwise I couldn't do magic." She explained. She was so smart and caught on quickly.

"Yes, you are part elf, a large part." She paused, unsure if she should tell the little girl the truth. The Banri wouldn't tell her, but there was really no reason she couldn't know as long as she kept it secret. "Can I tell you a super big secret? You must promise me that you will only talk about it with me, no one else." She explained. The little girl analyzed her and shook her head in agreement. "I'm your aunt." Tanilly smiled wide.

"We're related?"

"Yes, but no one can know just yet because you are not pure-blood elf. The Banri is fighting for you to have full rights as a royal child, but no one can know before that is complete, does that make sense?"

"Yes Ma'am."

"Perfect." She hugged her again, lifting her through the garden.

They spent the rest of the day learning control of different kinds. Alveen did not teach her to use fire, but explained she can help plants grow, she can move water and air and other little things for her to practice on.

Dinner was prepared for them, and they ate with The Banri, as usual in silence. Alveen ended their day in the library, this time with a slew of guards tagging along.

"I don't know about you, but I love books and I love learning." Hilfyro stood at the back of the library, smiling when he saw them.

"My, Tanilly you look beautiful in your gown." She spun around for him, giggling.

"Why don't you go pick a book for us to read?" Alveen suggested. She ran off in search, Griffith on her tail to assist her and ensure she wasn't alone. Alveen shot him a quick appreciative smile. "Hilfyro, do you have any instructions from The Banri on magic training for Tanilly?" he looked surprised at her.

"No, I was unaware she possessed the ability."

"She has a very strong ability. Dare I say equal to my own. She needs to learn control at the very minimum, the basics, the guidelines. She is innocent enough that we can instill good values in her."

"She's so young."

"I know. I only just found out today, she was terrified of her magic. That's going to cause damage. I understand possibly wanting to keep it quiet but, she needs to learn control, beyond what I can teach. Will you do that for me when she is with you next?" He nodded immediately.

"Of course, I agree with you. Uncontrolled magic is dangerous, especially in the hands of a young one." Tanilly was heading back with a book in her arms. Hilfyro nodded and walked away, giving the area to The Princess and the young girl.

"What did you find?" Alveen asked with enthusiasm. She knelt down and Tanilly held out a large hardcover children's book. A book about talking alicorns. "This looks exciting! Let's go over here." Alveen had them sit next to the large window, trying to stay cool as the fire was still burning bright.

After reading two books, fog appeared before them as they sat in the chair.

"Are you ready to meet a friend of mine?" Alveen asked the girl on her lap. She nodded excited. "Proper Princess, remember?" Tanilly placed her hands folded in her lap and sat up tall.

"Good evening, Princess Alveen." Luka looked confused for a moment, looking between the two girls in his vision.

"Good evening. Tanilly, this is my friend King Luka of Bulgrakta. Do you know where that is?"

"Yes, it's all the way at the top of the world. It's very cold there." Luka laughed. She turned to Alveen and whispered "He's handsome." Alveen pretended to analyze Luka.

"I suppose he is, isn't he?" She whispered back.

"Yes, it can be a little chilly up here. What did you beautiful girls do all day?" Tanilly blushed and whispered to Alveen.

"He just called us beautiful." She giggled. Alveen wrapped her in a small hug, smiling at her innocence.

"Do you want to tell him what we did?" she looked at her mentor, unsure if he was safe to tell about her magic. Alveen nodded to her.

"We did magic." Tanilly whispered.

"Oh, did you now? I bet you're pretty good, aren't you?" Tanilly smiled and sat up again, getting a positive answer. She nodded.

"This one is very strong." Alveen admitted. Tanilly sat up proud. "Why don't you return these books where you found them while I talk to King Luka?" She suggested with a smile. The girl hopped off her lap grabbed the books.

"So.." Luke said, waiting an explanation.

"So, your good with children." she stated, flattered to see yet another part of his hard facade had fallen. "So, what?" She asked seriously.

"There is a miniature girl that looks almost exactly like you that you're reading to, and you ask me what?"

"She's not mine if that's what you're wondering."

"I was defiantly questioning the possibility." He thought for a second before continuing, "Zakarian's?" He asked as if he knew already. Alveen's eyes went wide. "I know of him and the fairy. It explains the pink eyes. This is why you were questioning non-purebloods coming into power the other day, wasn't it? That's your niece." Luka smiled large, excited by his discovery. "This is certainly some good information."

"You cannot say anything. She doesn't know everything yet."

"So, what does she think?"

"She knows who her mom is, but they opted not to tell her about her father. Not yet, but I did tell her that we are related, hopefully that will help her want to stay close to me so I can help protect her." Luka nodded. "What?"

"Nothing. She just looks a lot like you."

"Why did you summon me? I told you I had a date today. You said we'd talk in a few days. Did you miss me already?" she asked sarcastically trying to change the subject.

"No, well, sort of. The Banri just summoned my advisors and informed them you were attacked last night, by Zakarian none the less, and that we are to expect an attack. I summoned to get your side of the situation and to make sure you were alright. I see you are fending fine for yourself."

"I am. It just happened to be the one night my guard had off, but I handled myself just fine. Until he literally vanished into thin air in front of me. He confirmed my parents are alive, he said he gave into the evil to be with them if that tells you anything. All he said was there is an attack coming, and it will be everywhere and it will be soon." Alveen tried to laugh, "I didn't get many specifics. Actually, I nearly killed him because I let my anger get the best of me." Alveen admitted, a little ashamed in herself. Luka sat and listened, not sure how to answer at first.

"But you didn't, right?" he tried lightening the situation.

"No, I didn't. It was actually me thinking of not getting enough information about the next attack that held me back." He still sat quiet, he could tell there was more, "that and, I couldn't figure it out. Why did he come to me? Why did he warn me? If he actually wanted to warn me, why would he be so vague?" She let out a quick breath and smiled. "Doesn't help me any to dwell on it now. I might as well just try to be as prepared as I can."

"You took out your big brother?" Luka asked with a smile.

"Do I not look like I can hold my own?"

"No, you look strong. But it's just surprising that all."

"He didn't look like himself. He looked weak, and scared." She pushed the image out of her head as Tanilly came back.

"King Luka, do you like to read?" She asked as she hopped back on Alveen's lap.

"I most certainly do. Look at this." He gestured to the bookshelves behind him.

"Whoa. Princess Alveen, we should go visit your friend."

"Yes, Princess, you should come visit me. I have many books and shelves for you to explore." Tanilly looked at her excited.

"He is cute, you should go visit him." She said with a smile. Alveen blushed.

"Maybe someday soon, okay? You and I both have training to finish, right?" Alveen nodded her head waiting for Tanilly to admit it. She leaned back into Alveen, admitting defeat. Alveen placed her hand on Tanilly's head. "Anyways, I have combat training again in the morning so I do need to get this beautiful princess to bed, and then head into my own bed."

"I may talk to you soon then?" King Luka asked.

"She will summon you tomorrow." Tanilly said for her.

"Oh I will?" she nodded. "I will think about it."

"Sleep well, Princesses. Princess Alveen, I hope to hear from you soon."

"Maybe after training tomorrow."

"Hey Alveen?" He said in a voice that was sweet but rough. She looked at him not sure what he was going to say. "That dress. It compliments you well. I like it." He gave a smile, telling her he was being serious and not messing with her. She smiled and ended the connection guiding her guards out of the library so they could send Tanilly back to her room.

"I had fun being a princess today. Thank-you Princess Alveen." Tanilly pushed herself on her tiptoes to give Alveen a hug.

"You are most certainly welcome."

"I will give you your dress back." She promised, with a worried look on her face.

"I don't think it will fit me. I think you should keep it." Her eyes got wide and she grasped fistfuls of the skirt.

"Are you sure? It's okay?" They reached Tanilly's chambers.

"Yes, of course." She walked into her own room where Mysti waited for her to help her into bed. "Good night. I'm sure I'll see you soon. Be careful" Alveen lifted her hands to show her that she meant with her magic. Tanilly nodded in understanding. She was bright for such a young girl.

"You do well with children." Caspian noted as they made their way to her chamber for the evening.

"Thank-you." Alveen said in a tone that ended the conversation. She didn't want anyone saying how good of a mother should would be someday or how someday she would have that for herself, because that day would never come for her.

Sleep was hard on her that evening. She couldn't get Zakarian's warning out of her head. She tossed and turned until morning.

She had her usual breakfast with Mysti and her guards, and was instructed to dress for combat. Her guards led her through the village to the training field. Nikoli trained her today as the other left to try to get some rest.

Swords clashed above Alveen's head as she swung her blade up to block her opponent. Centaurs were known for having amazing strength, making her training with Nikoli even more advanced. She took a step back, collecting herself and gaining her footing after she nearly stumbled.

"Don't hesitate" Nikoli encouraged her. With his words she lunged forward, keeping her footing as she gracefully advanced toward her mentor, connecting blades yet again. She had been on the ground more times than she cared to share with anyone. Being in the training grounds however, had gained her an audience. She did her best to block them out. They began circling each other again. She swung her blade methodically in a figure eight, feeling the weight of the carved wood and steel in her palm, allowing each muscle to gain familiarity with the weapon. As she regained grip on the hilt a roar erupted from the forest beyond Nikoli.

He turned to face the unknown and she jogged up to his side. Creatures rushed out of the trees, screaming. Taking a look back in the direction of their fear, one by one she could see the trees falling, crashing into the ground in the distance. The beautiful view of the mountains beyond was clouded as dust rose from the ground.

"Nikoli?"

"Princess, Go to the palace. Now."

"And leave you alone? You must not know me at all." He didn't meet her eyes but he smiled as she shook his head. The world below them began to shake as the forest fell to the soil, sending its pain through the ground like screams of agony.

"I don't think there is much we can do here." As he spoke the ground shook violently, knocking Alveen on her back. Nikoli collided with her. Using each other for stability, they managed to make it back to their feet. Dust erupted from the ground. They couldn't see over the edge of the mountain now; the ground was being ripped out from under them. With a single glance Nikoli grabbed The Princess by the arm and swung her on his back, racing away from the danger behind them. Alveen looked around. Buildings were collapsing and crumbling as the root systems were shredded underground. She thrust her arms out in different directions, moving her citizens out of harms way.

Another violent shudder caused Nikoli to lose footing, tossing Alveen from him. Her skull connected with the cobblestone street leaving her unable to move or think for moments. Moments that she needed. She pushed herself up on her arms, still sitting on the ground trying to find her friend and mentor, but it was too late.

One of the falling natural pillars crushed Nikoli, forcing dark blood out of his lips. Alveen's eyes ran over with tears as she clutched her chest, the pain of yet another loss on her heart. She wanted to run to him, to save him. She could have saved him if she had just been paying attention. She could have caught herself, or moved him out of the way. *You don't get the luxury of grieving. This is not about you.* The words repeated in her head until she saw the others around her that she could save. On her feet again, she raced around the village, using her powers the best way she knew how.

"Princess!" Caspian galloped towards her as if he could protect her from whatever was happening to her kingdom and her tribe of citizens.

"Caspian! Oh, Thank Vines."

"Yes I'm fine. Are you harmed?" He questioned with haste, looking over her for wounds.

"Caspian.." She trailed off. "Nikoli.. He didn't..." She couldn't finish the sentence and compose herself. That was simply asking to much of her in this moment. His eyes shined over with what she swore would have been tears. He tilted his head for a moment before pulling her toward the palace. "Caspian, I can save people. Let me help!" She demanded her guard. He looked at her debating on how he could best protect her.

"Stay close by." The shaking had stopped. The village was covered in a thick blanket of dust and fog from the disturbed forest floor below them. She covered her nose and mouth trying not to breath in the airborne particles. "Princess! On the edge of the mountain." Caspian called her over. Multiple citizens hung by roots protruding from the newly eroded cliff. Below them, three bodies lay broken and contorted from their drastic fall. Alveen couldn't focus on them, she had to focus on those she could save. Caspian was shouting orders and reaching for supplies that were now reaching him. Before he could lower the rope someone brought him, Alveen extended her arms reaching for the creatures hanging on for their lives.

"You need to let go. I will bring you to safety." Some couldn't hear her over their fear.

"I will get those too afraid, you bring up the others." Caspian instructed. Him and multiple other guards tied to downed trees and lowered each other, allowing them to wrap around or grab hold of those that didn't trust magic. Meanwhile, Alveen made eye contact with others, instructing them when to release their grips once she was certain she had their full weight in her grasps. She curled her fingers, calling on the magic of nature to fill her. One by one the creatures were brought to the edge and met with healers and anyone able to assist getting them away from the edge.

"Banphrionsa! Sir Caspian!" Sir Magnus yelled from behind them as they brought up the last of the survivors. "The palace! I can't find The Banri!" He panicked. His voice was demanding. "Part of the palace is in ruins. We can't get through." Caspian glanced at Alveen, giving her an encouraging nod. They rushed off to the palace. Magnus was right, the entrance was blocked and the main corridor was covered in downed branches.

Alveen stepped forward thrusting her arms forward. "I'm only worried about getting in right now, not fixing anything." She made sure her intentions were clear to The Queen's guard. He nodded in agreement. Breathing deep she caught a burst of energy, her eyes radiating white as she pushed the trees and branches aside enough for one person to slide through. Alveen led them in, heading towards the throne room. The golden doors were knocked off the hinges and the room was a maze of pillars. Caspian jumped on one, leaping and bounding across the room. Alveen followed, sliding under branches.

"Banri! Banri are you here?" Caspian called. No answer. Alveen could sense her grandmother's presence though.

"Caspian. She is here. I can feel her." They were over halfway through the room now, nearing the staircase to the throne. A trail of red under the leaves caught her eye. "Caspian, hold on!" She crouched down like she was doing a squat and pushed with all her magical might, forcing the trees off the ground in the rest of the room. Caspian stood beside her now, ready to grab The Queen. Once the trees were cleared, Caspian ducked under the maze and within moments was back with Banri Vailion in his arms. Crimson liquid covered her bodice, though she was still breathing. Her eyes fluttered as if she were going in and out of consciousness.

"Magnus! Get Leigheas NOW!" She began barking orders. "Excuse me?" She yelled to a passing staff member who was surveying the damage. "Is there any room undamaged?"

"Your chambers, Your Highness. The Banri's are inaccessible. She nodded her gratitude before casting a knowing look at Caspian, who understood where they were going immediately. Her healer met them on the way to Alveen's

● ● ●
242

chambers. As they entered, it appeared as though her room was untouched. Caspian laid The Queen on Alveen's bed and they stepped out allowing the healer to do her work.

"We should return to the village. See if there is anyone else we can help. I will return shortly to check on her." A thought burst into Alveen's head. "Wait. Where is Tanilly?" She faced Sir Magnus, hoping for an answer. He opened his mouth as if he were about to talk, but no words came out. "Speak! Where is she? Do you not know where she was supposed to be?"

"I..I'm not sure Princess. She normally is in the village with the children or in studies with Hilfyro." He said shaking.

"Send guards to search the library and Zakarian's old room. Finding this girl is of the utmost importance." She paused. If this was a deliberate attack and Zakarian or Malika returned, there is a very good chance they kidnapped her, taking her to the valleys with them. She was powerful. She could very well do damage like this if her emotions were not in control. She turned back toward the guard, "Retrieve me the moment she wakes." Alveen ordered Sir Magnus. He bowed in acceptance.

"We will find her Princess." Caspian comforted her.

"We need to find her now." Alveen said with authority. They ran back through the palace and toward the entrance, Alveen moving what she could.

"You are acting Queen, Your Highness. After we survey the damage, you may want to consider calling upon our allies for support or possible shelter for our citizens until we are repaired and can figure out what happened." Alveen must have look dumb founded. She had not even thought of that. She had not been taught much about diplomatic necessities since there hadn't been any councils held or any meetings other than celebrations. Caspian could sense her stress and rested a hand on her shoulder for comfort, but gave no words, just a friendly smile.

"Thank-you. I will figure this out. Let us help the others and try to find my niece." Caspian ordered multiple guards to search the palace for Tanilly. Surely if she was out in the village, they would find her.

Caspian galloped to the far end of the village to see what assistance he could give and assess further damages. Alveen heard a soft cry, so quiet she was unsure if it was just her ears playing tricks on her. It didn't repeat itself, but Alveen entered the first building she came to, Masgo's butcher shop. One of the many towering trees had collapsed down the center of his roof, leaving little room to walk in his shop.

"Masgo! Are you alright?" She waited for a response. Particles still hovered in the air creating a curtain of cloudiness through her vision. "Is anyone here?" She yelled again. She heard heavy footsteps from behind one of the walls.

"Banphrionsa! Oh, you've come! Please help!" The bald butcher was smeared with his own blood covered in dust.

"Masgo, are you alright?"

"Do not worry about me, I will survive. My wife. She is.." he looked at the gigantic tree trunk laying horizontally in his shop. Tears began to stream down his dirty skin, leaving trails in the dirt. "I hear her. There is nothing I can do." He was reaching for her to help, desperation in his eyes. She squeezed his hand and turned. As she tried summoning her magic, she realized how exhausted she was from the feats she had already managed. The tree wouldn't budge. Frustration overwhelmed her. She placed her hand on the tree, leaning against it as she thought about how she could accomplish this.

As though her magic gave her the answer, her hand began to glow. Her magic expanding and crawling like vines along the tree trunk. She pulled her hand off and the magic still radiated in front of her. Masgo had come to stand beside her. They watched as the solid tree trunk slowly turned transparent, and then vanished before their eyes in glittering sand. His wife lay on the other side on the wooden floor.

"Caspian!" Alveen screamed. Masgo was on his knees by his wife, she was unconscious. Alveen could still feel life pulsing in her. The familiar guard burst through door, surveying the scene before him.

"Princess! What's wrong?" He rushed to her side, giving her something to hold onto as she stumbled.

"I'll be fine. Get her to the healers." Alveen pointed to the fairy on the floor with obvious broken bones.

"Your Highness, you must rest. You have saved many today." She reached up, allowing him to assist her onto his back before he took the butchers wife in his arms and headed back to the palace. "

"You may follow Masgo, I believe she will rest in The Banphrionsa's corridor." The butcher looked to them with grateful eyes, following them into the palace that was being cleared out by palace staff members. The injured were moved to the throne room that was now completely cleared out. Caspian checked with a healer as they walked in and placed her where he was directed.

Masgo reached up and squeezed Alveen's hand. "Thank-you, Banphrionsa. I am forever grateful." He leaned down and held his wife's hand, stroking her cheek with his other. Alveen gave a tired smile and she laid against Caspian's back.

"Now for you." He smiled walking to the entry room. "I find this room to be comforting." He knelt down making it easier for her to descend.

"Thank-you Caspian. Please let me know of any developments. I need to contact the others." He nodded, still wearing an expression of concern as he backed out of the room. Was this the attack Zakarian had warned about? Alveen sat back in front of the fire, before she was able to summon anyone a fog formed in front of her giving way to Queen Karolyn's face, soot and ash marks across her cheeks and forehead.

"Queen Karolyn! Are you alright?"

"Is Banri Vailion alright? I was unable to reach her."

"No, actually she is currently with a healer. Our kingdom has undergone a disaster of sorts. An earthquake that led to an avalanche." The Queen looked at her confused. "Violent earth shaking, then the edge of our kingdom crumbled down the mountainside." Alveen elaborated trying to remain professional.

"Oh my. I suppose that puts you as the acting leader for now. Though I fear you may not be able to help me. Loxley has undergone fierce random fires in the forests surrounding the palace. We were able to extinguish many, but the kingdom. We are in ruins. It will take time to repair." An attack everywhere. This had to be it.

"I understand. We are in a similar position. How coincidental that such disasters happened at the same time though, wouldn't you agree?"

"Most curious if I do say so myself. I will contact Irielle and Krumvite."

"I will contact Foresi and Bulgrakta and see if any other kingdoms were involved in this phenomenon. I shall reach back out to you once I have news." She nodded and ended the connection. Alveen waved her hand to summon Willow, nothing. She tried multiple times, pushing more of her magic into her connection and nothing happened. She did the same with Hunter multiple times. Neither of them were reachable. That could not be a good sign. From everything she learned, the only time that happened was in death and unconsciousness, such as her grandmother now. She reached out to Luka next. His face appeared before her, his beard covered in snowflakes and his cheeks and nose a pink color from the wind chaffing at his skin. As she was ready to begin her conversation, Caspian entered the room.

"We found her! She was in the library. No injuries." They found Tanilly. Thank vines. Alveen rested a hand over her heart, grateful that that weight had fallen from her shoulders. The little girl ran into Alveen's arms, tears streaming down her face.

"Are you okay beautiful What happened?" she didn't say anything. She was shaking.

"I believe she is just scared and shocked Princess. The library was in shambles when they found her. She has been checked by healers for injuries." Alveen petted her nieces head, holding her close for comfort on the couch.

"Thank-you very much Caspian." Alveen looked down and spoke to Tanilly. "It's alright. Everything is okay. You can stay with me now."

"I.. I used the magic you taught me." She finally whispered. Alveen thought for a moment, did she actually cause all this accidentally?

"What do you mean?"

"The shield you taught me in the garden. I used it to protect Ollahm and me from all the branches falling down." She whispered as if what she was saying was an important secret. Alveen felt relief in her chest. It wasn't Tanilly that caused this damage. She protected them.

"I am so proud of you. It's a good thing you learned that, isn't it?" Alveen smiled at her. The little girl nodded. "Why don't you go warm up by the fire. I'll be right here, I promise." She walked away and Luka was still in the cloud that formed in front of them.

"Hi King Luka." He waved to her without a smile as she left his vision.

"Princess? Are you alright? You look awful."

"Why Thank-you King Luka, as always it's a pleasure. No, I am not. Our kingdom has undergone a disaster causing half our kingdom to crumble below us and slide down the mountain side. Casualties are unknown, though I know for certain there were a few. Banri Vailion is injured. I am looking to send my people somewhere while we undergo repairs and figure out what is happening. Loxley was surrounded by fire. It seems they managed themselves, but they are in a similar situation."

"Something is most peculiar. I am away from the fortress at this time, many of my seaside lying citizens have experienced waves that wiped out the entire villages. We are bringing the remaining people to the fortress for safety. When I reach there, I will be able to more accurately let you know if we can accommodate anymore."

"Three natural disasters? Something is wrong. I am unable to reach Princess Willow or King Hunter either. Luka, I fear this may just be the beginning of something far worse. Zakarian said the attack would be everywhere, but how can a single sorceress do something of this magnitude?"

"I have to say for once, I agree Princess. Allow me to reach out to Foresi and see if I get different results. I will contact you soon. Stay safe Princess."

"Be careful, King Luka." They held eye contact for a moment before the connection broke. Almost immediately after, Queen Karolyn was connected to her again.

"There is still some good news in this world" She started with. "Krumvite was unaffected. They are willing to take in as many citizens as they can. However, Irielle has experienced raging storms off the seas. They are undergoing repairs and many of the underground housing is flooded. They too will be traveling to Krumvite until repairs are made. What of Bulgrakta and Foresi?"

"Something is most defiantly wrong. Bulgrakta has experienced overpowering waves that have wiped out entire villages along the shore. King Luka is transferring the remaining survivors to the Bulgraktan fortress. He will contact me upon his arrival to let me know if he is able to house any others beside his own. By all means, get your people to Krumvite. Foresi is unreachable. It has me worried, Queen Karolyn. King Luka is trying them now but I fear something horrible has happened." A cloud appeared, Alveen accepted the connection. Queen Karolyn's eyes widened as King Luka's face appeared.

"Princess, how did you do that?"

"Is this not normal?" She asked referring to the multiple connections.

"Um, no. Definitely not." Luka chimed in.

"I'm not sure then. It just happened. Anyways, King Luka, any news?"

"I had no luck reaching Foresi. Upon my guard's overview of the survivors, we should be able to accept some Cosaintians into the fortress." Alveen let out a relieved sigh.

"Thank-you King Luka. I am grateful." She paused. "I should fly to Foresi, being the closest to them, and see if I can find The King and Princess." Luka and Karolyn nodded. "I will leave Sir Caspian in charge of gathering survivors here and preparing them for the trip to Bulgrakta. I will be in touch." Queen Karolyn nodded and ended her connection.

"Too bad it took such unfortunate circumstances for you to come visit me, Princess." Luka joked.

"I've only just begun my training again, I would have made it once I finished a few more sections." She explained convincingly.

"Are you sure you're prepared to have me in your kingdom, Your Majesty?" He gave her an admiring look.

"I assure you, I am." They held eye contact for a moment, "I will be sending my transportation to you. Alicorns unfortunately are not very well adapt to ice storms and blinding snow."

"What kind of transportation do you use?" Alveen thought back to when he arrived in Cosaint. She hadn't seen him arrive then. Nor had she seen him arrive in Krumvite or depart from Loxley.

"You'll see soon enough." He smiled. "See you soon, Princess." She sent him a tired smile before the connection dissipated. She knew for a fact that she needed rest, and then she needed to clean up before she would take on such a journey.

~Chapter XII~
Finding Foresi

.

The Banri had taken over Alveen's room, though she was allowed in and out as needed. The Princess took Tanilly and made her way into Alveen's room, trying to get sleep on her couch as she often did, instead of the couch in the entry room that was barley long enough to lay on. Tanilly curled up in a chair with a pile of blankets, falling asleep fast. Alveen actually had to carry her from the entry room, where she fell asleep in front of the fire. Alveen hardly slept. She couldn't seem to get comfortable no matter where she laid. She also felt uneasy with her throne room full of injured citizens, but she knew her healers were doing everything they could.

Alveen had learned a little of potions and healing spells but hadn't practiced them much yet. Either way, she did not have the strength last night to preform anything more.

A long shower was how she started her day, allowing the steam to relax her and the scalding water to unknot her muscles. Today would be a day of helping repair homes and assisting in any way she was physically able until Luka arrived to transport citizens.

"Good morning, Your Highness" Mysti was standing by the closet at this early hour. Alveen jumped, not expecting anyone except a few guards to be in her room.

"Mysti! What are you doing here at this hour?"

"One of the guards informed me that you had woken, I wanted to be sure I was here right away. I know you're going through a lot, I thought you may need company or assistance of some kind." Alveen thought about everything that was to transpire in the coming days.

"Actually, yes. I need to prepare for a journey to Foresi. Only a day or two. And upon my return I shall need to pack for a few days in Bulgrakta as well."

"You're finally going to visit the fortress, Your Highness?" She spoke excited, understanding that meant Alveen and Luka would be spending time together.

"Yes, but I am actually transporting citizens whose homes are in ruin. With our palace half in ruin also, we can only house so many people. I will be requiring as many that are able to help with repairs to stay back to ensure the kingdom is back to full strength as soon as possible. I will return once I assure my citizens are safe and I will be doing a day or two of research before my return." Mysti nodded, understanding that now was not a time of romance, but of political necessity and business. She was the acting Queen now. This was her chance to prove she could handle this. If The Banri didn't wake up or heal, she may very well have to handle it. "Mysti, do you think you could keep an eye on Tanilly while I am in Foresi? I will take her with me to Bulgrakta, but my trip to Foresi is not one for a child." Alveen had promised to take Tanilly with her, and she would rather have her by her side than far away.

"Of course, You Highness." Mysti bowed.

As she began to think, a small groan came from her bed. The Banri was moving around under her covers. Alveen rushed to her side.

"Grandmother?" she asked to see if she was actually awake. Her eyes fluttered open. Her face was swollen on one side and bruises covered her jawline. Those were minor injuries to be healed later.

"Alveen? What happened? Why am I in your chambers?" Alveen reached out to hold her hand as she spoke to her.

"I'm afraid we may have seen the beginning of Zakarian's warning, though I am not sure how. We experienced and earthquake resulting in an avalanche on the far side of the kingdom. We have yet to see the extent of the damage today. Many of the citizens homes are destroyed. I plan on working with others to repair as many as possible, but Bulgrakta has graciously opened it's fortress doors to citizens in need. However," she paused giving The Banri a moment to take all of this in, "we are not the only one's who have experienced such disaster." She tried to sit up but Alveen gestured for her to rest. "Loxley is in ruins from wildfires,

Bulgrakta took on powerful tsunamis, Irielle was hit with a hurricane and Foresi is unreachable, both Hunter and Willow. Krumvite is the only kingdom unaffected. They will be hosting Loxlians and Iriellites if they need it." Alveen took a deep breath after explaining the main information that she needed to.

"How many casualties here?" she asked quietly.

"We're unsure of exact numbers, but there were a few." Alveen paused, closing her eyes to hold back her tears, "Nikoli being one of them."

"What of other kingdoms?"

"Bulgrakta took on the highest casualties. The waves washed away entire villages, taking their occupants with them. King Luka said they found a small number of survivors and will be hosting them and a few surrounding villages in the fortress."

"You were unable to reach both King Hunter and Princess Willow?" She asked with a stern expression.

"Yes. That's the other thing, I decided to travel to Foresi to see what has happened there. I fear the worst has happened since none of us can reach them, but someone needs to check on them. We happen to be closest." The Banri shook her head in agreement.

"Yes. Yes, I agree with you Princess. They are one of our closest alliances and they are good people. We must not leave them alone at a time like this." The Banri leaned back in the pillows, staring at the ceiling as if she were thinking. "When will King Luka be here?"

"I will be confirming with him later, but if I remember correctly it's a few days journey?"

"It's a few days by any of our transportation. Bulgraktan transportation is the fastest though. So, he may arrive yet today. When do you plan on leaving?"

"I was hoping to leave this afternoon or tomorrow morning. I wanted to be here when our citizens were transported. I planned on going with them to ensure they are housed safely and I have been wanting to access Bulgraktan libraries for some research." She nodded, understanding.

"You seem to be doing very well on your own, Princess." She smiled.

"Sir Caspian has been my wise advisor for the time being. He has helped tremendously." The Banri stared at her for a moment, analyzing her.

"You will remain as acting Queen until I am to full strength." Alveen's eyes widened, not expecting that sort of response.

"Are you certain? Surely you will do a better job than I would, even from bed." The Banri chuckled, coughing with pain in her chest.

"I'm positive." She smiled, "You will need to decide soon who you will be leaving in charge and which guards will go along with you." Alveen thought for a moment. She knew Caspian would be staying back as her most trusted confidant, also because she knew he would ensure that repairs were made quickly. With Nikoli gone, who would she trust enough to take as her guard? Ruslan and Griffith have been around her the entire time, perhaps they would not be bad options. Stella was a strong guard as well.

"I suppose I should prepare for the day and talk to our citizens." She stood. "Mysti, please fetch Leigheas to and let her know The Banri has woken."

Alveen hurried to her closet, dressing in durable warm clothing, fully knowing a gown would be inconvenient on a day like today. "Good luck Princess Alveen. I have confidence in you." Alveen nodded to her grandmother and walked out the door, being trailed by Ruslan and Griffith.

The throne room was lined with injured creatures. Some had obvious broke bones, others bruises that showed possible internal bleeding. If these creatures had been human, over half of them would not have survived. The magic in their bodies must have begun healing them, getting them past the fatal stage. Alveen wanted to tend to the village first. The less people she had to transport back and forth from Bulgrakta, the better. She searched out her mentor to discuss the real numbers of their situation.

"What is the reality of our situation?" She asked when he finished speaking with a few creatures that were leading the work on repairing buildings. He did not have a pleasant look on his face.

"The entire far side of the kingdom in gone, slide off the mountain and into the valley below, including the training grounds. Most of the businesses on the main area of the village have been damaged, along with their homes. It will take many days to fully restore." He explained. "We've got a dozen elf cross breeds working on repairs. You are really the only one who can speed this up."

"I know, I will do everything I possibly can today. Tomorrow morning, I leave for Foresi. Tanilly will remain in the care of Mysti, my attendant, until my return. Upon my return we will see how many of our citizens need shelter. King Luka has graciously opened his doors for our citizens. I will be traveling with them and will return within a few days. Then I will fully be able to help with repairs."

"I understand."

"What of casualties?" She didn't want to ask, but she needed to know the truth.

"Twelve dead, just shy of one hundred injured, including minor injuries." As horrible as it was to lose anyone, the numbers were not as bad as she had expected. She nodded.

"Alright. Where is best for me to begin?"

"Follow me. I would recommend starting on the homes and worry about the businesses later. If we can fix enough homes and clear out and repair the palace, we may not need to send our citizens all the way to Bulgrakta."

Caspian led her to the area of Cosaint where dozens upon dozens of cottages once stood, now a field of rubble lay before her. She decided to speak with Luka and then begin.

"You have not left yet, correct?" she asked The King.

"I will be shortly, why?"

"We are repairing homes and I plan on doing as much to the palace as possible. We may not need Bulgraktan assistance, but I won't know until tonight."

"I'm coming either way. My kingdom is under control, my citizens are warm, fed and sheltered. The least I can do is help another. And I really don't think anyone should make the journey to Foresi alone if we have no idea the state of it."

"I plan on leaving in the morning, will you be here by then?" She asked, unconvinced that he would make it on time.

"I most certainly can be. I'll see you in the morning." The cloud disappeared and Alveen focused back on the task at hand.

"That was a simple conversation." She took deep breathes in and closed her eyes, forming the building inside her head. Slivers of magic shot out around her, towards separate piles of rubble. Her arms stayed extended towards two buildings at once.

Snapped branches healed back together, lifting up to their original positions. Leaves floated upward toward the branches they fell from, reattaching themselves. Roots dug deeper into the ground and the soil crawled back over them, keeping them securely in place.

Alveen walked around to each large tree that had fallen, thrusting her magic underneath them, one by one, to place them upright and hold them until the magic in the world repaired their roots. By lunch they had repaired five homes and cleaned up many of the debris from the trees above. The inside of the homes were still a mess, but the homes now stood upright and could be worked on by anyone, with or without magic.

Caspian led Alveen to the front lawn of the palace over looking the bay. Many had gathered there to eat lunch. The palace had much stored up and some creatures were able to crawl in and out of damaged homes for food and ingredients. Small croissant sandwiches were made with elk meat and layered vegetables for Alveen and the other creatures who were focused on repairs in order to keep their strength and protein intakes high. The other creatures who, together, managed to roll a few of the large trees out of the streets and repair another home. Alveen had confidence that they could all come together and repair the palace before the day ended. She wouldn't be concerned about the palace if it were not for the fact that it could house over half the kingdom. It would be the quickest repair and provide many with shelter and access to food and rooms. The palace had an entire wing of thirty rooms for situations like this, for guest staff members and for large events.

Some of the entry corridor had been cleared away, but not much. Alveen slowly began twisting her hands and creating a field underneath the branches. She lifted them up, shooting magic into each little branch, ensuring it would attach to its original spot and heal correctly. Alveen stood tall, her arms extended above her head, holding the weight until the ceiling had reformed together. With a final shove, the field of magic below the branches crawled up and mended each of the broken sections. She dropped her arms, wiping sweat from her face and neck.

They repeated this procedure multiple times as they walked through the corridors, cleared out the dining hall, and repaired the few rooms at the back of the palace that were damaged. Alveen was forced to take multiple breaks as others worried she would work herself unconscious since she pulled all her energy from herself and the ground below her.

"I am quite impressed. You work harder than any monarch I've seen in my lifetime." The rough, charming voice behind her brought a grin to her sweaty, flushed face.

"How in the world are you here so fast?" she asked as she embraced her Bulgraktan friend.

"I told you, my transportation is unlike any other. Now," he paused and looked around, "where will I be of the most help?"

"I probably shouldn't be doing much more, but we have many homes in need of repair. If you wish to help this evening, I'm sure we can find a few others that still have energy left."

"It's fine, really. Show me where and I will begin repairs." She pointed toward Caspian who gestured for him to follow. "Do you mind holding these?" Luka handed her his cape and crown, after he rolled up his sleeves. He wore jeans and a long sleeve black thermal shirt, both which fit his body perfectly, accentuating the muscles that years of blacksmithing had given him. She looked him over, taking in his perfectly groomed beard and hairstyle, falling into the liquefied gold that caressed his irises. "Princess?" He asked with a half-smile. She snapped back to reality.

"Of course. I'll go check on your room and I'll leave them there." He bowed, holding eye contact, the hint of a blush touching his cheeks.

Alveen was figuratively intoxicated by the smell of his cape. Why did he have to smell so good? She focused on her feet, trying to just make it to the royal guest wing, which no one had thought to check. Pillars had fallen down blocking the hall way. Alveen's frustration swirled, giving her a little more strength. She held one arm out palm up, forcing the pillars back in place. Once the hallway was cleared, she nervously opened the room Luka normally stayed in. She had never actually been in the rooms, but each door had the symbol of the guests' kingdom.

His was much like her newly remodeled room. Stone floor, large dark engraved bedframe. His room only had a few narrow tall windows. She didn't want to dwell long, so she set his crown and cape on the blankets before heading to her room for the evening to freshen up.

The Banri's room had been repaired, allowing Alveen her bed back once they changed the bedding. Tanilly insisted on staying in Alveen's room, which she didn't object to. Tanilly had gone to the library with Mysti to fetch books to keep her occupied over the next few days while she was to stay in Alveen's chambers and be under watch.

Alveen walked the halls one final time, stopping to sit in the entry room for some privacy after multiple hours. A sliver of the weight her shoulders held was relieved as she fell onto the couch.

"Do you come here often?" The familiar voice asked.

"I do actually. Good memories in here." She winked when she turned and faced Luka. "How are you doing?"

"I am exhausted. I cannot imagine how you are still standing." He walked over and sat next to her on the couch.

"Well you look fantastic, if that makes you feel any better. I bet I look like…"

"Mesmerizing?" he said in a low tone, his head leaning against the back of the couch as if he would fall asleep. "You make it look so easy."

"In case you've forgotten I do have a little bit of an edge on you." She said referring to the extra magic she absorbed at birth.

"That is true." He slouched in his seat, and closed his eyes.

"You know your room is ready, right? You don't have to fall asleep here." He didn't answer. "Why are you really coming with me tomorrow? You know I can handle myself." He turned his face and looked at her for a moment before responding.

"The world only just got their lost princess back, I'm not about to let them lose her again. I saw the hope and the faith in their faces when you appeared in every kingdom. It's been a long time since they've had that." He explained, "and because we have no idea what you are walking into. I don't think going alone would be the best option, for anyone. And as I said, my kingdom is as well as it can be, I can be of more use elsewhere." She didn't respond.

They sat in silence, Alveen drifting off next to Luka as she relaxed in the heat of the fire. When she woke, she was laying on Luka's shoulder. She sat up quickly, to see him looking at her.

"I am so sorry. That was wildly inappropriate."

"It's really okay, Princess. You deserved to rest, that's why I didn't wake you."

"I should have rested in my own bed. How long was I sleeping?" she asked.

"Over half the night." She grunted in disapproval.

"So, I still have time to sleep?" She asked.

"Well, you could, or we could get an early start." He suggested. He stood and stretched in front of the fire, Alveen purposely kept her eyes averted in order to avoid another chance that she would zone out while admiring him. She looked out the window, it was still dark but the light from the suns were visible beyond the mountains.

"We might as well get an early start." She left and went to change.

Tanilly was sprawled out in her bed, mouth open and snoring. Alveen chuckled at the site. Mysti had stayed in the room as well, along with a few guards.

"You are all packed and ready to go, Your Highness." Mysti gestured to a backpack for her to take to Foresi. "And when you return, you and Tanilly are already packed for departure to Bulgrakta."

"Perfect, thank-you. I suppose I should still go and show support to his kingdom. Plus, I need to get more research done." She wiped the sleep from her eyes and dressed for the day of travel ahead. The emerald cape she wore one of the first days she was in Cosaint would cover her identity well should they run into anyone. Alveen hugged Tanilly and let her know she would be back as soon as she could and went to The Banri's room to let her know of her departure.

The stone floor continued into her chamber, towering trunks from trees made up her canopy bed and burgundy curtains and comforters accented her room perfectly. The fireplace in her room was hand carved from multiple trees, extending to the ceiling.

"Heading out early?" She asked from her bed. She had been changed into clean clothes and her face had healed nicely.

"Yes, I will summon you with whatever we find out." Alveen bowed respectfully.

"Stay safe, Alveen." She nodded in understanding as she walked out of her grandmother's chamber and headed to the stables to ready Allicent.

Luka waited in the stables for her, watching as she approached. She wore tall riding boots, warm lined jeans, a fitted long sleeve shirt and vest, gloves and her emerald cape.

"He is magnificent." Luka commented turning his attention from her to the black and teal alicorn in front of him.

"Yes, he is. That's Beastil." She lowered her voice, "He was Samual's." Luka continued to pet him.

"May I?" he asked. He had said they didn't ride alicorns often in Bulgrakta, other than for trail riding and border patrol. He was going to need one to make this trip. Alveen felt a tinge of pain in her chest. Was it wrong to give the man she now had feelings for permission to bond with her first loves alicorn? She wasn't going to over think it, Beastil needed to be flown.

"Of course. This is Allicent, he's mine." They led the alicorns out of the stall and Cordelia started to fuss. "It's okay girl, we will be back soon."

"She is beautiful, but I'm sure Queen Karolyn would throw a fit if she knew you let anyone else ride her." He was right. She was very possessive and protective. They led Beastil and Allicent out of the stables and to the street where their guards already waited.

"We will need to fly high," Luka explained. "This is when Dorcha are active. We can't risk them seeing us." She understood. She realized she had never really seen them or their civilizations, other than the attack. Alveen petted Allicent's face and mane as they readied for departure. A running start was enough for them both to lift off the ground. They soared low over ground that soon became cracks and holes, and then dropped off below them. Alveen could only see with her heightened senses that the buildings and training grounds had been torn apart when they slid down the mountainside. She looked back for a moment, mourning the section of kingdom she lost.

Looking ahead she saw a glow in the deepest crevice of between the mountains. Luka nodded, telling her that was the Dorcha. They directed their path higher in the sky. Looking down Alveen could see the glow from the camps below, like rivers of torches glowing through the trees between the mountains that separated Foresi and Cosaint.

The suns rose, allowing them to fly lower. Alveen knew they would be getting close to Foresi now. A few more mountains to wrap around and then, they would be there and hopefully soon after, figure out what was going on.

They didn't get the chance to enter Foresi. Where the streams poured into the lake that had once been the entrance to the ally kingdom, nothing was in front of them. The streams ran off a cliff side that extended far down where the mountain of Foresi once stood.

Luka and Alveen exchanged a glance, this had not been anywhere near what they were expecting. They both flew out over the edge of the newly formed cliff, investigating where an entire mountain could have gone. The streams and rivers poured over the side that appeared to go on beyond their field of vision. Roots swung in the wind off the dirt and rock wall being eroded by the falling streams.

Alveen created a protective bubble around her and Allicent, slowly descending into the mist from the wall of waterfalls that now existed. Luka followed her lead.

The mist made it difficult to see, but they were certain there was no land down here. They finally reached the water below, flying level with it even further south. The mist finally gave way, when they turned around, it was confirmed. Foresi was gone. The whole kingdom missing. It hadn't sunk into the sea, it hadn't crumbled, it was ripped from the mountain range.

"How is that even possible?" Luka questioned as they hovered near one another, both staring at the anomaly.

"I have no idea." Flying over the mist, they headed back to the break in land. They landed back on the nearest peak, overlooking the void. Alveen held her arms out, palms up and summoned every royal she could think of. Viktor, Lovisa, The Banri and Karolyn all appeared before her in separate clouds.

"I really must know how you do this." Karolyn asked. "Is King Luka with you?" he said nothing. Back to his stoic appearance.

"Yes."

"Have we any news? Where is Willow?" Viktor asked impatiently.

"We have no idea. This is what we flew upon." She backed out of the way, pushing the cloud forward to give them a view of the void where a kingdom once stood. She flipped it around to speak again. "We flew below to see if possibly they had a similar situation to Cosaint, there is nothing below. The kingdom looks as if it were ripped from the mountain range."

"How is that possible? Even with sorcery. Where would an entire kingdom go?" The Banri asked irritated at the unknown.

"I wish we knew."

"I will send the sea guard to evaluate below, maybe there is some evidence there." Krumvite had an underwater guard that could investigate better than they could.

"In the meantime, there is nothing more you two can do there." The Banri spoke.

"We'll be on our way back to Cosaint within the hour." Ending all connections, Alveen stood by Luka, thinking about all the research she had done. None of it prepared her for this possibility.

~Chapter XIII~

Bulgraktan alliance

They witnessed no gatherings of the Dorcha tribes during their flight home. They both remained silent, thinking of solutions and explanations. The fallen mountainside came into view, the fallen trees leaving a perfect landing strip down the center of the village. Beastil and Allicent's hooves clapped against the stone walkway as they came to a halt. It had only been a day, but it seemed many of the citizens were up moving and cleaning the interior of shops and homes. Not all homes were rebuilt yet. The citizens were still working on them when Alveen looked over.

Her hood still above her head as she looked around covered her from the strong breeze that now came from the fallen trees no longer providing a barrier. They guided the alicorns to the stables.

• • •

"Beastil is quite magnificent." Luka said petting his neck. The alicorn lifted his head as if asking for more.

"He is a character that's for certain. I'm glad he was finally able to get out. It's been a while. He took the loss hard. Wouldn't eat for a week." Luka brushed him down before returning him to the room him and Allicent shared. Alveen kissed Allicent's snout, causing him to lean into her. "Oh yes, you love attention, don't you?" she spoke aloud to him while rubbing his neck and side.

Alveen headed into the palace, grateful to see how much work had been done in a single day. Stella stood guard, bowing and opening the door for the on coming acting Queen and Bulgraktan King.

"Princess!!" Tanilly ran to the door as Alveen swiped her hood off her messy hair she had tied back in a low bun.

"I told you I would be back soon!" She laughed, leaning down and holding her niece. She gasped quietly when she saw Luka.

"He's here. With you." She whispered, blushing.

"He is. He went with me to keep me company."

"And to help keep you safe." She noted with confidence.

"Maybe a little." Alveen joked. "Are you going to say hello?" The young girl wore a burgundy, long-sleeve, knee-length tulle dress with black leggings. She ran around with no shoes on, and her hair done up nicely in a formal ponytail.

"Nice to meet you, King Luka. I'm Tanilly." She curtsied to the intimidating man that towered over her. He knelt down so he was closer to her height. He reached out for her hand and placed a small kiss on the back.

"It is a pleasure to meet you." She giggled and ran back to her books she had laying out on the floor in front of the fire. "Is she coming with us?" he asked after she walked away.

"If that's alright? I told her I would take her to see your libraries."

"Ah, a girl after my own heart." He jested. "Of course, she's welcome. After all, it's best to keep her close, is it not?" she had forgotten that Luka knew the extent of her magic and how important she was. Alveen nodded and tried to get Mysti's attention.

"Yes, Your Highness?" she said as she approached. "Nice to see you again, Your Majesty" she bowed to Luka.

"Have our bags been packed for the journey?" she asked politely.

"Yes, packed and already awaiting you."

"Mysti, would you like to join us? I have much research I'd like to get done and it would be a great help if you could assist me with Tanilly while we are there. I'm sure she will want to wander." Mysti's face was covered with surprise.

"Me, Your Highness? Are you sure? I've never traveled before and I'm afraid I may not be the best choice."

"Only if you want to go. I'm not going to force you to do anything. I trust you, especially with her, and I thought you may enjoy getting out of this palace." She smiled at her attendant. They had become close friends since her arrival. "I'm here to stay with Tanilly, you have the rest of the evening to pack and get anything in order that you need to." She looked back and forth between Luka and Alveen until she finally smiled and shook her head, acknowledging that she was going to pack now.

Alveen went and sat on the couch, wrapping herself in her elk skin blanket that she loved so much. Luka sat in the chair near her.

"So, what did you learn today?" Alveen asked. Tanilly jumped up and brought her a book, sitting along side her.

"I learned all of this. Hilfyro taught me about the map today. And we counted. And I am working on all the kingdoms colors!" She spoke excitedly.

"Do you know Bulgrakta's colors?" she asked pointing to Luka. She nodded excited.

"Black and gold. And Cosaint is dark red and gold."

"Do you know where we're going tonight?" Alveen asked. Tanilly pinched her brows together confused. She didn't know they were leaving.

"We are going to see King Luka's libraries! We are going to Bulgrakta, to see his home."

"Really!?" She asked with wide eyes and an open mouth, excited. Alveen knew she had to be getting restless. "Are you going to dress up like me?" she asked twirling in her dress.

"Maybe not to travel, but when we get there I might."

"You will be fine to dress up during the travel portion. Our transportation is comfortable and shielded from the weather." Luka interjected. He wouldn't admit it out loud but he thought she looked magnificently regal when she wore a gown. Her confidence was even greater. He would see her and think he preferred her in her casual appearance, then she would dress up and wow him yet again, leaving him to love every look she had. She gave him a playful glare before allowing the young girl to pull her into the closet.

"Alright, alright. Which gown shall I wear today?" She sat in her chair and waited for her to choose one. She was a little indecisive today, but ended up choosing another organza ballgown. This one was an emerald green with only a few folds in the skirt, and glittering designs of faux lace scattered across it. The neckline was deep and the straps hung off her shoulders. She would defiantly need a fur cape or wrap with this. "Okay, while I put this on, I'm going to need something to keep me warm. I really like fur." She said to the little girl who ran excited to the area where the covers were hung. She pulled down a black and grey fur cape with three Cosaint golden clasps to protect her torso from the cold. Alveen walked over to the island and picked out a silver and emerald tall standing crown, with a matching set of dangling earrings. She put only minimal eye makeup on and headed toward the room.

"No, wait! Let me announce you!" Tanilly said excited. Oh no. Alveen laughed to herself. Tanilly slipped through the door and Alveen could hear her talking to Luka, telling him how beautiful she looked. "May I present the beautiful Princess of Cosaint, Princess Alveen." She heard muffled through the door, she dramatically opened the doors and spun for the little girl.

"I have to agree, a beautiful Princess indeed." Luka sat with his legs crossed over the arm of the chair so he was facing the closet. He clapped and gave her a charming smile.

"Why Thank-you, Your Majesty." Alveen did a deep curtsy, batting her eyes at him as if she were a courtier trying to win him over. He rolled his eyes at her. "Alright, now that we are finished with that, are we ready to leave?"

"Yes, of course Your Highness." Luka jumped to his feet, holding the crook of his elbow out. Alveen reached down and held Tanilly's hand after she pulled on her shoes and coat.

Leaving the palace, Alveen wanted to ensure Caspian was on schedule. "How goes the progress?" She asked as she approached the tall centaur outside the throne room.

"Well. We are actually ahead of schedule. You have some very dedicated and compassionate citizens Princess."

"They have been working extremely hard. We must thank them some way when I return, do not let me forget." She told him, "Are you going to be alright in charge? The Banri is still here, so you are not alone. It will be days before she back to full health."

"I will over see all repairs, and make sure all creatures are attended to and have a safe place to sleep, if that's what you mean. I will leave the diplomatic stuff to you and The Banri." He chuckled.

"Of course. Thank-you for being so loyal." She hugged his torso, then pulled away bowing with a fist over her heart.

"Hurry back Princess." He joked as he gestured her away to avoid being sentimental.

Alveen wasn't sure where, or what, Luka's form of transportation was. She followed him trustingly with her niece in tow. They headed to the far north side of the village, where many fields spanned wide open across the kingdom. When they reached a clearing, Alveen almost laughed outright. There in the center of the frosted over field sat black train cars with gold accents around every embellishment. There was no head to the train, simply the cars she was use to seeing in the middle. Alveen looked around and took note that there weren't any, nor did she ever remember seeing, any kind of tracks.

"Now you've sparked my curiosity." She said as they approached. They had more space than necessary since there was no need for her citizens to travel any longer. They proved to be more productive than she anticipated, and over half of the injured creatures had recovered, giving them more able bodies.

"Just watch and see." Was all Luka said as he lifted his hand, pulling the doors open with his magic. Alveen stepped into the car and was taken aback by the luxurious décor. Tanilly was behind her, still holding her hand.

"This is fancy." The young girl said to Luka, letting go of Alveen's hand and running to one of the few oversized chairs. The interior was dark but elegant. Dark brown fabric covered the walls, golden curtains hung, folded stylishly out of the way. The floor was carpeted with a material she didn't recognize. A fireplace sat at the center of the far wall, dark brown suede and leather like couches strewn about to provide the best seating options. A wrought iron chandelier hung in the center of the car, providing a warm light.

"I'm more interested to see how this thing moves without tracks." Though she was also impressed by the interior.

"Tracks?" Luka questions. Of course, he wouldn't know what those were. She waved it off as if to say never mind. Luka approached the front of the car they were in and slid open a drawer in a bookshelf, bending it down like a tablet. She saw him scan over a map of Beannithe on the screen. He zoomed in and clicked on a spot on the very top of the map. The car shook minimally, then all the doors locked. Alveen's guards were in the car one down from them, along with any that Luka had brought along, which she assumed wasn't many, if any at all. Alveen walked to a window. Without even feeling it, they had lifted off the ground and they we soaring through the sky. She felt no motion at all from the inside.

"It's magic" Luka twisted his wrist and made it snow for a few seconds when he saw Alveen's astonished face. She looked out the window to see they were traveling faster than any alicorn would possibly fly.

"This is how you got here so fast. Impressive." She said as she sat by Tanilly in front of the fire.

"Are you ladies prepared for this weather?" He asked, though he seemed far too excited to get back to the frozen tundra.

Tanilly fell asleep on Alveen's lap, trapping her until they arrived. Luka had joined her, joking and keeping her company. She couldn't help but cherish her conversations with him. He ignored the other royals unless there was an important need to converse. He held minimal conversations with anyone outside his kingdom, yet when it came to her, his laughter and conversations were endless. His flirting and joking were unusual for him. She remembered seeing him the first time as they sat in front of the fire. He had even tried ignoring her, he tried being rude and pushing her away. She supposed it was a fortunate thing that she was stubborn.

"We're nearly there." Alveen woke Tanilly and stood up to stretch her legs and look out the window. The snow came down slowly and gracefully, still allowing a view of the snow-capped mountain range they flew through. She was amazed how warm it managed to stay in there while they were at high altitudes and in no doubt freezing temperatures.

The kingdom soon came into view. It reminded her of Irielle, in the way that they were both completely in mountains though Irielle was more carved out of the edges and open to the warm air, Bulgrakta had a towering bridge with a frozen waterfall beneath it that led to a massive iron arched doorway. Had it not been for that and the guard stations you could see positioned throughout the mountains, the kingdom was hard to spot. The cars lowered themselves, lining with the runway that led into the doors.

Two dragons pushed on the inside of the iron doors, holding them open for the cars to slide by. They looked much like Alveen would have pictured. The dry scales covered every inch of them. Long heavy muscular tails dragged on the solid stone ground behind them and their teeth nearly matched the sharpness of their talons. These dragons were both solid black and stood over halfway up the height of the doors into the mountain. Giants, to say the least.

"Are you okay?" Luka asked as Alveen gapped at the creatures.

"Yes, I've just..." she gestures to the beautiful creatures, unchained aiding in the kingdom. "never seen a dragon before. I knew they existed here, but.." she trailed off, admiring them.

"Yes, they are coming close to extinction though. I have extended my generosity to the few remaining in my kingdom. I provide food, shelter and company as long as they be involved in the kingdom and help us with warmth. They are strong creatures, but they are stronger together. Too many of them lived alone. I have tried to help them rebuild their colony within our kingdom. They are grateful creatures. Great allies to have." He explained in detail.

He guided them into the kingdom, torches, and hearths lined the corridors and staircase that they climbed. The natural stone clicked with each step anyone took. The hum of conversation entered Alveen's ears. Tanilly squeezed her hand. A small voice spoke to Alveen.

I'm nervous.

Alveen tried not to look alarmed or concerned, but the voice she heard was Tanilly's. The little girl next to her. She wasn't sure if she was doing it on purpose or how she was even doing it. Alveen tried to communicate back, just thinking her thoughts and looking at the girl.

Can you hear me, Tanilly?

She was not as good at hiding her surprise. She looked up to her aunt and smiled. Alveen put a finger over her lip, advising her to keep quiet, it was their secret for now. Alveen had never even heard of anyone having the ability to communicate like that. She wondered how far it extended. She let go of her hand and tried again, no reaction. She picked her up and held her to make her feel better about their situation and sent her thought,

It's going to be okay. King Luka is a friend. All kingdoms are very different. You will learn that soon.

She looked at her aunt and nodded that she heard her. They must have to have physical contact for it to work. She wondered why she had never noticed it before.

As they reached the top of the gloomy, but warm staircase, the view before them impressed both of the girls. They were above the kingdom. The lower half of the mountain looked to be almost hollow, filled with streets and stone buildings and beautiful lights as far as the eye could see. They saw very little sun here, but it was bright as day.

"This is the fortress. It is where many come to seek shelter in Bulgrakta, however there are many villages within the mountains arounds us, in the sun with their own yards and property. This has become more of a refuge for those who have lost loved ones, family, and need a place to reconnect and know they are worthy. They have created their own community."

"Did you do this?" Alveen asked, wondering if the dark king had a heart that was not yet frozen solid.

"My grandfather." He looked at her. "I'm sure you've heard the stories of how my father was ruthless, cunning and horrible to his citizens. This was nearly empty for a long time. He would kick those out who weren't willing to work themselves to death. We lost many citizens to his selfishness." Alveen knew him well enough to know the rumors about him being like his father were far from true, but people, monarchs even, still feared him because of things his father had done and the legacy his father left him to follow. "Anyways, I should show you ladies to your chambers while you're here. We can start in the libraries first thing in the morning." Tanilly grabbed Alveen's hand and sent a thought letting her know she was hungry. They hadn't eaten dinner yet, but it was late.

"Any chance you can show us to the kitchen?" Alveen asked with a chuckle looking down at the girl next to her.

"Right this way." They entered the staircase again, climbing even higher. Atop the civilization below was the actual castle formed to the peak of the mountain. Windows allowed in the last bit of sunlight. The kingdom was not entirely dark as she would have expected. Much of it was a grey and tan stone, the décor all dark stained elegantly carved woodwork, no doubt from Foresi, and iron work from within the kingdom.

Alveen would never be able to find her way out of this place. They turned so many corners and went down so many hallways that she was certain they had gone through a maze. Finally, they entered the glamorous and oversized kitchen. It had to be larger than her own chamber at home and she knew their kitchen was not that large. Luka walked over to a cabinet and pulled out a small basket of snacks.

"I doubt we'll find a warm meal at this hour, but these may be just enough to get us through the night." He pulled out a few glasses and filled them with a steaming beverage from a warm barrel. He handed Alveen a glass.

"Is this alcohol?" Luka looked confused by the words again. "Will this make me make a fool of myself?" she asked more specifically.

"No, not at all. This is actually a seasonal beverage here." He poured Tanilly a small cup, handing it to her.

"Mmmm, it makes you so warm inside." She said sitting on the counter, kicking her legs excitedly.

"Alright now, off to bed." She picked her up and carried her toward the door, following Luka. She was happy to learn they were not far from the kitchen.

"This is where you lovely ladies will reside while you are visiting." He pushed open a solid wood door with scones on each side of it. Two fires burned in the room, one between the windows and one just right of the entrance, keeping the room cozy and warm. Much like the castle the walls were carved from the stone in the mountain. The hearths were stones stacked neatly together, and much like the one in the library, the mantel stood shoulder height to Alveen, allowing for them to provide most of the light in the room as well aside from scones that lined the upper half of the wall. A bathroom was off to one side with a free-standing golden tub and a wood carved sink. The bed looked larger than hers, the frame a black wrought iron, old world design, was covered with gold silk sheets and numerous blankets, topped with a large dark animal pelt. Tanilly changed quickly and Alveen tucked her into the bed.

"I will be right back." She kissed her forehead and followed Luka out of the room. He stood waiting expectantly outside the door, she nearly ran into him. "I just wanted to say, from what I have seen so far, this place is magnificent. It's beautiful and strong."

"I appreciate that." They stood in an awkward silence for a moment before he continued, "I'll see you in the morning then?"

"Yes, where is Mysti staying?" he pointed two doors down from her.

"Your guards should be finishing their orientation of the kingdom, but I will assure they are placed outside your door."

"Much appreciated." She wanted to ask where he would be, but that would come off far too straight forward. This having a crush thing was not going well for her, she just wanted to be able to say she had feelings and know how things would play out.

"I'll only be down the hall if you need me for anything." He pointed down another corridor that rounded. She couldn't see a door if he was pointing to one, but she assumed it was the only one down that hall. "Sleep well, Princess."

"Same to you, King Luka." She batted her eyes at him, catching him off guard. She turned and walked into her room before she could embarrass herself further.

"Did you kiss?" Tanilly's voice came from the pile of blankets on the bed.

"What? No, of course not. Why would we kiss?" She questioned the girl far too smart for her age.

"Because he likes you. And you like him. And you're a princess. And he's a king." She explained as if it were the easiest thing in the world.

"I'm not sure that he likes me. But I appreciate the confidence." Alveen closed the door to the bathroom and went to change out of her gown. A set of black and red plaid flannel pajamas were hung, waiting for her with a note.

'These are much more comfortable than Irielle's'

She giggled to herself. She couldn't believe he actually remembered their conversation about the pajamas that Lovisa had given her. The did look extremely warm though.

Alveen crawled into bed and Tanilly curled up next to her, already half asleep.

Mysti walking in their room startled Alveen awake the next morning. The sun had begun to pour through the windows, but the fires were still certainly needed to keep the temperature tolerable.

"I apologize, Your Highness. One of the attendants here showed me the kitchen and I thought you and Tanilly might enjoy breakfast after the long night of traveling." She set down the food at the table by the fire.

"You are always so kind." Alveen slipped out from under Tanilly, letting her sleep as long as possible, while she ate breakfast.

"Luka will be here to show us the libraries. You are welcome to take her to any of them or in the room, beyond that I don't know much about this place so I would keep her to those areas." Mysti nodded in agreement. Alveen changed quickly into casual clothing. She wore black leggings with warm socks and ankle boots and a knee-length button up black and blue plaid dress with a scarf and vest to help her stay warm. She tied her hair up in a messy bun, knowing she would be doing research today and had no reason to look particularly nice. Tanilly had woken up and dressed, nearly finishing her breakfast by the time Luka made it to their door.

"Good morning sleeping beauty." Alveen remarked, realizing he wouldn't understand the reference.

"You have your strengths, I have mine." He rolled his eyes waiting for Mysti and Tanilly to come to the door and follow him to the library. Another hall curved around, wrapping the interior of the mountain, but only a single door was on the right side of the wall. Luka led them in, lighting all the scones and the fireplaces, strategically placed throughout. The three levels of shelves and books stacked taller than herself appeared with the light. The center of the mountain was the library.

"Top floor is where you'll find educational and children's books." He gestured to the staircase that wrapped around all three levels. Mysti and Tanilly ran off in the direction he pointed.

"I might just stay here." She laughed, eyes still wide and she took in every detail on every shelf, railing, pillar, desk and lighting fixture.

Much of the day was spent in the lower level, researching magic and sorcery as they had been before. They didn't talk much other than to suggest crazy theories that would help them. Tanilly ended up retreating to the room with Mysti to take a nap shortly after lunch, leaving Luka and Alveen alone again. There were no more awkward moments though. They sat in comfortable silence, reading and educating themselves on things that probably wouldn't help with their current predicament. The clocks rung, telling them the day was at a near end. Luka chivalrously offered to walk Alveen back to her room for the evening, making her laugh the whole way there. Once they reached the door, he wasn't so sure he wanted to leave her yet.

"Well, one day down, only a few left." She said innocently. "We found nothing today and my brain feels like mush." He wasn't really listening to her ramble. He grabbed her hand.

"The day isn't over yet. I want to show you something." He guided her down the curved hallway with sporadic windows that led to a giant iron door, guards lining the hall on both sides. He pushed the door open, revealing his chamber.

"Um are you sure this is where you meant to bring me?" she said nervously. It took him a moment to catch on to the fact that she was trying to be flirtatious.

"I would at least court you first, Your Highness. I am not as immoral as other may have you believe." He rolled his eyes at her, watching her for a moment as she admired the room. His canopy bed sat atop a short staircase with a large fireplace and a window overlooking the mountain range. The odd material covered the floor again, she assumed as a form of insulation against the stone. A couch sat in front of another fireplace, directly across from the door. A rustic theme took place in this room. Antlers and mounts of animals covered the walls, pelts hung in stylish angles and there was more carved dark wood furniture in his chamber than she had seen in the entire fortress so far.

"Good to know." She said looking back at him with a sweet smile. He met her gaze for a moment, getting lost in her unique eyes. He stood in front of a smaller set of iron doors she hadn't paid attention to until now.

"I had to show you this. I knew you would have an appreciation." Luka unlocked the iron doors, pressing against them until they gave way, slowly creaking open. With a wave of his arm, warm light filled the wrought iron scones wrapped around massive pillars revealing aisles of stacked books. Alveen cautiously stepped into the secret room, admiring the hand crafted desk that sat in the middle facing the door.

"Is this your study?" She asked as she stared around the room in wonder.

"Well it's a little elaborate for a study, but I suppose that's the best word for it." She walked around for a few minutes. "I have collected many books. Knowledge is key to me. I thought maybe this would be a good place to look for any kind of spells, magic, historical events that would help us."

"That sounds perfect. Let's start with history, if something like this has happened before we need to know." Luka moved past her, brushing his hand with hers causing a chill to crawl up her arm.

"We'll start over here." He grabbed a pile of books titled *The History of Beaanithe, Historical Events, Bulgrakan History, Cosaintian History*, and a few others specific to Foresi. Alveen sat on the floor and reached up for him to hand her a few. "We have a desk." He gestured toward the scroll designed piece of furniture.

"You can use the desk, I prefer to sit here. It's closer to the books." She bent her fingers in an encouraging way, asking for the books to be handed to her. Luka looked at her with an admiring smile and sat down next to her, handing her two of the books. She stared at him, curious, before flipping through the pages of the first one.

It was hours before they found anything useful. History proved to be unhelpful since nothing like this had happened before, but studies of magic seemed to have quite a bit more information.

"Here!" Luka proclaimed. "Look at this. I don't know why none of us thought of this before. Magic is literally what holds our world together." He leaned closer to her, moving his finger along the words as he read. "The first realm. Any destruction happening here has to come from something not holding it together there. Any disruption in balance there.."

"..would upset the balance here." She continued to read. "So what do you think is happening there?"

"There's only one way to find out."

"We need to find something on transfer spells and sorcery. The upset may have started there, but it wouldn't have just caused a kingdom to vanish, would it?" There were so many different issues they were trying to solve.

"I suppose you're right." He thought for a moment before jumping up and searching for a certain book. "This is the one I found my other information in." he flipped through it, searched for the information he found before, flipping past it slowly, reading the spells. One of them caught Alveen's attention.

"Wait" she stopped him from turning the page. "What is this?" she read quickly over the worn page of bleeding ink. "Remobortica?" She whispered. "Do you think this could help?"

"I think it would most certainly be useful to you. I'll let you take this one with you." Alveen stood and reach for another book.

"*Dark Magic*. Maybe this is where we should have started." She joked at the plainly named book. Flipping through the pages she saw rituals, sacrifices and magic done by moonlight and darkness. "I feel like we are headed in the right direction." Flipping through a few more pages, she found exactly what they had been looking for.

"Look!" she nearly yelled. She read over a spell that required the harnessing of moonlight, as Luka had previously found, and a blood sacrifice that would give the spellcaster the ability to transfer an object to a different realm.

"You don't think it's possible that they could transfer a kingdom though, do you? This says an object, not a mountain." Luka analyzed.

"I'm not sure. But if they harnessed enough moonlight, and had a strong enough sacrifice, who says the object couldn't be that large?" Luka raised his eyebrows, thinking it could maybe be a possibility.

The excitement that they may finally have a lead spread through them as their eyes met. Alveen's head leaned in and before she knew what she was doing, her lips crushed against Luka's. The kiss consumed her, relaxing her instantly. She pulled back, her eyes flying open. Why did that feel so right? With Samual she had sparks and passion, but with Luka it was comfort and security. With Luka there became a peace inside her from no longer fighting what everyone else said to be true.

"Oh no..." She said covering her mouth, not believing what she just did. "I am so sorry. I don't know why I did that."

His eyes remained staring at her, not letting his gaze break from hers. She was helpless under the golden eyes that were staring into hers. "Don't be." He hesitantly reached out to her wrapping his flawlessly constructed arms around her, pulling her close. She melted under his embrace.

She pulled the open book to her abdomen, making sure to save the page, barley allowing her lips to leave his. Her fingers wrapped behind his neck as she pulled herself onto his lap, facing him, still consumed by The King's kiss. He pulled away slightly, resting his forehead on hers. It was relaxing, calm and innocent. It was as if a weight lifted off her shoulders and she felt for the first time in her life like someone actually wanted to protect her and cherish her. He tipped her chin up towards him with his finger.

"Are you alright?" He asked with a perfect smile, white as the snow that swirled across the frozen tundra just outside the walls.

"I'm not sure." She laughed, falling against his chest, letting him hold her, resting his chin on her head. "I thought we were just a mutually beneficial alliance." She said. "Best friends." She sat back, looking at him.

"I think there is no better person to spend the rest of your life with than your best friend. And a marriage *is* a mutually beneficial alliance."

"Marriage?" She asked shocked. "You actually...You want to be with me? Forever?" He thought for a moment before answering. Had this been any normal relationship, she could have made the comment of moving too fast, but they were royalty and there had been so much talk of an engagement between them that the idea didn't seem nearly as far fetched as it normally would.

"Yes. I do. I probably should have been properly courting you this whole time, but.." He paused, "I wanted to make sure you had time to grieve." His serious composure broke letting out an adorable grin. "I didn't plan on enjoying your company as much as I do. Nor did I expect to be able to trust you." She smiled.

"I'm impressed. I didn't have to beg for an explanation." He rolled his eyes at her reference to his stand-offish personality and silence.

"Normally you would, but I need you to know these things because I have been holding them in for a very long time, waiting." Alveen moved off his lap, sitting against the shelf across from him. Her face no longer reflected happiness. She looked deep in thought. "What's wrong, Princess?" He reached for her hand.

"Nothing. I just hadn't really ever thought about us. I hadn't thought about another person courting me, or thought about the possibility of marrying someone since Samual." She tried smiling, but she began to cry as the reality of her secret weighed on her. "But I need to tell you something before you decide if this is really what you want. Something that might make you change your mind." His smile didn't leave his face. What could she possibly tell him that would make his feelings for her change?

"I…" she had a hard time saying it out loud. Someone telling her was one thing, but taking in the reality of her situation was a hard pill to swallow. "I can't have kids." Luka's eyes widened as he straightened up against the book shelf. He thought for a long minute before his face relaxed. "Say something please. I understand if you change your mind. Being the last of your line it would be more than understandable that you need an heir."

"How do you know for sure?" he asked.

"That first syragon attack, I hurt myself pretty bad when I summoned my magic. After multiple healing sessions, my healer let me know. It was actually the day of the royal walk that I found out. At the time I didn't think much of it, because even Samual and I hadn't talked about it. And Zakarian had an heir already so I wasn't worried about my line dying."

"I was with you most of that day. You hide your emotions well." He stated. "It amazes me how much you go through, and how strong you manage to be." He stood up and reached for her hand, pulling her up with him. "We will get through it. We can try healers and warlocks-"

"No, you cannot become involved with me assuming this problem can be fixed. What if it can't!?" She interrupted, frustrated that he didn't seem to take this as a permanent problem. The last thing she wanted to do would be disappoint him.

"If that doesn't work, then we'll adopt. Or we'll figure something out. All I care about is you. I just want to be with you. Any relationship that is worth it will never be easy and will take work." He walked her over to the desk, giving her a little more room to move around if she needed. "I want to make this work Alveen. You have no idea how long I've been waiting for this." He lifted her up so she now sat on the desk in front of him with his arms wrapped around her. "Do you know that I love you, Princess? With everything in me?" He asked her as if he'd said it a million times before. He loved her?

"I didn't." she reached up pulling his head down to meet hers. "but now I do." She smiled, planting a longing kiss on his lips.

"Life seems easier with you." He pushed a strand of hair out of her face, taking in her features and falling into her golden rimmed teal eyes. "Though you can be the most difficult woman I have ever spoken to at times, you are honest and straight forward and yet somehow still considerate." He took a breath in like he wasn't done but wasn't sure what else to say. "You inspire me." He said at last.

"Why are you so amazing?" She asked, now trying to conceal the salty drops from trailing down her cheek. His words warmed her heart and gave her a sense of certainty. He had been with her through everything that had gone on. He was the one who consistently checked on her, no matter how rude she came off, he was always there for her. Even when he was in a different kingdom he made her a priority in his life, and that was what she needed. She needed to be someone's first choice because when she ruled a kingdom, she was always going to have to put herself last.

"Because I now have someone that makes me want to be amazing, and be better than what I was." He gently rubbed his thumb along the back of her palm before holding her hand.

"So it's official? You are courting me then, King Luka?" She asked trying to lighten the mood.

"Actually.." he trailed off, looking down at her hands. "Alveen, I would like to be officially engaged to you. I want to marry you. Maybe not soon, necessarily, but I know I do not want to give any other man the opportunity to take away the treasure I have found." Alveen stared at him, his golden eyes serious, gazing into hers waiting for an answer. There was no ring, he wasn't on one knee, but somehow everything in that moment was everything she hoped she would feel. Though it hadn't been official, they did act as if they were courting. They could be official now.

"You really want to be my husband? To deal with me?"

"It would be my greatest pleasure." He cupped her face enjoying one more long-awaited kiss.

"Then yes. I will be engaged to you Luka." She leaned her forehead against his, enjoying that she no longer had to hold back the mysterious feelings, and knowing finally that he really did feel for her what she had been feeling for him. "We should really get back to our research.." Alveen whispered when they parted.

"Right." He whispered in return, backing away from her, blinking as if he needed to focus. "We've determined, purely on theory, that there must be some kind of destruction or balance upset in the first realm, which would lead to less magic leaking into our world and Beannithe literally falling apart. There is also the theory with this, that Foresi could have vanished into thin air somehow through first realm magic, or we have the very faint possibility that the entire kingdom was transferred to a different world entirely."

"I think that sums it up nicely. So, what should our first step be?" She asked standing by his side looking over the open books laid out with all the information they found.

"We travel to the first realm. Assuming the portal still works if there was any upset in balance. We need to figure out what changed and try to fix it."

"Then we leave tomorrow morning for Cosaint. Are you able to travel or should I do this with my guards?"

"I'll be fine to leave. I will just need to make it a quick trip." He said beginning to put books back that we had left laying out.

Luka walked her out to her room, holding her hand, in silence. "Well, Your Highness, this is where I bid you good night. I look forward to seeing you in the morning my dear." Alveen blushed. His attitude had changed from stoic and harsh, even with her, to something more relaxing. It was as if he were in the same position as her, frustrated to be holding back feelings and now that they were free to express themselves, they were becoming better versions of themselves.

"Good night, Your Majesty. I will see you bright and early?" She joked. He rolled his eyes, telling her that he would most defiantly be sleeping in, especially since they had stayed up so late. Luka gently raised Alveen's hand, placing a gentle kiss on the back before releasing her to her chambers. She closed the door behind her, rushing to change into her sleepwear. Even though she stayed up far later than she was used to, she couldn't help but sit in front of one of the fireplaces, thinking, before making her way to bed, having to pull some of the covers from Tanilly, who was sprawled across the bed as if she were a flying eagle.

~Chapter XIV~
The Unexpected

The remaining day in Bulgrakta proved to be useless as Alveen tried desperately to research more in her chamber, paging through the books Luka had given her. Luka had much to attend to for his own kingdom since he had been away for a few days and planned again to be away from his duties. The advisors didn't seem to mind and Luka never complained about how they handled affairs in his absence.

Alveen had found nothing all day and her impatience grew more as she thought about how they could be traveling home. A mix of emotions filled her as she would get excited thinking that she was actually engaged. They had agreed to keep the engagement quiet until they had finished with their current investigation into the missing kingdom.

"Tanilly, we need to get your things together so we can depart tonight." Alveen informed her niece. She wasn't listening at first but with a little encouragement the young girl began to pick up her books and nicely pack away her cloths. Mysti had stepped in to make sure everything was folded properly so everything would fit.

"Your Highness, I can do this for you, really." She insisted.

"It's quite alright, Tanilly can learn to clean up after herself, right?" she asked the little girl. She rolled her eyes with a smile. "So, you never did tell me, what did you ladies do yesterday? Did you stay in the library?"

"We went and wondered The Foretress! Princess, it was so beautiful. There were so many lights and everyone was so nice. They even had a skating rink. It made me feel warm and fuzzy inside." Tanilly explained loudly with excitement.

"Oh, is that so?" She responded, happy that they had gotten to chance to explore a little. She had wanted to go down to The Fortress and meet some of the citizens and see what the community was like, but her research would not allow the extra time. "I'll have to remember to make my way down there when I come back."

"You intend to come back?" Mysti asked with an overly excited smile on her face.

"Yes, I have every intention of coming back here."

Guards helped the ladies carry all of their luggage down to the train cars where Luka stood, arguing with an advisor. His face pinched together and his expression was much like the first time she had seen him, completely unreadable, though he certainly didn't look to be having a good conversation. When he turned and saw Alveen walking towards him he ended the conversation with the advisors bowing to him.

"Good evening. Are we ready to venture on home?" He asked. Tanilly and Mysti curtsied to him and expressed that they would miss his kingdom, making him smile, as they stepped onto the train. His hand swung around Alveen's waist after the guards and others had gotten on the train. "And good evening to you, beautiful."

"I thought we were being quiet for a while?" she asked with a smirk.

"We shall see how long we can keep that up. I would like to take advantage of every opportunity with you that I can though." His hand slid down to entwine with hers as he placed a gentle kiss on her forehead. He released her hand as she walked up the steps, joining the others and warming herself by the fire.

She only watched out the window while they departed, admiring the dragons yet again and getting lost in the lure of the mountains. She slept most of the way there, making herself comfortable in one of the oversized chairs by the fire. When she woke, Luka was sitting in the other, watching the flames. When she opened her eyes, she took a moment to appreciate her fiancée. The flickers flames warmed his eyes of liquid gold and the shadows accentuated his jawline.

"We're nearly there." He said not making eye contact with her for a second. When he looked at her, she could see his admiration for her shining, though he quickly hid it when Caspian approached as they were landing.

The entourage went directly to the palace, King Luka and his men heading toward the dining hall for dinner and Alveen leading Tanilly to The Banri to see her condition. Alveen ensured her guests that she would be with them promptly.

"How is she?" The Princess asked as she approached her grandmothers chamber.

"Well. Slowly improving." Sir Magnus stated as he opened the door for her.

"My dear! How was your trip?' She asked.

"Eventful. We believe we found some useful information and wish to follow up on a theory we have." Her grandmother sat upright in her bed, placing her cup of tea on the side table.

"And what might that theory be?" Alveen exhaled, not sure how her grandmother would take it.

"We believe there is a chance the sorceress may have been harnessing moonlight this entire time, and with a sacrifice, she could have transported the entire kingdom of Foresi to another realm.. like the first world perhaps, which would explain all of the phenomenon's destroying the other kingdoms." She waited as she watched her grandmother ponder the theory laid out in front of her.

"There are many theories I have thought of while resting, but that was not one of them." She stared at her granddaughter, her face unrevealing to if she approved or not. "It's reasonable. How do you wish to follow up on this?"

"We wish to take the portal to the first world and see if we can find the Foresi Royals or any clues to anything in regards to this as well."

"We as in you and your guards?"

"Yes, and King Luka and his guards. With his kingdom under control and many of his citizens out of harms way, he wishes to contribute as much as he can." She stared at her granddaughter with disbelief.

"When is that man going to properly court you?" she asked with a chuckle.

"Why would you say that?" Alveen asked, trying to be as unaffected by the comment as possible.

"Because he has never once wanted to be involved with the other kingdoms. He has been isolated and though he is a good ally, he doesn't show his face unless absolutely necessary. We have all seen more of him since the royal walk than we have probably his entire life." Alveen wondered if she should say anything, she knew her grandmother would make an announcement so she waited.

"Well, maybe someday soon then."

"I approve of the journey. And I hope you find Hunter and Willow." With a bow Alveen expressed her gratitude. "You best be off to dinner. King Luka is very appreciative of promptness." She smiled to The Princess.

Alveen entered the dining hall, forcing everyone to stop eating and stand. Everyone except King Luka. Though she knew he didn't have to, it was still a sign of respect. Her guess was it was him trying to play tough yet again in front of his guards. She sat at the head of the table, away from The King to make a point to him that his gesture was not appreciated.

Much of the dinner was quiet. Most of the guards returned to post while Tanilly and Alveen finished dinner together.

King Luka had gone to his chamber for the evening. She had no idea if they intended to leave in the morning or tomorrow at all. She calmed her emotions and allowed herself to enjoy the moment with her niece while everyone else was away. Alveen wasn't sure how the trip to the first world would go, there was a very strong chance it may end horribly or she may not come back. She wanted to be with her niece as much as she could. Tanilly and The Princess joked and played games at the dining table under the watchful eyes of Caspian, Mysti and another guard.

"King Luka, Your Highness." One of the guards announced as he was entering.

"Your Majesty. To what do we owe the pleasure of you rejoining us?" She asked professionally.

"I've come to confirm our travel plans. I wish to make this a hasty trip so I may return to my kingdom without delay." Alveen hoped there was no irritation in his reasons to go home. She realized with all the recent trips, he had to be needed back home by now.

"Of course, The Banri has given her blessing and we will head out early in the morning. Should everything go as planned, you will be able to return home once we've finished our task." Alveen spoke as she stood making eye contact with The King. Even now he tried to intimidate her with his size and position, but she would have none of that. She could be far more intimidating if she needed to be. The King bowed to her and exited the room.

"Where are you going Alveen?" Tanilly asked from her chair.

"King Luka and I have a special trip to make to see if we can help find Princess Willow and King Hunter."

"Can I join you?" She asked excitedly. She had thoroughly enjoyed her trip to Bulgrakta.

"Not this time my dear. We don't know what we're in for and it is important you are kept safe." Tanilly hung her head. "Let's get off to bed, shall we? I know I'm tired." The young girl walked hand in hand with The Princess toward her chamber. Alveen had come to enjoy all the time she spent with her niece. Once in the room they found Mysti had already begun preparing the room for them. Alveen often slept on her couch with her pelts and Tanilly slept in the large bed. Sleep found them both quickly after the hours of traveling.

Alveen tiredly opened her eyes, pulling the pelts closer to herself as she sat up to check on Tanilly. She was still asleep in bed. Alveen noticed the sky was beginning to lighten outside her balcony, telling her the time to leave was soon. She took a warm shower and dressed warmly, grabbing her pre-packed backpack and heading out the door. She wore tall boots and thick jeans with a dark brown coat lined with white fur and a tan wrap around her ears, allowing her to pull her hair up in a bun yet stay warm. She glanced back at Tanilly and didn't want to wake her. This trip would prove to be useful, she had to believe that. As she pulled her door closed behind her and stepped out into the corridor, King Luka was already on his way to get her.

"You're running behind a little don't you think?" he asked. Alveen had had enough of his rude persona. She walked quickly towards him, standing in his way and not allowing herself to get lost in how beautiful his eyes were.

"I've had about enough of this. If this is how you treat other royals, no wonder no one likes you. It's one thing to be rude in the morning since I know you are not a morning person, but it's another thing to outright disrespect me in my kingdom in front of my guards and family." Her cheeks had grown a rosy shade of red as she flushed with anger. How dare he act compassionate one day and then turn around and treat her so rudely the next.

"Your Highness, how are you this morning?" He asked sarcastically.

"I could be better." She glared at him for a moment before leading the way to the portal that was now exposed to the mountains and valleys toward where Foresi once stood. "Let's get this over with." She said as she held out her hand. Their few guards were also with them so they knew this would take quite a bit of magic to get them all through this portal.

They began the incantation in a whispered tone and the swirling pool appeared above, waiting for them to dive in. The guards entered first, leaving Luka and Alveen for last. He gestured for her to go first, squeezing her hand and tossing her an entrancing glance now that everyone had gone. She tried to keep from smiling, but it proved useless. She let a grin expand over her lips as she jumped into the portal. The wind jerked and slammed her body into what felt like rocks, her body was thrust into invisible walls, cracking her bones and slicing her attire. She became nauseous as she was finally spat out the other side, landing on a what felt like cold slop, soaking her.

She laid for a moment, sending slivers of magic into her hip and shoulders where she was certain there was damage. Her eyes finally opened and she was looking up into falling snowflakes and a shining sun. After moments of letting her eyes focus, beyond the snowflakes she witnessed the trees covered in yellow, orange and red leaves sprawled across the branches with blooming flowers. Wait, snow? Blooming flowers? Fall leaves? Alveen sat up quickly, looking around at the faces peeking out from behind the sparkly trees. Observing the ground below her she quickly stood realizing she had landed in icy mud and crunching leaves. Her attire had become soaked and tore from the travel. She had been to the first world before and this certainly was not it.

"Banphrionsa?" The guard near her called out, rushing to his feet to ensure she was well. "Have you been hurt?"

"Only a little, but I'll be fine. Where is King Luka? And the other guards?" He pointed around to the guards strewn about the ground, some bleeding, others throwing up, and King Luka standing and taking in his surroundings.

"Your Majesty, are you alright?" She called. He looked to her and nodded, once again not giving a verbal response. "What happened? Where are we?"

"I would have to say we are not in the first world. The portal may be inaccessible from all the damage done. It looks like we have been rerouted, thus the rough travel." He pointed towards everyone else. Alveen looked around.

"Luka." She braced herself for an attack. Surrounding them were bears and wolves of monstrous sizes. Atop their backs rode what she could only swear were pure blood elves carrying guns. She hadn't seen any guns since she left Earth, and these were certainly tactical weapons of the highest caliber. Alveen had her hands on her daggers in her thigh holsters, realizing how ridiculous they must think she is for thinking she had a chance.

"What are they holding?" Caspian asked as he approached her. The elf in charge seemed to have the bulk similar to Luka's, which was substantial for an elf. The leader spoke loudly to them in a demanding tone, though their language was foreign to all who stood together now from Beannithe.

"Those are very modernized weapons. Your armor will not protect you from those."

"How do you know this?" Luka asked her without taking his focus from the army around them.

"I grew up with them. Don't tempt these soldiers." She warned, then turned to the leader upon a white bear. "We mean no harm. What is this world?" She raised her arms from her weapons and spoke clear and slow. "I am Princess Alveen of Beannithe. What is your name?"

The leader again shouted, saying something about Beannithe, though none of them could understand. King Luka stepped forward, copying her formality of a peaceful venture. "King Hunter? Is he here? We search for a friend." The weapons were raised again and they began to close in on the group. The guards and royals went for weapons but realized they would be soon be overtaken.

"We must leave." Alveen ordered Caspian and her guards.

"We will go nowhere, we will fight." Luka spat back.

"Luka, we are not in the first world, we have no idea where we are or who these people are. They clearly do not welcome us."

"Most of them are not healthy to travel again. It will be too much for them."

"It won't be if we reach out and protect them. We need to go. Now." She grabbed his hand and started the incantation quietly as not to disturb the threat around them. The portal opened and the warriors backed away as each of the unwelcomed guests dove through, ready for a rough ride.

Alveen felt the wind wiping her hair again, but this time, she felt no pain. She reached her magic out to each of her travel companions, feeling for injury. There were none, this travel was normal. As the other end of the portal opened, everyone landed promptly on their feet. Alveen stood in the grassy field, waiting on Luka who burst past and stood in front of her.

"We could have found information there."

"You're welcome, King Luka, for saving your life and your guards. We can return later if we feel it is necessary but we first have a kingdom and friends to find. If we return, we need to know their realm and language so we can communicate with them before we get our faces shot off and our entire guard murdered." They stood arguing nose to nose, being watched by those in their guard. They knew to stand back and not interfere with royal disputes.

"Research." Luka said plainly, exhaling.

"Yes. We need to do our research. We know something kept us out of the first world, that is information. That is a clue helping us come closer to a solution. I will be in the library tonight if you choose to join me." She walked away with Caspian and the others at her side, heading for her chamber to clean up and get her clothing repaired.

With the travel to the first realm failing, it had Alveen worried that this could be a far greater problem than all their theories had come up with.

In the library, Alveen sat on the floor of the second level, surrounded by books about magic and dark arts and sorcery, most of which she had paged through multiple times now. Answers seemed to be a great distance away.

She retreated to her chamber, spending more time on the books Luka found information in before, referring back to a few spells that she thought may be helpful. She heard clicking footsteps advancing down her corridor toward her chamber. The door flew open without a knock.

"Alveen! You're here! We were looking for you!" Mysti trailed behind her, out of breath from chasing the young girl.

"And it seems you have finally found me." She smiled, greeting Tanilly with a hug.

"What are you working on?" she asked with innocent curiosity.

"Magic. I'm doing some research and studies." Tanilly nodded that she understood. Alveen thought for a second, re-reading one of the passages. "Would you like to help me with a spell?" she asked her niece as an idea formed in her brilliant mind.

~Chapter XV ~

Rembortica

"How is she?" Alveen asked the healer who stood at the end of The Banri's bed.

"Worse. I do not understand it though. She was healing, her body was assisting the recovery and now it is as if it has given up."

"Do you have predictions?" Alveen asked holding her sleeping grandmother's hand in hers. She didn't look at the healer when she asked the question.

"If her body doesn't fight back soon, we are looking at a week at the most, before it fails. I will continue to do what I can and figure everything out possible."

"She always told me you were the best, so I will stand by that statement and trust you will find something." She stood and smoothed her gown. "Retrieve me if she wakes please."

There was no way that The Banri would fall back that quickly after she had seemed to be healing so well. Something else was happening and she was going to find out. The Princess, or acting Queen now, marched out of The Banri's room, Caspian awaited her down the corridor. She would not let another die, especially her Queen and grandmother, without trying everything she could think of. Right now, her only idea was getting information from a certain palace guest.

"Bring the intruder to the throne room immediately. I have some questions I wish to ask." She demanded, her voice like an angry growl. Caspian was taken aback by her tone, but complied with her orders as he nodded and took another guard with him to the dungeon where the stranger was held. She was acting Queen. That gave her the right to do what she felt was necessary, and she knew he was a key component. She flicked her wrist, forcing the golden doors of the throne room to fly open. The centaurs that stood guard straightened their stance as she walked by, exchanging a glance of concern. Tanilly stood inside with Mysti against a side wall. The girl stood tall, fearless as her aunt barged in full of frustration.

Alveen and Tanilly had practiced the spell multiple times and gone over everything. They insured all the necessary ingredients were collected, though they tried to do it mostly in secret since everything they were doing was based solely on theories and a letter. Clattering echoed down the hallway as Caspian and Griffith escorted the man toward her.

The stranger was forced to his knees at the center of the throne room. He didn't look up at her. Tanilly stood at the back of the throne room, walking toward him and Alveen has instructed.

"I am tired of playing games. I will not allow more in my kingdom, especially The Banri, to die." The man looked at her, exhausted and confused. She let out a sigh. "This may hurt a little, but we need to know." Was all Alveen said before she reached out resting all of her fingertips on the man's skull. Tanilly did the same from behind. Alveen gave her an encouraging nod, letting her know it was okay. "Rembotrica!" They exclaimed with power in unison.

The room filled with static and the air above them darkened. The static charges connected like striking lightning bolts into each spot where their fingers touched. Alveen was forced across the room as if she had been kicked in the chest.

Images and scenes flashed before her eyes. She was seeing the memories of this man, though they flashed by so fast Alveen could only make out certain parts. She hoped Tanilly didn't see everything that see did. Caspian ran to her side, but she held her hand out relaying that she was fine. Tanilly was on the floor on the other side of the room, already standing up with Mysti and Griffith at her side. Thankfully, she wasn't hurt. Alveen looked at the stranger, glad she was the one facing him. His face warped, blurring like a demon in a horror movie she had once seen. The brunette color of his hair washed away revealing the blonde hair, a notable feature for an elf. His previously unmatching eyes of pink and brown switched with a blink to peridot green and his round face slimmed into more striking and sharp features.

Alveen stood back up as the man before her came to his senses. She watched as he looked around the throne room, unaware of how he came to be there. His hands patted his clothing, unfamiliar with the material. The man's eyes lifted to her, now standing in front of him near the throne.

"Alveen." He whispered with wide eyes, recognition in his tone. His expression made it confusing to determine weather he was happy or upset to see her with tears threatening the rims of his eyes.

"Killian." She said back as if greeting him in a hallway with a masked expression. Everyone else in the room, which was only a few others, gasped in recognition of the name. They stayed silent watching the scene before them unfold.

"You..you knew?" he asked, still on his knees and his voice shaking.

"I had my theories." She said bluntly. She hadn't smiled yet. The emotion inside her surged like a storm, it took a lot of strength to hold all of it back. Confirmation that her father was indeed before her, alive. Curiosity overwhelmed most of her feelings. She wondered so much about him, and so much about his involvement in everything that had been going on. "Now that that is handled, I have a few questions for you."

"Anything." The man before her looked broken and weak. The longer she stood there not speaking, the more clearly, she could see some of his oldest memories growing up in this very palace, she saw herself as a young girl running through the halls and the village and a blonde-haired woman she could only assume was her mother.

"With your memories back now, I'm sure you are aware that Zakarian has decided to betray us." He nodded in understanding. "Why were you sent through the portal on the night of the attack? What is your purpose here without your memory?" The man thought for a second.

"I guess it was more of a taunt from the sorceress. Wiping my memory and concealing my identity to ensure I would not get treated well, ironically in my own kingdom." He looked at her, "You have become a beautiful young woman." She ignored the last part. They would have time to catch up, even if it was in a dungeon cell.

"Why did she wipe your memory in the first place?"

"I refused. I refused to do what she demanded. I betrayed her, in her eyes."

"What exactly was it she wanted you to do?"

"Sacrifice. Sacrifice those whom I love."

"By supporting her, you supported the death of King Bowen, King Ronan and many others." The man began to cry out of regret.

"King Hunter." He bawled, nearly inaudible.

"Where is King Hunter? What happened to him??" She had a dozen questions about Foresi, but overwhelming him was not the way to get it, she needed to speak strong and clearly and get every bit of information, one at a time.

"She sacrificed him as part of her plan. Poisoned him." Alveen wouldn't hold back the tears, she controlled her tone but the tears still fell from her eyes as she waited for her father to continue. "She's been harvesting moonlight since she gained rule of the Dorcha tribes. With a sacrifice strong enough, she could send an entire kingdom to the first realm, long enough to destroy all the kingdoms without her needing to do it herself."

"A sacrifice like a genuine elven monarch." She whispered, covering her mouth. "What do you mean when she came to power."

"Your mother. She left here out of anger towards you. Somehow when she gave birth to you, all of her magic was transferred to you. All of her natural abilities, now yours. Which is why you are so much stronger than others. She held a grudge for that and insisted that she could learn by the hands of the sorceress through potions and spells and learning different abilities. She didn't know it was going to make every once of darkness in her grow. She just wanted her magic back. But she grew to hate you for what happened. She murdered the last original sorceress, the one who had taken her on as an apprentice, and took her place reigning above the dark lands." Alveen tried to take in all of that information. The letter had given her theories, but her mother being the main evil force they were fighting against made everything a whole lot more complicated.

"Where is Foresi? Where is Princess Willow and her citizens?" Alveen demanded. She would deal with her family drama and emotions later, right now there were only a few very important questions she needed answered.

"Stuck. In the first realm. Foresi was transferred there through the strong transfer spell, there is a portal open in the syragons lair, eventually it will close if not given another sacrifice and Foresi will return to it's previous state." He explained.

"Where is the lair?"

"Bottom of the world. Underwater."

"Why should I believe anything your saying?" She asked. He was giving his answers way too easily, which made her very uncomfortable. Everything he said made sense, and some of it lined up with her theories through her endless hours of research.

"Because.." he slowly got to his feet, trying to stand tall. "I betrayed her in saying I wouldn't sacrifice you and Zakarian. You two were supposed to be gone, protected. Zakarian went of his own will, but I protested and refused to help her assassinate the only other heir this family had. I only went because I loved her, I would have done anything to make her happy, but that's where I drew the line."

"Well I do appreciate that, Killian. What a noble act to not want your children murdered." Alveen reigned herself in, noticing she was letting her emotions take place where reason and logic should. She needed Luka here to help her through this.

"Alveen.."

"It's Your Highness." She corrected him. "You have not gained the monarchs trust back, so you will not come back here and expect to rank as highly as you did. You will earn your way back." He nodded. "You forfeited your right to the throne and to this kingdom."

"Your Highness, her goal is simple. To assassinate you. That is why the attacks became more frequent when you returned. When you were gone, she sat and plotted and waited for your return."

"I've warded off many assassination attempts thus far, as I'm sure you're aware."

"Where is my mother? Shouldn't she be here during this conversation? How do you have the right to interrogate a prisoner?" He asked with concern in his voice, not distain.

"I'm acting Queen right now. She is unable to be here and I will do whatever I find necessary to protect my loyal family members and my kingdom."

"What happened?"

"The avalanche. That your wife caused. The palace collapsed. Thankfully she's working on recovering. Don't worry yourself with that."

"She would have recovered by now."

"Her body isn't fighting it. We have our best healers working on it."

"The poison."

"Excuse me?"

"The poison. The one Lyra's minion gave to King Hunter. He was not injured but it forces their bodies to give up, it pulls the strength from them, the life. There is a connection between the poison and her sacrificial alter, as the poison works it transfers the life it takes to the alter."

"What does that mean for us?"

"It means my mother, your grandmother and Queen, is her next sacrifice."

THE STORY CONTINUES WITH

NEW FOUND
LEGACY

~Chapter 1~

"Caspian. Guard The Banri's door. Explain the situation to the healer, see if there is anything she can do if it is poison causing her ailments. We need to figure out who she all has working within the kingdom."

"Your Highness, Zakarian was in the palace only days ago. It could very well have been him." Her trustworthy guard mentioned. He had a point, they had done a ridiculous amount of security checks and if any of her minions were still here, it was surely a suicide mission if they believed they could hold the portal open long enough to destroy all six kingdoms.

"You're right. Just relay the message to her and see if there is anything she can do to find out if this is what's happening." She turned to her niece. "Tanilly, you did wonderful. Mysti please take her back to my chambers."

"You have a daughter? Are you married?" Killian asked.

"No, I am simply mentoring her."

"She looks just like you."

"So, everyone keeps telling me." Alveen was frustrated and unsure what to do about her father in front of her. The last thing the kingdom needed was another potential threat running around. "Griffith." The guard snapped to attention, walking toward The Princess. "Take Killian back to the dungeon. Give him a clean cell, a more comfortable one if possible. Until we know his intentions, I don't want him roaming freely. Ruslan, assist him please." The guards escorted the chained former Prince out of the throne room, leaving Alveen to her thoughts. She sat in the throne, resting her head in her hands, trying to finds solutions to everything. Sitting back, she took a moment to enjoy the comfort of the throne. If the poison was caught before it was too late, The Banri would soon be back. Alveen was fine waiting for her chance to reign.

She waved her hand, summoning her fiancé for advice.

"What a beautiful surprise." Luka answered. It only took seconds for him to see the stress on her face.

"It worked. The stranger that came through the portal was my father, also known as Prince Killian."

"And?"

"And he had a lot of information."

"What's wrong Alveen?"

"King Hunter... he said he was sacrificed. He's dead." She cried. "Apparently our theory was correct. With enough harvested moonlight and a strong enough sacrifice, they could transfer an entire kingdom to a different realm."

"We don't know if he's telling the truth though. This could be another part of her plan."

"What are the chances that she actually expected us to figure out the memory spell though? I don't think his placement is part of her plot. He said, and you could be right, he could be making this all up, but he said the reason she threw him through the portal and wiped his memory was more of an ironic torture, having him killed in his own kingdom by his own people, or in our case locked away since he wasn't murdered on site as she might have expected. He said that her goal, through all of this, is to get to me. To assassinate me. And he claims he refused to assist with any part of her plans that had anything to do with harming Zakarian or I."

"A lot of help that did Zakarian."

"He went of his own will though, that's not something he could have helped with. I just don't know if I should trust him."

"I wouldn't not yet. Where is he now?"

"Back in a new cell."

"Good. Keep him there for a while. You can still go talk with him but you have enough on your mind without him wandering around doing who knows what."

"Have you told anyone of our engagement?" she switched gears, going back to a less pressing matter. It was nice for her to focus on troubles that didn't end in life or death.

"I spoke to King Viktor. He wanted to tell me that his underwater guard found no remnants of Foresi. Did you know he and Willow had just gotten engaged?" Her eyes widened.

"No, I didn't. I would have thought she would have mentioned something like that."

"He said he was there the day before all of the disasters happened. I guess they had been courting in secret because they didn't want anyone to interfere. He's a worried mess as you can imagine."

"Willow should be in the first realm. With all her citizens. According to Killian."

"But we can't get through to bring them back."

"No. but he mentioned that there is a portal, in the syragons lair. The sorceress keeps her sacrificial alter there, the more sacrifices she feeds it, the longer the portal remains open, doing more damage to our world and closing the portal between ours and the first realm. He suggested that if the sacrifices were warded off for long enough that the portal will close and Foresi will return to its previous state."

"So, what are we supposed to do? Go charging into the syragons lair and fight off the entire dorcha tribe and the sorceress herself for an unmentioned amount of time until the portal closes?" he asked with a tone suggesting she might be crazy.

"That might be exactly what we have to do."